Airship Daedalus

Assassins of the Lost Kingdom

By E.J. Blaine

FIRST EDITION

ISBN: 978-1-7349293-8-6

Copyright © 2016 E.J. Blaine & Deep7 Press
All Rights Reserved Worldwide

Edited by Nina Sullivan and Dan Heinrich
Cover art & design by Todd Downing
3D ship model by Hans Piwenitzky

Based on the *Airship Daedalus / AEGIS Tales* setting and characters by Todd Downing and published in various media by Deep7 Press. *Airship Daedalus™* and *AEGIS Tales™* are trademarks of Deep7 Press.

WWW.AIRSHIPDAEDALUS.COM

Deep7 Press is a subsidiary of Despot Media, LLC
1214 Woods Rd SE Port Orchard, WA 98366 USA
WWW.DEEP7.COM

- CHAPTER 1 -

New York City, July, 1926

On the day he died, Eamon Cobb surprised his staff and left work early. It was a humid, muggy summer in New York. The air hung still and heavy in the streets and tempers were short. Cobb looked out over Manhattan from his office on the 50th floor of the Cobb Tower and could see the whole city seething. He suddenly felt very tired. Cobb Industries was doing better than ever. But Cobb could feel himself growing old. He'd planned to work late tonight, then stay at his apartment in town. But suddenly he wanted nothing more than to get out of the city, to his estate on the Long Island Gold Coast where a refreshing breeze would blow off the water.

The union men would be downstairs, of course. They'd been raising hell on the sidewalk outside his building for a month now over some accidents at his mines in West Virginia. As if he knew the first thing about mine safety. He had foremen for that. That's what the rabble refused to understand. Cobb was an idea man. His mining subsidiary was a financial machine, inputs and outputs on paper. Nothing more. The yokels were barking up the wrong tree.

And of course the police were useless. They'd move them along, but they never arrested anyone so the rabble just came back. Cobb was sick of it. If he left early, maybe he could avoid the worst of it.

MacGinty and Coyle were waiting in the outer office when he emerged. They were huge men, muscles straining at their suits. Both were former Pinkertons; expensive, but worth it. They fell in on either side of him as he walked to the elevator.

"I'm in no mood today," he said. "Let's see if we can't slip out before they notice us."

"Yes, sir," said MacGinty. "The car's out front."

The express elevator deposited them in the lobby, and the two Pinkertons led the way outside. Cobb was dazzled by the sudden brightness, and the muggy air felt like walking into one of his steel plants.

"There he is!" someone shouted. "The butcher!"

The crowd of union men was bigger than he'd expected this time of day. In front of them, nearest to him, was an emaciated, one-legged man on crutches. He wore ragged coveralls with the empty leg pinned up and he gawped at Cobb like he was the King of the Faeries.

"Look what you did to a working man!" someone shouted. There were more shouts, overlapping into a chaos of noise.

Then a stone flew out of the crowd. It grazed Cobb's cheek, and he felt the sting. His hand flew to his cheek and came away wet with blood.

Coyle roared and waded into the crowd. Cobb saw the brass knuckles on his right hand glitter in the sun. Then it was chaos. Everyone was shouting and pushing. Somewhere, a police whistle shrieked. His Cadillac was a dark shape ahead of him. He headed down the steps toward it, but someone broke from the crowd and leapt onto the stairs. The man was red-faced and roaring with incoherent, animal rage. He grabbed at Cobb's briefcase, and Cobb nearly fell as he tried to yank it free.

MacGinty appeared out of nowhere, swinging his blackjack. Cobb saw it snap the man's head back. A mass of bloody spittle flew from his mouth and spattered Cobb's suit. The man fell to the sidewalk, and then MacGinty hauled Cobb down the steps and threw him into the back of the Cadillac. Cobb landed on top of his briefcase on the back seat. The door slammed shut, and the car sped away.

Cobb looked out the back window as the police swarmed the scene. He saw truncheons swinging, and blood.

He collected himself. He was Eamon Cobb, a titan. This was no way to react. Cobb sat up, controlled his breathing, and smoothed out his rumpled suit jacket.

"The mob's a bit testy today," he said to his driver.

"Yes, sir."

The Cadillac drove Cobb out onto Long Island, a world away from Manhattan. Maybe he should withdraw from the city entirely, he thought, and leave it to the ingrates. Let them starve in the streets without his companies to give them work. But of course he wouldn't give up the business. Still, he might set up an office in his mansion and run it from there. He was so fed up with people's expectations, their strange demands, their death threats. To hell with all of them.

Cobb's staff weren't expecting him, but they reacted quickly. A servant took his coat and tutted over the bloodstains. Then Cobb walked into his study and shut the door behind him. He opened the French doors that looked out over Long Island Sound and let the breeze in. He rolled up his shirt sleeves and opened his private bar. Inside was a self-contained electric refrigerator that kept ice frozen. It was the latest thing. Cobb imagined how astonished his mother would have been if she were here to see it. He dumped a few ice cubes into a heavy glass and poured in three fingers of scotch.

Then Cobb settled into his favorite leather wing chair, drank his scotch, and looked out at the trees along the shoreline.

When he felt the first flash of heat he took it for a hot breeze from outside and thought to close the French doors. But he couldn't stand. He got partway up before his muscles quivered and trembled, and he fell back into the armchair.

He was so hot suddenly. His skin began to tingle, and his heart beat like a hammer. Was this a heart attack? A rush of fear overtook him, and he called out for his butler. But only a faint squeaking sound came from his throat.

Cobb felt shooting pains through his limbs. He watched in terror as dark tendrils crept down his arms, his blood vessels swelling and turning black. And then the agony crushed him. He tried to scream, but couldn't. He could only watch in horror as his skin blackened and swelled. His wrist strained against his watch band until the skin split. The pain was like being burned alive. He reached for the cold glass and knocked it to the floor. The scotch spread into a thin pool on the hardwood.

He slid from the chair onto the floor, his eye a bare fraction of an inch from a fallen ice cube. He lay there immobile, drowning in agony, unable to move or call out. He heard the footsteps of his butler pass by outside and prayed for him to open the door. But the man was under orders to never disturb Cobb here while he enjoyed his afternoon scotch.

Eamon Cobb was the 17th richest man in the world. He owned railroads, mines, and steel mills. He had decided the fates of thousands. When he died, he died alone on the floor of his study and was grateful for the release of oblivion.

℈

Jack and Doc took the Ohio State Limited into New York, where Thomas Edison's driver was to pick them up. But as they stepped down onto the platform at Grand Central Station, there was no sign of him.

Jack McGraw was a handsome man of about 30 with a lean, muscled build and a shock of sandy blonde hair that he struggled to keep neatly combed. At his side, Dorothy "Doc" Starr was a striking brunette with fierce green eyes softened by a mischievous smile. The couple made heads turn as the passengers and porters flowed around them. They scanned the sea of people surging through the station.

"It's not like we'd miss him in the crowd," Doc observed dryly. Edison's driver was an enormous Slav named Stefan. He was a perfectly capable chauffeur, but his real job was to be Edison's bodyguard, and at that he was unmatched. They'd seen Stefan handle an attack on Edison once. His response had been quick, brutal, and very effective.

"Look at all these people," said Jack. "I almost forgot what New York is like."

"Did you miss it?" Doc asked. She took his hand in hers and gave it a quick squeeze.

"Not a bit," said Jack, turning to smile at her. "I had all I needed. Ah! Here he comes!"

Stefan hurried toward them parting the flow of humanity like a steamship making full power upstream. "Captain McGraw!" he said as he reached them. "And Doctor Starr! How wonderful to see you again! It's been too long. AEGIS hasn't been the same without you."

"I don't know," said Jack, "I hear they're growing like mad."

"It's been quite a year," Stefan agreed. He apologized for being late as they collected their luggage. It had been a busy day, he told them, with a lot of major AEGIS personnel arriving for high-level meetings with Edison.

"And he's asked us to come back," Doc said. "What's going on?"

"It's hard to say," Stefan said as he loaded their bags into the back of a Model L Lincoln. "Maybe it's nothing. Just a run of bad luck. But nothing good for sure."

They got in, and Stefan pulled the Lincoln out into traffic. They drove through Manhattan, crossed the Hudson, and headed into New Jersey.

A year, Jack thought as they rode. Apparently it had been a big year for AEGIS, the organization Edison had created to combat the darkness he saw taking root in the aftermath of the Great War. Well, it had been a big year for him, too.

Jack glanced over at Doc, looking out at the passing scenery. Part of him still couldn't believe they had a daughter. *He* had a daughter! One he never would have known if fate hadn't twisted back on itself.

He didn't blame Doc for that, not for any of it. He certainly didn't blame her for turning him down in Paris in 1918. There was a war on at the time, and Jack was a fighter pilot. Marrying him was a bad bet. A few days of happiness together was all they could hope for, and back then it had seemed like enough. None of them really expected to survive the war, but somehow they'd done it. By then though, Doc had married Dirk Starr and they had a daughter, Ellen. Jack left them to their happy life and got on with his own.

When Dorothy Starr reentered his life, she was a widow working for AEGIS, and she wanted to recruit him to fly their new proto-type airship, the *Daedalus II*. So Jack had gone with her and a band of their old companions from the war, and they'd managed to strike a few blows for good.

But then Doc had changed his life yet again. He had always believed Ellen was Dirk Starr's daughter. Starr himself went to his grave believing it. But Doc revealed that she was actually Jack's child, from that brief time in Paris. It was a lot to take in.

They'd spent the last year together, away from the constant action and danger of AEGIS, learning to be a family in their odd way. Jack had thought he and Doc might marry finally, but Doc had let him know she wasn't ready. She'd rejected Jack for fear of losing him. But she'd lost her husband anyway. Dirk Starr had been poisoned on a mission for AEGIS and took months to die as Doc fought in vain to save him.

That loss was still too close to her, Jack knew. She'd told him the truth about Ellen. She'd let him into their lives, and they'd traveled the world together for the last year. But the solidity of a wedding ring was more than she could handle.

Jack could live with that. She was in his life, and so was his daughter Ellen, now being looked after by Doc's aunts. It was more than he'd dreamed of. For the rest, he could wait.

"Where've you gotten to, Jack?"

He looked up in surprise. Doc gave him a teasing grin and pointed forward. "Can't believe you're missing this."

The Lincoln drove down an approach road to an AEGIS airfield in the New Jersey countryside. A huge, sloping wall of steel and concrete rose ahead of them. The airship hangar. Jack felt his heart race a bit. He'd missed this.

The car pulled up in front of the gaping doors at the end of the hangar. Jack and Doc got out, and there she was. The *Daedalus II*. It was such a graceful design, Jack thought. The ship was a low, sleek lozenge almost two hundred and fifty feet long, with a gleaming skin of vulcanized canvas and aluminum fibers. Her cockpit was slung beneath the bow, and he could see the ducted propeller nacelles on either side and the rudders at the rear. He couldn't wait to fly her again.

As they went inside, Jack noticed the forward canopy had been removed, leaving only the aluminum frame. He'd heard they were replacing the glass with a lighter, stronger kind that had new anti-glare and anti-fog coatings. Most of the internal skeleton was being replaced with a lighter foamed steel too. Some of that weight reduction would translate into improved flight characteristics, while some would be traded back for new gear loadouts.

AEGIS was endlessly updating the ship. After every mission there seemed to be a new advance to be installed. Jack knew there was talk of just decommissioning her and starting over from the keel up. But not yet. Not yet.

"Well, if it ain't Captain Stratosphere!" someone shouted. Jack winced at the nickname he'd picked up during the war. He was convinced it was meant to tease him, no matter how much his friends insisted otherwise.

Carl "Rivets" Holloway, the ship's mechanic, walked out of a storage shed at the side of the hangar, hefting an armload of what looked like heavy steel beams. Rivets had a stocky, grizzled look, capped off by salt and pepper hair and an unruly, bristly moustache. He wore coveralls and an oil-stained cap. It was the same outfit he'd been wearing the last time Jack saw him.

"Good to see you, Doc!" Rivets called out happily. "Check me out, Jack. The Amazing Rivets. World's Strongest Man!"

"Always thought a shaved head and a bearskin would suit you, Rivets," Jack said.

"Nah, these are that new foam steel," Rivets explained. "Stuff's light as a feather."

"Uh, yeah, I figured that," Jack said. "It's good to see you, Rivets. Are Duke and Deadeye around?"

"Nah, big AEGIS confab up at Edison's house. All the bigwigs are talking strategy."

"You didn't go?"

"Nah," Rivets answered once again. "I'd just open my mouth. And then before you know it there's a fistfight. Besides, someone had to stay here and put your ship back together. You know, these are pretty light, but if I stand here holding them long enough..."

"Right, sorry." Jack took several of the beams and followed Rivets up a wooden access ramp that led through a section of the ship's frame where the outer skin had been removed. Scaffolding was set up on the ship's skeleton, piled with tools and structural beams.

"Mostly done," said Rivets. "Have her back in the air in a day or two. Put them up here, okay Jack?"

"How's she doing?" Jack asked as he helped stack the beams.

"Well, the new frame of course, and you saw the canopy's off. New electrics, new gimbals for the engine mounts. Hell, new stove in the galley. You name it, somebody's got a better one to swap in."

"But does she fly any better?"

"She will now that you're here," said Rivets. "Nothing against Duke. Fine pilot. But you and this ship were made for each other."

"Duke" was Edward Willis, a British soldier and sometime intelligence agent. They'd become friends during the war, and when Jack joined AEGIS, Duke was already there. Along with Charlie "Deadeye" Dalton, another old friend Jack had recruited for his courage and his sharpshooting skills, they formed the *Daedalus II*'s first crew. Duke had taken over in his absence. Jack hoped there wouldn't be any awkwardness about him coming back now.

They heard the telephone in the hangar's comms shack ring. A minute later, Doc shouted, "Jack!"

They hurried back down the ramp to the hangar floor.

"What's the matter, Doc?" asked Rivets.

"That was Mr. Edison," she said. "One of his friends has died. Murdered apparently. He wants us to come right away."

"What about me?" Rivets asked.

"I asked him. He said he wants the ship ready to fly as soon as possible."

Rivets looked relieved. "Best place for me," he said. "She'll be here when you need her."

It was dark by the time the Lincoln pulled into Glenmont Manor. The house was brightly lit and cars lined the driveway. Men patrolled the grounds with tommy guns.

Two familiar figures met them as they approached the front steps. Duke and Deadeye looked like they'd taken good care of themselves in the last year. Duke still had his pencil-thin moustache, and his jacket and tie strongly suggested a military uniform even though he hadn't been in the military since the war ended. His ever-present officer's cap was perched at a rakish angle atop his dark hair. Doc used to say that Duke dressed the way he did solely to justify wearing that cap, which she claimed was the source of his matinee-idol good looks. Without the cap to pull his look together, she joked, he'd actually be kind of plain. Duke tolerated teasing from Doc, but from no one else.

Charlie Dalton, on the other hand, was wearing a crisply pressed suit. He even looked at ease in it, though Jack knew perfectly well that he hated it. Deadeye was of Cherokee ancestry, lean and wiry, with dark hair and faintly olive skin. When the two of them had been in Italy a few years ago, fighting fascist militia groups, Deadeye had been able to pass for Italian. At least as long as he kept his mouth shut. Jack knew his calm exterior was a mask. Deadeye would be restlessly scanning the surroundings, looking for threats. If something happened, he was usually the first one to spot it and react.

Together, they made a heck of a crew. He'd enjoyed his time away from the hustle of AEGIS operations, getting to know his new family. But he'd missed these men too, good friends and trusted companions. They traded hugs and handshakes all around.

"Glad to see you both back," said Deadeye. "We can use you."

"That we can," Duke agreed. "We'll catch up later. Mr. Edison wanted to see you the moment you arrive."

They all went inside, and Duke knocked on the doors to the main parlor. Jack heard what sounded like a contentious meeting going on behind them. After a moment, Thomas Edison himself emerged, and Duke and Deadeye went in and closed the door.

"Let's go across the hall," said Edison. "I could use a break from in there. Nobody can agree on what to do."

"What's the crisis, sir?" Jack asked.

"Soon enough," said Edison. "Soon enough. It's good to have you back with us, Jack. Dorothy." He led them into a side room and closed the door. Jack thought he looked tired, noticeably older than he had a year ago.

"Eamon Cobb died this afternoon," said Edison.

Jack knew the name. "I'm sorry to hear it, sir," he said.

"He was murdered," Edison said. "Poisoned, they think, though no one's identified the poison."

Jack glanced over at Doc, and her expression told him all he needed to know. Poison was a sore subject with her.

"And he's not the first," Edison said. "There have been three other deaths while you were away. All important industrialists or financiers. And Eamon Cobb was a friend. God knows he could be a stubborn old bastard, but he helped AEGIS. His company made that foam steel that's going into your airframe."

"What do you want us to do, sir?" Jack asked.

"AEGIS can't be a tool for my personal quests," Edison said. He walked to the wall, lined with photographs of himself with famous and powerful men, the men who had helped him build AEGIS. "But these were friends of mine. And Dorothy, I know your expertise in rare poisons all too well. I want you to investigate this. I want to know who's doing this, and I want them stopped."

"We're on it," Doc said, her voice firm.

"It's the right thing for AEGIS to do," said Jack.

Edison turned to face them. "Thank you," he said. "The Bureau of Investigation is handling this. They're at the estate now. I pulled some strings, and they've agreed to brief you as a favor to me. You can use the Lincoln. Find out what you can, and take whatever action you feel is appropriate from there."

"Understood, sir," said Jack.

"As you can imagine, this has thrown a wrench into AEGIS business," Edison added. "I should get back in there and keep everyone on course. But I want to know what you learn."

Outside, they walked back down the drive toward the Lincoln.

"Are you sure about this?" Jack asked. He'd missed the excitement, but they had a daughter to think about now.

"Positive," said Doc. Her voice was tight, but Jack heard her determination. "I'm sure I'm not the only one with a hunch about who we'll find behind this."

"Let's keep an open mind," Jack murmured. "See what the facts say." But he knew what Doc was thinking because he'd thought it himself. And if that hunch turned out to be right, well, then they both had scores to settle.

- CHAPTER 2 -

It was almost midnight by the time Jack and Doc made it back across the city again and out to Long Island, but the Cobb Estate was a bright beehive of activity. At the gates they identified themselves to a patrolman who called up to the house then passed them through and told them where to park. The place was packed with police cars, ambulances, and unmarked vans. Portable floodlights swept the ground as a long line of uniformed policemen moved slowly across the front lawn searching for evidence. Jack parked the Lincoln where he'd been told, and another officer was waiting to take them inside.

They followed him through the open doors and into a large room off the front hall. Gun cases and the mounted heads of wild game lined the walls. A group of men in suits and trench coats were clustered at the far end of the room. They stood beside a heavy mahogany billiards table and argued in hushed voices. They took no notice of the new arrivals.

"Agent Shelby," the officer said after a few uncomfortable moments.

The men turned as one and stared in annoyance.

"Who's this?" said one of them—Jack assumed he must be Agent Shelby.

"Edison's people," said the officer.

"Yeah, all right." He sighed and gestured them over. "Come on, then."

The others drifted off with a few incurious glances at Jack and Doc, and the cop followed them out. Clearly they weren't wanted here. Jack could sympathize. These men had a job to do. In their place he could understand why they'd be annoyed to have a pair of civilians thrust on them to humor some distant bigwig. The best thing to do, he decided, was to be polite and helpful and not waste their time.

"Agent Shelby," Jack said, offering him his hand. "Jack McGraw. This is Doctor Starr. Thanks for agreeing to see us."

"Wasn't my idea," said Shelby. "Word came down to show you every courtesy. So here you are. And let me say that's a really nice tie you're wearing."

Jack laughed it off. "We're not here to get in your way," he said. "We may be able to help. Doc here is an expert in rare poisons."

"We also have some thoughts about who might have done this," said Doc. "Can we see the body?"

"Coroner's already got the body," said Shelby. "And we know who did it." He picked up a sheaf of papers from the billiards table. "Cobb's company was having a dispute with the miners' union in West Virginia," he read. "There was an explosion a few months ago. Some miners were killed. Few more maimed. The labor unions have been up here raising hell ever since."

"Is there evidence connecting that to Cobb's death?" asked Doc.

"Looks pretty clear to me," said Shelby. "Bunch of trade unionists up here, mixing with intellectual socialists. Probably being used as a front for International Communism."

The way he said it, Jack could actually hear the capital letters.

"So he was poisoned by communists?" Jack said in disbelief. "How did they do that?"

"We're working on that," said Shelby. "Two possibilities. One, he was known to make himself a scotch on the rocks every day when he arrived home. His habit was to shut himself in his study with orders not to be disturbed until he finished his drink and came out. That's where he died."

"So they poisoned his scotch," said Jack.

"Or the ice," Doc added.

"Except the bottle was half empty," said Shelby. "So it wasn't poisoned somewhere else and sent in here. He'd drank plenty of shots from it already. That means whether it was the scotch or the ice, they would have had to get into his study to plant the poison, and there's no evidence they did that. No signs of a break in, and the staff hasn't seen any strange characters hanging around."

"Well, that's conclusive," Jack muttered under his breath.

Shelby rolled on without noticing. "Second possibility. There was a scuffle outside Cobb's office when he was leaving. He was hit by a thrown rock. Broke the skin. We're thinking the poison was introduced that way. Coroner will tell us for sure."

Jack couldn't believe what he was hearing. "I just want to be sure I've got this. Your theory is that communists threw a poisoned rock at him?"

Shelby looked at him, his lips a tight line across his face.

"Not really their style, is it?" Jack added. "They'd lean more toward shooting him or blowing up his car in my experience."

"We're Federal agents, Mr. McGraw," he said at last. "We know what we're doing. This isn't the first of these murders we've investigated."

"Mr. Edison said this is the fourth?" Doc offered.

"That's right," said Shelby, keeping his glare on Jack. "And what they had in common was that all of them were major league businessmen. What does that tell you? Who'd want to kill America's leading capitalists? Trade unionists and socialist agitators, that's who."

"May I offer an alternative theory?" Doc said softly. Jack recognized that tone, and he knew what it meant when she started speaking so formally. He prepared to rein her in if she seemed about to get them both arrested.

"By all means," said Shelby. "Educate me, Doctor."

"The victims had something else in common," Doc said. "They were supporters of an organization called the American Enterprise Group for International Security, or AEGIS. Thomas Edison formed it to protect America and promote world peace following the war. Henry Ford was a founding member, Harvey Firestone. So were the other victims, and so was Eamon Cobb."

"Yeah, I'm sure these guys all go to the same parties," Shelby offered.

Doc ignored him and went on. "AEGIS has enemies. Chief among them the Astrum Argentum, or Silver Star, a secret society founded by a British occultist named Aleister Crowley. The Silver Star has immense resources and an equally immense thirst for power. We've thwarted their plans on numerous occasions, and eliminating AEGIS is their first priority."

Jack put a hand gently on her forearm.

"And while exotic poisons may not be a major weapon in the arsenal of the United Mine Workers, I can assure you, Agent Shelby," Doc said, slowly and distinctly, "from direct personal experience, that they are very much part of the Silver Star's."

She fell silent and leveled a defiant glare.

"Thank you, Doctor," Shelby said after a moment. "We'll keep that in mind. Did you have any other questions?"

Doc started to say something, but Jack squeezed her arm and she let it drop.

"Can you tell us the time of death?" Jack asked.

Shelby flipped through his papers. "Cobb arrived home about half past four, went straight into the study, and shut the door. When he hadn't come out by a quarter to six, the Butler knocked and let himself in. He found the body. So sometime between then."

Jack nodded. "Thank you, Agent Shelby. We'll get out of your way. If we have anything to offer, we'll be in touch."

"You do that," said Shelby. "Have a nice night." He slapped the sheaf of papers back down on the billiards table and walked out of the room. "Make sure these two make it back to their car okay," he said to an officer in the doorway.

After the officer saw them outside, they walked back to the Lincoln.

"Bureau of Investigation," Doc said in disgust. "What an idiot! You should have let me take him apart."

"He's the idiot in charge," Jack observed. "We want anything out of them, we need to get him on our side."

"I don't want him on our side! He's a liability!"

Jack shrugged. "It doesn't exactly sound like they're on the verge of a breakthrough," he admitted. As long as Shelby and his agents remained obsessed with their communist agitators theory, he doubted they'd turn up anything useful.

"We need to call the Coroner's office," Doc said as Jack started up the Lincoln and headed back down the drive. "At least the autopsy should tell us something."

∞

The next morning Doc called the County Coroner, who proved eager to consult with someone with Doc's experience with poisons.

They parked around the corner from the nondescript brick building and met an orderly who led them through the offices and downstairs where the morgue and the autopsy rooms were located.

"This is as far as we go," the orderly said at the bottom of the stairs. A beige hallway stretched ahead of them with double doors on either side. But the hallway was blocked by an empty gurney with a hand-lettered sign that read "Danger, Keep Out."

"What's going on?" Jack asked.

"Doc Finley will take you back," the orderly said. He shouted, "Doc! They're here!" Then he retreated back up the stairs. Jack thought he'd never seen someone so eager to get out of a hallway.

A pair of doors on the far side of the gurney opened, and a figure stepped out into the hallway. It took Jack a moment to realize what he was looking at. The County Coroner looked like some medieval plague doctor in a floor-length rubber apron, rubber gloves, and a gas mask.

"Doctor Starr," he said, his voice an eerie drone through the mask. "Glad you could come. Edwin Finley. Good to meet you." He stopped at the other side of the gurney and took off the gas mask. Finley was a man of about forty, Jack estimated. He was stocky, his hair just starting to go gray at the temples. He looked like he hadn't gotten much sleep.

"Doctor Finley, what in the world's going on?" Doc asked. "Is this that dangerous?"

"I have no idea," said Finley. "So I'm not taking any chances. Whatever we're dealing with...well, you wouldn't want to get it on you. You'll find aprons and masks on your right there. Suit up and I'll show you what we've got. Got to warn you, it's not pretty."

As promised, they found more gas masks and protective gear in boxes in a small room across the hall. Jack and Doc quickly put them on and rejoined Finley. He led them into the autopsy room.

Jack's peripheral vision was lost to the mask. It smelled of chemicals and felt hot and sticky against his skin. Men had worn these in the trenches while they waited, wondering if a gas attack would come, and whether the mask would really protect them if it did. It must have been torture.

The body was on a table in the center of the room, but it took Jack a moment to realize that. "Oh," Doc said suddenly. "Oh, that's horrible!"

The body of Eamon Cobb was a deep purple, almost black. His clothing had been removed, and he lay on his back. Jack saw long, deep cracks in his extremely swollen skin. He looked like something that had been cooked over a low fire. Jack had seen his share of horrible things, both in the war and elsewhere. Not much frightened him. But the thought of something that could do that to a man from the inside out..."A poison did this?" he asked.

"That's what the government people tell me," said Finley. "But I don't know what to think. Apparently he went from perfectly healthy to this within about an hour at the outside. That's no poison I ever heard of. Not that we deal with a lot of poisonings around here, accidental or otherwise. But if it's not, honestly, I can't even tell you why the man's dead."

"There's no localized focus of damage?" Doc asked. "It had to be introduced to his body somewhere and then spread from there, right?"

"Heh," Finley let out a breath. "Abdominal cavity looks like a bomb went off in there. Organs are practically melted." He turned to a wheeled side table nearby and read from a notebook that lay there. "Massive, generalized tissue damage prevents identification of point of origin. Extreme metabolic acidosis with subsequent internal and external blistering."

"Acid buildup in his tissues," Doc translated for Jack. "That might explain some of the swelling, but not that much."

"Look at his wrist," Finley said. "Swelled around his watchband until his skin tore. We had to cut the watch off him. I'm assuming massive hyperthermia as well. Though I don't have a reason for it."

He flipped a page of the notebook. "It spread through the circulatory system. One of the few things I can still make out is hardening and discoloration of blood vessels, right down to the capillaries. But it had to be a lot faster than the speed of circulation."

"So it wasn't physically carried through the bloodstream to new parts of the body," Doc mused. "It...it cascaded! It was a chemical process. That's how it worked so quickly."

"I don't follow," said Jack. He noted that Doctor Finley said nothing.

"Most poisons only harm tissue they come into direct contact with. That can still be fatal, of course. Cardiac agents shut down the heart. Muscle relaxants can paralyze the diaphragm and stop breathing. But those are secondary effects. The poison itself is very localized. Think about a snake bite. The damage is worst at the bite site, and it spreads slowly from there."

"This didn't work like that," said Finley. "I mean look at him. This wrecked his whole body, and it did it fast. So you're saying it's a chemical reaction. In the body itself?"

"It's got to be." Doc was getting into her subject, Jack saw. She was pacing back and forth as ideas spilled out of her. "That's the only way it could happen so fast. It sets off something in the victim's body and then that reaction spreads on its own. My god, a fatal dose could be microscopic! So what happens next? There would be an initial heat flush. Maybe nervous system convulsions."

"Or maybe outright paralysis," said Finley. "This much acid unleashed in his tissues, it had to hurt like hell. He should have been screaming bloody murder but nobody heard anything. So I'm thinking he couldn't."

They fell silent. Like him, Jack assumed, they couldn't help imagining what a horrible death they were describing. Jack didn't like to think that someone would deliberately do that to another human being. Unfortunately, he knew of people who were all too willing to use something that awful against innocent victims. He was more convinced than ever that they would find the Silver Star at the bottom of this.

It was Doctor Finley who finally spoke. "I don't like to admit it, but I'm out of my depth here. I was really hoping you folks could help. Have you ever seen anything like this, Doctor Starr?"

"I'm sorry," said Doc. "Believe me, I'd remember."

"I bet," said Finley. "I know I will."

"Can we have a copy of your report, Doctor?" Doc asked.

"Of course. Though I don't know that it's going to do you much good. But I'm done here. Government wants me to box him up and ship him off to the Army Hospital in Washington. They can deal with him."

They left the room behind and removed the protective gear. When they came upstairs to Finley's office, they found him on the telephone. He waved for them to come in.

"Yes, sir, here they are now," he said, "just a moment."

He put his hand over the receiver and said excitedly. "It's Thomas Edison! He wants to talk to you!"

Jack took the phone. "Yes, sir, what is it?"

"Jack, I'm glad I caught you," said Edison. "I just got a call from a friend of mine, J. Elling Ponderby. Owns West State Chemical. Can you get over to his place right away?"

"We're just wrapping up here. What's going on?"

"He heard AEGIS has investigators on the case so he gave me a call," said Edison. "He says he's the poisoners' next target."

- CHAPTER 3 -

The Ponderby estate wasn't so different from the Cobb estate, Jack thought. It was just a little farther out on Long Island and a little farther back from the road. At first glance the grounds looked like forest, but Jack soon realized the place had been carefully designed by a landscape architect to give the illusion of wilderness. It was art whose whole purpose was to conceal itself.

The house looked like a castle set in a clearing. It was gray stone with peaked roofs and intricate leaded windows. The lawn around it was perfectly manicured, rolling gently past scattered topiaries until it blended into the landscaped wilderness.

"Quite a place," said Doc, looking up at the gargoyles on the roof. "Maybe one day we'll have a place like this," she added with a grin.

"Oh don't talk like that," said Jack. "We've got plenty of good years left."

Doc laughed and slapped his arm affectionately. "It's not a tomb, Jack."

"If you say so," said Jack.

Ponderby's butler answered the door and led them through cavernous halls to a pair of closed doors. He rapped, and a thin, reedy voice came from inside.

"Who is it?"

"Captain McGraw and Doctor Starr, sir," the butler called out. "Mr. Edison sent them, as you requested."

"Did he? Did he just? So you know Edison then? Know him well?"

"I think so," Jack shouted back.

"Well, then. If you know Tom Edison, tell me about his tattoo!"

Jack looked to Doc and mouthed, "tattoo?" Doc sighed and nodded.

"Five dots," she called back. "Four in a square with the fifth in the center, like a die. On his right forearm."

Jack looked at her in amazement. Doc just shook her head in exasperation. "Long story."

"Where'd he get it done, then?" came the voice.

"Did it himself," Doc shouted back. "Experimenting with his electric pen."

Jack heard the door latch click. "You can let them in, Phipps."

The doors opened into a library lined with floor to ceiling bookshelves. At the far end French doors looked out onto the back yard. A large desk sat near the doors, and various chairs and smaller writing desks were scattered around. Jack liked the room. It looked comfortable, lived in.

J. Elling Ponderby stood near the bookshelves, pretending to read from a book he'd taken down. He turned as if just noticing them. As if none of that strange exchange through the library doors had taken place.

"Ah, you must be Captain McGraw and Doctor Starr," Ponderby said, returning the book to the shelf. "So good of you to come. Welcome."

Ponderby was in his 60s, Jack thought. A reed thin man with sparse, gray hair. He moved with a delicate grace, and though Jack was hardly one to keep up with fashion, he recognized that Ponderby's suit was well out of date.

"Most charmed, Doctor, most charmed," Ponderby said, taking Doc's hand in his and performing a slight bow before releasing it.

"Mr. Edison said you're in danger, sir," Jack said. "What can we do to help?"

"I didn't realize there were others at first," Ponderby answered. "When Carter died, I wondered. And when they got Wolcott in Pittsburgh, then I knew. But what could I do? The police are useless. Couldn't find a lost hat. But when I heard Edison had his people on the case. Well..."

"Maybe if you started at the beginning, Mr. Ponderby," Doc said gently.

"Yes, yes, of course." Ponderby paced around the room as he spoke.

"I received a letter nearly a month ago. Unsigned. But full of dire warnings of a horrible, agonizing death if I didn't do as it said. They claimed they had created a terrible poison. Colorless, flavorless, undetectable by any chemical test. More deadly than anything heretofore known. Terrible agony and certain death if I didn't meet their demands."

"What did they want you to do?" Jack asked.

"They wanted to dictate the management of my company!" said Ponderby. "They knew all about certain research projects that I'd thought were secret. Still need to work out how they're getting their information from inside my company. But they said if I didn't abandon those projects and destroy all the associated research, I'd be murdered."

"And did you do what they said?"

Ponderby looked shocked. "Heavens, no! Let those scoundrels tell me how to run my company? Where would I be? Where would it stop?"

"Then they didn't follow through on their threat?" said Doc.

Ponderby snickered. "Oh, I don't doubt their intentions, my dear, but I'm too clever for them! All sorts of things can go wrong in this world. Fires, earthquakes, civil disturbance. All sorts of trouble. A wise man's always prepared."

He grinned at them, then dashed to the bookshelves and pulled out a particular volume. There was a grinding noise, and a whole section of books slid backwards and out of the way.

"Look," said Ponderby. "Look how I fooled them!"

The hidden door revealed a bare-walled chamber stacked high with crates. "My emergency cache," said Ponderby. "Preserved food and clean water from a spring in the Catskills. Enough to sustain me for months. I've been living off these supplies since the letter came.

Nothing else has passed my lips. There's no other food in the house now. The staff eat elsewhere. They're under orders to let nobody in. Ha! Let them try and poison me."

Jack decided Ponderby was about half crazy. But he had to admit he was clever too.

"But that won't last forever," said Doc. "We have to stop them."

"Indeed," said Ponderby. "I was relieved to hear Edison had someone on this. Tell me what you know about this business."

"Not much, I'm afraid, sir," Jack said. "Mr. Edison brought us in last night. We went to the Cobb estate."

"Poor Eamon," said Ponderby. "You've seen the body then?"

"We have," said Doc. "They're not bluffing. Whatever killed Mr. Cobb...it wasn't pleasant."

"We didn't have a chance to learn much more," Jack added. "The government has agents on the case. They seem to think it was socialist agitators."

"Bah," Ponderby sniffed. "Bureau of Investigation. I have a letter from them somewhere. No better than the police."

Suddenly Jack heard the thundering report of a shotgun. The French doors exploded inward and showered the room with glass.

Jack ducked and drew his .45 automatic. He glanced over and saw Doc diving for the floor, unhurt.

Ponderby stood in the middle of the room with a surprised look on his face.

"Are you hit?" Jack shouted.

"No, I don't think so," said Ponderby softly. "Just a nick from the glass perhaps? Oh...oh my."

He turned to face them, and Jack saw a hypodermic dart sticking out of his chest. Doc saw it at the same moment. She gasped and looked to Jack with a horrified expression.

Jack ran to the wreckage of the French doors, shattered glass crunching beneath his feet. Peering around the ruined door frame, he saw two figures vanishing into the woods.

"Stay with him!" he called to Doc. Then Jack sprinted across the lawn in pursuit.

He crossed the lawn until it gave way to forest, then he dodged between trees and ran down a grassy path marked out by carefully placed shrubs. For all its apparent wildness, this place was a park, designed to be easily navigated. After a few hundred yards, he broke into a clearing around a pond. The two men were there on the far side of the water. Jack snapped off a shot but missed. One of the assassins spun and leveled a Thompson gun at him. Jack's reflexes took over, and he dove to the side. He hit the ground and rolled as bullets shredded the foliage where he'd been. Then the gunner turned and vanished into the trees again. Jack sprang up and followed.

The landscape had been designed with such skill that Jack was surprised when he suddenly came upon the wall at the edge of the estate. The attackers had rolled a large stone against it to help them get back over, and Jack saw one of them atop the wall. He aimed and fired, but the man dropped off the other side of the wall, and Jack's shot only nicked the mortar where he'd been.

Jack jammed his .45 into his pocket and ran forward. He bounded off the stone and caught the top of the wall, pulling himself up. On the other side, Ponderby's carefully crafted forest gave way to a narrow roadway and marshy flatland beyond it. Jack levered himself over the wall and dropped down.

As he got to his feet, he heard a car engine roar to life, then tires on gravel. He dashed to the road just in time to see a dark gray Packard fishtail as it wheeled around. He emptied his .45 at it but only managed to punch several bullets into the bodywork as the car sped away.

Jack turned and ran back down the road toward the estate's main entrance. He remembered a garage set into the perimeter wall near the gate. He just hoped Ponderby had something there that was fast enough to catch a Packard with a head start.

He was breathing hard by the time he reached the garage. He sprinted across the pine needle-strewn ground and threw open a small side door. Inside he stopped, hands on his thighs, recovering his breath, and smiled to himself. A row of cars stretched out before him, each more expensive than the last. But what caught Jack's eye was the motorcycle right in front of him. It was a brand new Harley Davidson JD, olive drab with a low slung seat, teardrop tank, and the new V-twin engine. It looked fast, and Jack knew it was. Jack had no idea why it was here. He couldn't imagine Ponderby riding it. But it was exactly what he needed.

Jack slapped a full magazine into his .45, then opened the nearest set of bay doors. He was turning back to the bike when a mechanic ran in from behind the garage. He wore grease stained coveralls and gripped a heavy wrench.

"What do you think you're doing?" he shouted and advanced toward Jack, brandishing the wrench.

"I...Mr. Ponderby's..." Jack shrugged. "Ah, gosh, I sure am sorry," he said. "But I don't have time to explain."

Then he laid the man out with a solid right cross. The mechanic collapsed in a heap and the wrench clattered away across the floor. Jack started up the bike and took off.

The Harley's engine sang as he raced down the narrow road, past stands of pine. He passed a few small houses and a kid on a bicycle who whooped as Jack flew by. He didn't see the Packard, but he was pretty sure this road ran straight back to the city. That's where they'd be headed, Jack thought. They probably didn't think he could follow them. If he was lucky, they might even be driving slowly to avoid attention. They had perhaps a five minute head start on him when he set out. He opened up the throttle to see how much of that lead he could wear away. Several more miles passed, but Jack didn't see anyone else on the road at all.

Finally he glimpsed the Packard as he shot through a tiny village, past a post office and a handful of small stores. Heads turned as he roared by, but Jack's focus was on the car ahead. He was closing the gap. Past the village they came into a long, empty stretch of straight road with scrub pine forest on either side. He had them.

Jack drew his pistol and prepared to take them on. He remembered they had at least the Thompson and a shotgun in the car. He'd close fast, then take out a tire or perhaps fire at the driver. This would be tricky.

Then the car did something Jack hadn't seen before. The driver braked hard and deliberately threw the car into a skid. The back end slid out and the tires screamed as the car whipped around until it stopped dead in the road, facing him. Just as quickly, it accelerated straight toward him. Jack saw the passenger lean out with the Thompson. He opened up and Jack felt a round drill past him, too close. He fired back with his .45 and put a round into the engine compartment and another through the windshield. But he was outgunned, and the Packard was a ton and a half of mass charging straight at him. Suddenly, his plan didn't seem like such a good one.

Then a shadow overtook him on the pavement. He heard the stutter of Lewis guns and saw the bullets stitch a line down the pavement and rake the Packard. The Packard's windshield exploded into a storm of shattered glass and the engine gave off thick, black smoke. Jack braked hard and brought the bike to a stop as the Packard veered off the road. It ran into the woods and slammed into a tree with a sickening crunch.

Jack looked up as the *Daedalus* swept by overhead. Jack had never been so glad to see the airship appear out of nowhere. He got off the bike and ran toward the car. The engine had caught fire and the flames were spreading quickly. The driver slumped unmoving over the steering wheel, a bloody mess. But the passenger staggered out the other side and ran into the woods. Jack followed. He spotted spatters of blood on the grass.

Jack kept his distance and let the man run until he wore himself out. He was limping, and his long black coat dragged on tree branches. He'd lost the tommy gun, but he fired a pistol blindly over his shoulder. Jack saved his bullets. The man wouldn't get away from him.

Eventually the trees ended in a sharply drawn line, giving way to cleared fields. Perhaps twenty feet past the tree line was a wire fence. The assassin realized he was out of room to run. He whirled and fired at Jack, but his shot went wide. Jack's two shots didn't miss. The man stumbled back and collapsed into the fence.

On the other side of the fence, the *Daedalus* was coming in to land in the empty field. Even before the ship touched down, Deadeye sprang down from the cockpit hatch and sprinted toward Jack with his Winchester carbine ready. But Jack was focused on the body of the assassin. It began to smoke and bubble. There was a horrible chemical smell. Jack backed off and turned away.

"You okay, Jack?" Deadeye shouted. "Doc called and said you were in trouble. Lucky we found you out here!"

"I'm okay," Jack said quietly. "I owe you one."

"Another one," Deadeye replied with a grin. He flipped the safety on his Winchester and let it hang at his side. Then he noticed the body. Nothing was left of the corpse but smoking bones and clothes. The sleeve of the man's black coat blew in the breeze like some horrible scarecrow. Jack knew they'd find the same thing back at the Packard. Nothing would be left of the driver but this.

Jack and Deadeye traded a dark look. They'd seen this before, and it could mean only one thing. Once more they were up against the Silver Star.

- CHAPTER 4 -

By the time the Bureau of Investigation appeared on the scene, the Packard was a blackened, smoldering ruin. Jack and the crew had put out the fire as quickly as they could with the ship's extinguishers. But the driver had been dead even before the fire. There was nothing to recover from the car.

Jack checked the pockets of the other assassin's empty clothes. In addition to the gun, he found a wallet with some fake ID cards and a couple dollars, a pack of Lucky Strikes and a Zippo lighter, and a folded sheet of heavy paper that turned out to be the menu from a diner in Brooklyn. Jack knew the place. They made a really good cup of coffee. On the back of the menu, he found several rows of five-digit numbers, written quickly with a dull pencil.

He stuck it in his pocket. Duke was the codes expert. Maybe he'd be able to make something of it.

Then they'd called back a report to an AEGIS operator at the airfield. Some phone calls had been made, and more radio messages came back, so Jack knew what to expect. Doc was unhurt, but Ponderby was dead. The Bureau was on the scene, but the Agent in charge was on his way to Jack's location. Jack had a good idea who that would be.

When Jack saw the line of cars approaching, he and Deadeye were standing by the edge of the road. "Better let me handle these guys," he told Deadeye. "Get back to the ship and tell Duke to take her up to a hundred feet or so and stay there."

Deadeye raised an eyebrow. "Trouble?"

"I just know who's coming," Jack said. "If she's on the ground, well, I don't want him trying to commandeer the ship."

Deadeye nodded and vanished into the trees.

Two Bureau cars pulled up in a line, followed by Doc in the Lincoln, and another couple Bureau cars bringing up the rear.

Doc ran to him, and he held her. "Oh Jack," she cried, "it was horrible. There was nothing I could do. I just watched him die. It was so awful." Her voice caught, and she buried her face in Jack's shoulder.

Agent Shelby was striding toward them with a dismayed expression. Jack imagined Shelby thought a crime scene was no place for a woman, and that this display proved his point. But Jack knew how strong Doc was. He understood how hard this would have hit her. Her husband, Col. Dirk Starr, had become an AEGIS operative after the war. He'd been on a mission five years ago—a mission to retrieve the plans for the *Daedalus*' engines, in fact— when he'd been poisoned by Silver Star operatives. It had been a slow poison, and Doc had struggled desperately to save him, but in the end, she failed. She'd been forced to watch for months as her husband slowly succumbed, all her medical knowledge useless. Jack knew this case must be bringing up painful memories for her. The fact that the Silver Star's involvement was now beyond doubt would just make it worse. Jack wished he could spare her, but she had to know.

"We know who's behind this," Jack said over her shoulder to Shelby.

Doc looked up at him, and he nodded. Doc released her grip on him. She adjusted her jacket and stood beside him, resolute.

"We suspected after Cobb," Jack added. "But now we know."

Shelby studied what remained of the Packard. The front end was crushed against the massive tree. The fire had blackened its bark, but Jack and Deadeye had put the fire out before it could spread. The car was smoking and popping as it cooled. The paint had been burned away, and bullet holes could be seen in the bare metal.

"What the hell are you packing, McGraw? A machi..."

Then the huge mass of the *Daedalus* rose above the trees. Shelby and the other agents looked up, astonished. The ship hung just over the trees, gleaming in the late afternoon sun.

"That's the *Daedalus*," Jack said, trying not to smile. The ducted engines whirred softly. Vanes shifted and the ship slowly spun until she was facing them.

"Holy moly," Shelby said softly. "Edison's got his own airship?"

"AEGIS," said Doc.

After another moment, Shelby looked away and summoned back his air of disdain. Jack realized Shelby wore it like a suit of armor and used it to keep others off balance.

"Message said there were two," Shelby said. Where's the other one?"

"Dead," Jack said. "I'll show you."

"So you're saying I've got no suspect to question?"

"You wouldn't anyway," said Doc. "Nobody's ever taken a Silver Star agent alive."

Shelby sighed. "Okay, one more time. Who?"

"The *Astrum Argentum*," Doc said. "The Silver Star. They're an occult organization led by an English magician named Aleister Crowley. Crowley's a madman, and the Silver Star is his personal army."

"I'm sorry," Shelby said. "Did you say magician?"

"That's right," said Doc. "He started out in the Golden Dawn; that's an occult secret society. But they kicked him out, so he started his own. Its sole mission is to increase Crowley's power, both worldly and supernatural."

Shelby looked at them with blank incomprehension. "Maybe you should show me the other one. Becker, you're with me."

Jack led them into the trees. Doc, Shelby and another agent—Becker, apparently—followed. "And get a wire off to Albany for those plates," Shelby shouted to another agent.

"Crowley finds angry, desperate people," said Jack as he led the way through the woods. "The war left plenty of them around. And they're easy pickings. He offers them whatever they need most. Sometimes that's not much at all. He's got a lot of support in Germany, but he recruits around the world. Soldiers, occultists, engineers. And they're getting bolder. They've always worked from the shadows before. But this is an open assault."

Shelby sighed. "Okay, so this Crowley is a moon bat with a bunch of moon bat followers, and they all get together and dance around bonfires or whatever they do. Why do you think they're behind this?"

"Because both the assassins dissolved," said Jack.

"Dissolved."

"It's what happens when one of them is killed," Doc said. "They just dissolve, in seconds. Nothing's left but clothing and bones. We think it's Crowley absorbing their life essence to bolster his own power."

"Do you people ever listen to yourselves?" said Shelby.

Jack felt his temper starting to rise. "We know what we're doing, Agent Shelby," he said. "More than you do. This isn't a regular murder case, and it's not bloody…socialists. You're out of your depth here. You need our help."

"Uh huh." Shelby let out a long breath and shook his head. Jack was tempted to just punch him, but that obviously wouldn't help.

"Up here," he said instead. "By the fence."

"All right, keep back," Shelby said as they broke out of the trees. He looked up at the *Daedalus* again, then he and Agent Becker approached the remains. Jack and Doc stayed a couple steps back.

"What the hell?" Shelby muttered as he knelt beside the bones. He took a pen from his pocket and gently prodded the grinning skull with its tip. He looked back up at Agent Becker, and Jack could see he was badly shaken. This was obviously well beyond what Shelby was accustomed to.

"Some kind of acid, maybe?" he said quietly. "Those beetles Johnson's always talking about?"

Becker sniffed the air and shook his head. "No acid," he said softly. "Flensing...that would take days." He shook his head again. "I've never seen anything like it."

"Pictures," Shelby said. Becker took a Kodak Vest Pocket folding camera from a pocket of his overcoat and opened it up. He started shooting photos of the bones and the long black jacket blowing in the wind.

"And not a word of this to anybody," Shelby said. "I mean it."

Becker nodded and kept shooting.

Shelby approached Jack and Doc. He didn't seem to know what to say for a moment. At last, he said, "All right, let's say I'm prepared to believe your story. Which I'm not, let me be very clear about that. But for the sake of argument, what would the next step be? How do we find these people?"

Jack bit his lip. "We..."

"We don't know," Doc said. "They set up clandestine cells for a particular mission. They used to operate out of an airship that let them reach almost anywhere in the world."

"Used to," Jack added for emphasis. "Until we blew it up."

"But we don't know where they're based," said Doc. "We weren't even certain this was Silver Star until now."

"Enough," said Shelby. "Enough. You seem like well-meaning folks, and I'll admit there's things going on here that I don't understand. Maybe your sorcerer and his silver whatever are real. Maybe they're not. But right now it doesn't matter. None of this helps me. You can't tell me how to find them. Even if I do find one, I can't question him because he'll just go poof." Shelby mimed it with his fingertips.

Jack had to admit Shelby had a point. At the moment they didn't have much to go on.

"I can't do anything with this. So I'm going to go back to my office now, and I'm going to do what I know how to do. That's police work. Becker, get that bagged up, and we're gone. We're done here, folks. Thanks for your help."

Jack looked up at the *Daedalus* and gave Duke a signal. The ship silently receded into the sky, turning as it rose, and headed west toward New Jersey.

As they walked back, Doc gave Jack a sardonic grin. "That went well."

"At least he's not still going on about trade unions and poisoned rocks."

"Still," Doc said, "I think we've worn out our welcome with Agent Shelby."

Jack drove the Lincoln back toward New York City as the sun settled toward the horizon and the shadows lengthened. They passed small hamlets and scattered marshland in silence.

"He couldn't speak," Doc said suddenly a few miles outside Manhasset. "That happened quickly. Voluntary muscle control was compromised within thirty seconds of onset." Her voice was tight and Jack recognized the detached, clinical turn her words had taken. He reached over and gripped her hand but let her go on.

"Patient was agitated and fearful, in obvious pain. Attempts to speak...failed. Tissue necrosis proceeded with remarkable speed, beginning with the circulatory system, then proceeding to muscle and subcutaneous tissue. Visible symptoms appeared within ninety seconds of exposure. Time from visible onset to death, approximately three and half minutes."

Jack hated seeing her like this. She'd been badly shaken. And he'd run away to chase the killers and left her there with the dying Ponderby. He hadn't been there to keep her from seeing what she'd seen. It was settled, Jack decided in that moment. He would stop this. He'd find out what the Silver Star was up to, and he'd put an end to it, no matter what it took.

"All that time," Doc said. "He must have been in incredible pain. He kept trying to reach his desk. He was reaching for one particular drawer. He was looking at me and trying to speak. I opened the drawer for him, and he just...he just died."

"What was in the drawer?"

Doc pulled up the side of her blouse to reveal a sheaf of papers curved against her side. "These. I thought it best if we didn't mention them to Shelby."

Despite himself, Jack smiled. Even with what she was going through, Doc always kept her head and thought three moves ahead. She was amazing.

It reminded him of something. He pulled the diner menu from his pocket and showed her the scrawled rows of numbers.

"Great minds think alike," he said. "Let's go have a talk with Mr. Edison."

Once again it was dark when they reached Edison's home in West Orange. This time, Edison himself met them at the front door.

"I heard about Ponderby," he said. "You'd better come through and tell me about it."

Edison led them through the reception room to the conservatory. It was a long room with a wraparound wall of windows that ended in a rounded prow like a ship's. It gave an excellent view across the estate's grounds. Duke, Deadeye, and Rivets were already there. Edison poured them iced tea from a pitcher, and they both told him what they'd seen.

"I guess we'd best take a look at those papers," Edison said when Doc had finished her report.

He spread the papers out on a table and they all crowded around to look. There were memos and drawings, what looked like chemical equations. Jack recognized the AEGIS classification stamp on several of them. They reminded him of the dinner menu, and he took it from his pocket.

"Duke, can you make anything of this?"

Duke studied the menu, then raised an eyebrow. Then he plucked the sheet from Jack's hand and retreated to a chair in the corner.

"I recognize these," Edison said. "Ponderby was working on a project for us. He was looking for a way to combine hydrogen and helium into a gas mixture for your airship. We hoped the right mixture would reduce the fire danger while keeping most of the lifting properties of the hydrogen. It would let the *Daedalus* fly higher and farther, while carrying more weight. He was making headway, until this."

Then he discovered a folded sheet slipped in among the chemical formulas and opened it. It was a simple typed letter without a signature.

"We know you are working on a hybrid lifting gas for AEGIS," Edison read. "End this project immediately, and cease all cooperation with AEGIS or face your destruction. We have a poison more deadly than any known to your science. There is no place you can hide from us. There is no one we cannot reach. Destroy all work on the hybrid gas or you will suffer unspeakable agony and death. For proof, look to Carter and Wolcott."

Edison turned and looked at Jack and Doc. "Simon Carter. The Wall Street genius. He was the first victim. No one was meant to know he was the main financial controller for AEGIS. Wolcott developed the hydraulic fluids for high altitude flight."

"They're all working with AEGIS, aren't they?" said Jack. "All the victims."

"In one way or another, said Edison. "But that's true of most major industrial concerns in America. In Europe too, for that matter. But this clears up some things. In the last month, AEGIS supporters have started withdrawing funding and canceling contracts. I haven't been able to get a good explanation until now."

"The Silver Star's coming for them," said Doc. "They're terrifying them with this poison, or else just killing them outright."

"They're attacking AEGIS by hacking at our roots," said Edison. "We have to fight back. AEGIS won't fall right away, but we can't last forever without money and technology."

"But now we know how to find them," said Jack. "Those men who pulled out of AEGIS got letters just like Ponderby's, and it scared them so bad that they knuckled under. But the Silver Star has to keep an eye on them to make sure they keep doing what they're told. We know who they are. So we stake them out, and sooner or later we spot their operatives."

Doc nodded. "It could work. Especially if we can talk one of them into fighting back. If one of them doesn't do as he's told, that will draw out the Silver Star."

"We're going to ask one of these guys to be bait?" said Jack. "That'll be a tough sell. Especially after they got to Ponderby right in front of us."

"Don't blame yourself, Captain," said Edison. "You did all you could, and you've given us an avenue of investigation. But I agree we shouldn't pressure these men to provoke the Silver Star. They've got families to think of. I can't blame them for doing what they feel they have to do."

"As it happens, we don't need to," Duke announced from his armchair. "I know where they're going. Jack recognized the look of triumph on his face. "Thought I recognized this," he said. "German naval code from the war. They tweaked it a bit, but not enough. German High Command knew we'd broken it. But if I had to guess, I'd say that news didn't make it down to our friends in the Silver Star. It's this first number that gives it away. The five digit groups are pretty standard, but here the first number's always a factor of the—"

"That's great, Duke," Jack said. "What does it say?"

"Oh, yes." Duke shot him a momentary glare, then scribbled a few words on the bottom of the sheet. "Team 1," he read. "Surveillance pattern Schakal—means jackal—surveillance pattern Schakal, T.R. Dorner. Then there's an address in Manhattan."

"Dorner," said Edison. "He's one of ours all right. Corporate attorney, and a darn clever one too. He built a lot of the legal infrastructure. Holding companies, blind trusts, everything we needed to keep AEGIS's inner workings hidden from our enemies. Supposedly ill with some undefined malady that keeps him bedridden. Out of the office. No deputy to handle his affairs with AEGIS."

"Well, I guess we know why," said Doc.

"They're not sure about him," said Jack. "They're watching him. So we'll watch him too. Rotating teams of two."

"How long?" Deadeye asked.

"As long as it takes."

- CHAPTER 5 -

Right after he dove off the roof, it occurred to Jack that his plan was actually extremely risky, and that the direct consequences to him if it did fail would be quite severe. There was something of a pattern in that, he realized in a sudden flash of insight as he plunged through the night air. It went a long way toward explaining the unusual path his life had taken. Then he slammed into the wall, grabbed the drain pipe with both hands, and clung to it for dear life. Well, sure it was risky, he thought, but it worked. And if he kept getting away with things like this, how was he ever going to learn any better?

The roof, the drain pipe, and the wall all belonged to T.R. Dorner. The crew had been watching his Manhattan townhouse for more than a week, waiting for the Silver Star's watchers to appear. Jack had taken a position on the roof, while Doc hid in the shadows of the alley behind the house. It had been a long and boring vigil, but tonight the waiting had finally paid off.

A little after midnight, two men had come up the alley and stopped behind the darkened house. One of them carried a compressed air gun that fired a grappling hook up to the roof as a cable played out behind it. The other wore some kind of boxy pack strapped to his chest. They clipped the cable onto the pack, and with a whine of springs and gears, the man was lifted off the ground and pulled up the wall.

That was when Doc broke from the shadows and charged. The one still on the ground took off, and Doc followed. But the other one had committed himself, Jack realized. He was dangling helplessly from the roof while the device on his chest hauled him up past the first floor windows. Jack's instincts recognized a rare chance to take the man alive. With a little luck, he might be able to stop him from using whatever suicide gimmick Silver Star operatives used—assuming he could get to him before he reached the roof. And that was about as far as Jack had thought it through before he jumped.

The man had been watching his companion flee down the alley, but he looked up in surprise as Jack slammed into the drain pipe. Jack had hoped his momentum would tear the drainpipe free, but it didn't. Jack eyeballed the rising Silver Star agent, judged the angle, and kicked hard against the brick. The pipe ripped away from the wall and carried him downward. The Silver Star agent fumbled for a pistol at his belt but had just gotten it free when Jack collided with him. The gun flew free and clattered down to the alley below. The agent's pack groaned under the added weight, but it held, and Jack hung onto the Silver Star man for dear life as they were both carried up toward the roof.

☙

Doc sprinted down the alley and around the corner. The Silver Star assassin was a dark figure dashing down the street ahead of her, his long coat flapping behind him like a cape. He was making for the darkness and cover of Central Park, a couple blocks away. She kept pace with him.

He dashed across Central Park West, full of traffic even this late at night, and sprang around the hood of a taxi that barely avoided crushing him. The cabby slammed on his brakes and shouted an obscenity after him as Doc flew past behind the taxi. Then she was across the sidewalk and running down the path toward the reservoir. She heard her quarry's footsteps ahead of her and made out his shape in the dark as she rounded a curve. She was gaining on him, and she knew he could hear her coming up behind him.

At the crossing of West Drive, the agent stopped in the pool of light beneath a street lamp and whirled on her. Doc saw a knife blade gleaming in his hand.

She threw herself to the side as the blade flashed past and barely missed her. Doc drew her own knife from a scabbard inside her jacket and went into a fighting stance. They circled each other for a moment in the circle of light, both breathing hard. The agent feinted, then thrust for her heart, but Doc sidestepped and slashed his forearm. She felt the blade slice through his overcoat and shirt, and then the resistance of metal parting flesh. He cried out and jerked his wounded arm away.

Then he surprised her with a left hook. The punch connected with her temple, and she stumbled to one side. As she was recovering her balance, the agent dashed off the path and disappeared into the darkness.

⌘

Jack took another punch to the face as the whining gears hauled them over the edge of the roof. The Silver Star agent had fought furiously to dislodge him, but Jack had no intention of plummeting five stories to the sidewalk. Now they both instinctively clawed their way toward the relative safety of the roof. As they tumbled over the riser, Jack got tangled in the cable and fell on his back.

The Silver Star agent kicked him hard in the ribs, then shrugged off the pack and took off. Jack untangled himself from the cable, got to his feet, and ran after him.

The agent hurdled the riser onto the next house with Jack a few seconds behind. They sprinted across the roof of the next townhouse and then the agent soared over a narrow alley. He hit the roof on the other side, rolled, and was up and running in a heartbeat.

If he can make it, I can make it, thought Jack. Then he was airborne. The yawning chasm flashed by beneath him and he hit the roof and rolled. At the far side of this house, he saw the agent leap down a small drop to the next roof and keep going.

He couldn't keep this up, Jack realized. They were coming up fast on Amsterdam Avenue, and the Silver Star man sure wasn't going to jump that. He had him.

Jack kept up the chase across the roofs of two more townhouses, and then the assassin was out of running room. But he wasn't stopping, Jack realized. The man took something from his coat pocket. At first, Jack thought he was pulling a gun. But instead he cried out, shouting words Jack didn't recognize, and there was a flash of pale green light from his outstretched hand. He veered to the right, sprinting for the edge, and Jack realized he wasn't going to stop.

The Silver Star agent never even slowed. He reached the edge of the roof and leaped into the night, limbs windmilling as he soared through the air. He was trying to make it across the narrower side street instead of Amsterdam itself, and he was aiming not for the roof but for a second floor balcony on the far side. But it was still an impossible jump. No one could have made it.

Even so, the Silver Star man nearly did. Jack pulled up at the edge of the roof and watched in astonishment as the man sailed across the street and past the trees lining the edge of the sidewalk. He reached out for the balcony railing, and his hands barely missed it. He slammed hard into the wall, bounced off, and landed in a broken heap on the sidewalk. Jack watched as he began to smoke and hiss. In moments, a pile of bones and scorched clothes were all that remained.

C03

Jack found Doc a few blocks south at the edge of Central Park. She was walking along the sidewalk on Central Park West, shining her flashlight over the wall into the trees.

"Are you okay?" Jack asked. "What happened?"

"I'm okay," she said more loudly than necessary. "But I lost him." Then she winked and put a finger to her lips.

"Mine didn't make it," Jack said.

Then Doc came close and whispered, "He's heading south."

"All right," Jack said aloud. "Nothing more we can do here. Let's get back."

They waited behind a closed newsstand until a figure emerged from the park a block down and crossed the street. Jack noticed he was clutching his right arm to his chest.

"I cut his arm," Doc whispered as they set off after him. "If we lose him, look for blood."

They trailed him for blocks, past the south end of the park and beyond, into Hell's Kitchen. The wounded man turned down a darkened street that took him toward the river. Jack felt eyes watching them as he and Doc followed from well behind. This was a dangerous part of town. He was confident they could take care of themselves, but they didn't need the distraction right now.

Then their quarry suddenly turned off the street, into a rubble-filled lot on the corner of a narrow alley. He made his way into the wreckage of a burned out building and seemed to vanish.

Doc and Jack traded a look. Then they moved closer to investigate.

The building was a ruin, a collapsed pile of scorched stone and charred support beams. It was the sort of place that could only exist in Hell's Kitchen. Anywhere else in New York, the site would have been cleared almost immediately, and a new building would be halfway complete by now.

They found droplets of blood in a trail leading into the center of the rubble. But there was no sign of the man himself.

"Where the devil did he go?" Jack asked.

"He has to be here somewhere," Doc answered. Then she spotted blood on the stones, black spatters in the dim light. "This way."

They moved slowly, following the trail of drops across the wreckage. The trail led to the shattered remains of a wall and stopped. Beyond it was a massive pile of rubble. There was nowhere else to go. Jack and Doc traded a look.

"He went right through here," said Doc. "There's got to be some kind of hidden door."

Jack was probing the stone with his fingertips. "Well, I can't find it. Maybe in the daylight. We'll come back here with more people and tear this place apart if we have to."

They headed back out of Hell's Kitchen, before someone decided it was worth taking a run at them. Jack decided it was time to talk to Agent Shelby again. And this time, Shelby was going to listen to them.

○8

It was mid-afternoon when Jack and Doc walked into the BOI's offices in upper Manhattan. A receptionist directed them to Agent Shelby's office, and Jack stormed in, ready to settle their differences once and for all. Shelby was at his desk. As Jack and Doc came in, he put down the folder he was reading and stood up.

"Well, McGraw and Starr," he said. Then Jack cut him off.

"Listen, Shelby, I've put up with about all I'm going to from you. We've told you who's behind this, and what they're after. Now we know where to find them, and what you can do about it, so it's damn well time you started listening to us."

"Yeah, I guess it is," said Shelby, to Jack's surprise. "Why don't you two have a seat?"

"I...okay." Jack realized he was disappointed; he'd been eager for a shouting match. But Doc smiled and thanked Shelby and got them into the two chairs in front of Shelby's desk. Jack was still trying to figure out what had changed.

"Want to guess where I've been for the last week?" said Shelby as he walked around them and closed the door. "Washington. Turns out the Bureau has quite a file on your Silver Star. It was a couple levels above my clearance, but thanks to you I've gotten read in on it now. Kind of wish I hadn't. So thanks for that."

Shelby sat down behind his desk again. "So I take it you two are with this AEGIS group?"

Jack and Doc said nothing. The *Daedalus* might have been a clue. But apparently nothing was real for Shelby until he'd read it in an official file with "Secret" stamped on it.

Shelby let a moment pass, then went on. "Okay. So what is it you came here to tell me?"

They described what they'd learned over the past several days and laid out the Silver Star plan as they understood it.

"But we still don't know anything about the poison," Doc concluded. "We need a sample to study. If I can get it into a lab, I may be able to find an antidote."

"We've tracked them back to a secret base in Hell's Kitchen," Jack added. "That's where we'll find them. But we need manpower to go in there and root them out. We need your help."

Shelby nodded and let out a sigh. "And that's going to be a problem," he said, rather sheepishly. "Apparently the Bureau has a strict hands off policy with regard to this Silver Star bunch."

Jack snorted and shook his head in disgust. "You've got to be kidding."

"Hey, I'm with you this time. But there's nothing I can do. Orders are we observe, but we don't engage. That's straight from the Director himself. Like you said, we don't have the experience with this hoodoo stuff. There's no way I can send a team of agents on a raid into Hell's Kitchen against these people."

"Well, that's useful," said Jack.

Shelby bit his lip and took a long breath. "But I might know someone who can help you," he said. He glanced up at the closed door. "I'm taking a hell of a chance here."

"We understand," said Doc. "Nothing leaves this office."

"Go to the Cotton Club in Harlem. Guy that runs the place is called Owney Madden. Tell him Jimmy Franco sent you."

"Owney Madden the bootlegger?" Jack asked in surprise.

"That's the guy," said Shelby.

Jack was astonished. "The BOI's in bed with a gangster?"

"I wouldn't put it quite like that," Shelby said sourly. "Let's say he recognizes that it's in his interests for the Bureau to focus its time and attention on bigger threats than him. So he makes sure we know who those people are, and why they're worse than he is. Your Silver Star guys sound worse to me than someone who runs Canadian whiskey through Hell's Kitchen, just as an example."

"All right," said Jack. "So we go to the Cotton Club and we say Jimmy Franco sent us. What does that buy us?"

"Not a damn thing," Shelby replied. "It should get you through the door and in front of Madden. From there, it's on you. Whether he helps you or not, that's up to him."

- CHAPTER 6 -

Harlem was bustling as Jack and Doc walked into the Cotton Club. The air inside was hot and the jazz beat was thumping. Dancers packed the floor. As Jack and Doc came in, the brass section stood up and swung their horns in time with the music.

Doc was holding Jack's arm, and he could feel her respond. He wished they had time to dance. He knew how much Doc loved dancing, and he would have loved a chance to spend a night out with her, just having fun. But, he reminded himself, this wasn't that night.

He stopped a passing waiter and told him, "We need to talk to the manager."

"I'm sure I can help with anything you folks need," the waiter said with a smile.

Jack didn't smile back. "No, we need to see Madden." He noticed the waiter's eyes widen. "Jack McGraw and Dorothy Starr. Tell him Jimmy Franco sent us."

"Yes, sir," said the waiter. He guided them to a spot away from the doors. "If you'll wait here, I'll speak to the manager."

Jack thanked him. On stage, the band brought their song to a climax, and the announcer took the stage.

"Andy Preer and the Cotton Club Orchestra!" he said, sweeping his arm to take in the bowing musicians. "Let's hear it for them!"

The crowd cheered, and people started shouting requests from the floor. A moment later the band launched into "Sugarfoot Stomp."

Jack tapped his foot to the music until a tall, gaunt man in a tuxedo appeared. He looked Jack and Doc over dubiously.

"Franco sent you?" he snarled.

"That's right," said Jack. "Jimmy Franco."

The man gestured for them to follow. He led them through a side door into a corridor full of busy waiters and chorus girls running everywhere. The music faded to a distant bass hum as they made their way to the back of the club, then down a flight of stairs.

Doc said, "Thank you, Mr...."

"Frenchie."

At the bottom of the stairs, the showgirls and wait staff were replaced by muscled men in cheap suits. They lurked in the corridors and watched Jack and Doc with sullen expressions.

One of them looked Doc over and let out a low, appreciative whistle. Jack stopped and glared back at him. The man met his gaze and took a step forward. Jack squared his shoulders and waited for him to make a move.

Frenchie turned and glared at them. "This way, sir," he said coldly.

The mobster shrugged, stepped away, and leaned against the wall. They moved on down the hall to a heavy oak door with two torpedoes standing guard outside. One of them knocked, then opened the door, and Frenchie led them in.

Owney Madden sat facing the door from behind a heavy oak desk. He was a compact man, sharply dressed, with a slicked back haircut and a white carnation in his lapel. He looked them over for a moment, then said, "Jimmy Franco, huh?"

"That's right," said Jack.

Madden sighed and waved their guide away. "So you're McGraw. And Starr. All right. Thanks, Frenchie."

Frenchie left with one more dubious look at Jack, and closed the door behind him. Madden stood up and walked around the desk, his hands outstretched.

"I don't know what the hell Shelby thinks he's doing, sending goddamn strangers my way now," he said. The words sounded like they were meant to be shouted in anger, but Madden's voice sounded warm and friendly. "But it sure is a pleasure to meet you, my dear." Madden took Doc's hands in his for a moment and gave her a winning smile. "Welcome to the Cotton Club."

"I don't think Agent Shelby's going to make a habit of it," Doc said. "Ours is an unusual case."

"Well, have a seat," said Madden. "I'll pour us some drinks, and maybe you should tell me what's brought you here."

They sat down and Madden produced a bottle, glasses, and ice. A moment later they were sharing illegal whiskey with a notorious bootlegger. It was the good stuff too, Jack realized after his first taste. He supposed if anyone in town would have good hooch, this would be the guy. They gave Madden an abbreviated version of the events of the past several days. Jack left out the supernatural elements, but emphasized the strangers staking out territory in Hell's Kitchen. It had the desired effect.

"Well, I never heard of your Silver Star or this Crowley fella," Madden said at last. "But I've been hearing stories about people going missing in Hell's Kitchen. Nothing strange about that, but it's usually folks that you're not surprised to hear they tangled with someone, you follow? And eventually they turn up someplace. Floating in the river, most of the time. Lately though, it's different. This is people who wouldn't be in anybody's way. And nobody finds them. Folks are getting spooked. Starting to talk. So this burned out lot you tracked your guy to. On tenth, was it? Near the river?"

"That's right," said Jack.

Madden nodded. "I know it. I'm the one that blew it up." He grinned and raised his glass to them and took a drink. "Used to be Skinny Doyle's place. He ran whiskey through there. We had a disagreement."

"If this Doyle was running whiskey," Doc asked, "did he have a basement? Maybe a sub level under that?"

"Place wouldn't be much use to a bootlegger without one," Madden said with a laugh. "Sure, there was all kinds of rooms dug out under there. We cleaned them out once the roof came down. But they're still down there. I guess your Silver Star fellows could have moved in. They could use the old tunnels to move around without being seen."

"Tunnels?" said Doc. "Do you know where they are?"

"Oh yeah," Madden answered. "A few of Doyle's boys came over to our side. We know the place all right."

"So," Jack said, "we mean to go in and clear them out."

"The two of you?" Madden interrupted. He took another drink and winked at Doc.

"We could use some help," said Jack. "You know your way around Hell's Kitchen, and you've got the men and the firepower. I guess it all comes down to how you feel about interlopers setting up shop in your back yard."

"It could certainly complicate your business," Doc said sweetly. "I mean it's because of them that we're here. Who can say who might turn up next?"

Madden set his glass down and looked them over.

"Yeah, I get what you want," he said. He thought for a long moment. Then he hit a button under the edge of his desk, and the doors opened. Frenchie leaned in.

"Get the boys together," said Madden. "Tell them to load up. We're going to make some noise."

Frenchie nodded and withdrew. Madden stood up and opened a cabinet in the wall that proved to be lined with guns. "Grab what you need," he said. "And you better not be wasting my time."

◌

The boat steamed up the Hudson under the moon. There was a cool breeze on the water and Jack felt Doc lean close to him for warmth. Around them on the deck were a couple dozen gang soldiers armed with Tommy Guns, shotguns, and pistols. Near the stern stood Deadeye with his Winchester, and Duke with a borrowed Tommy Gun.

Madden moved around the deck giving orders. He'd split his men into two groups, one for each of two concealed tunnels that led into Skinny Doyle's old hideout. Duke and Deadeye would go with the first team, while Doc and Jack went with Madden and the second. The men talked quietly among themselves and smoked until Madden gave the order to put them out.

A few moments later, the boat pulled into a moldering pier along the bank. A crewman climbed ashore and hauled in a mooring line. Immediately, Madden's first team started leaping onto the dock.

"Give us ten minutes to get in place," Madden said. "Then hit them hard."

Duke and Deadeye were the last ones off. "Good luck, mates," Duke said with a casual salute.

"See you inside," said Jack.

Then they pushed away again, and the men on the dock were lost to the darkness as the boat moved downstream.

"We're next," Madden said. "Just like that. Don't waste any time. We get down the pier fast, before someone sees us. Then we move down the tunnel and take out anybody we see."

"Got it," said Doc. She was holding a Tommy Gun she'd borrowed from Madden's collection while Jack had decided to stick with his two .45s.

Madden laughed. "You sure you know how to use that thing?"

"She does," said Jack.

"Well, if you two are right about this place, I guess we'll find out."

It was barely a minute later that the boat bumped up against another neglected pier. Jack and Doc sprang out and trotted down the dock, surrounded by heavily armed gangsters. They moved under a rotting wooden shelter that covered a set of rusted iron grates. One of the men knelt beside a grate and slid away a metal cover to reveal a shiny new padlock. He nodded to Madden.

"New tenants all right. We didn't leave this here."

Someone produced a pair of bolt cutters and quickly snapped the lock. Two others hauled the grate out of the way and pointed flashlights down a shaft with iron rungs set into the side. The whole process had taken less than a minute. Jack was impressed.

After half the team had gone down, they sent Doc down, followed by Jack and Madden. Then the others brought up the rear. At the bottom, a long, roughhewn tunnel led off through the bedrock. Jack could easily picture men carrying heavy casks of whiskey down the pier from a boat in the dark, lowering them down the shaft with a portable winch, and then hauling them through these tunnels.

"Let's move," said Madden, and they set off with weapons ready, sweeping the tunnel ahead with flashlights.

Jack could feel the tension growing as they advanced. Then someone shouted, and a Tommy Gun roared in the tight space. Instantly, hearing became impossible. They were charging forward. There was a body on the floor ahead. Madden watched in amazement as it bubbled and vanished into a pile of bones. He looked at Jack in shock.

Jack nodded. Madden nodded back and gripped his gun tighter.

Then there was a bright flash, and an explosion rocked the tunnel. Jack saw one of Madden's gangsters kneeling on the floor, shouting in anger as he fired his Thompson. Madden moved forward, and they followed him. At least three of their men were down, Jack realized, taken out by what must have been a grenade. Doc knelt by one and checked his pulse. Then she stood up again and shook her head.

Communications had broken down. The tunnel filled with smoke. Muzzle flashes sparkled in the darkness, and the flashlight beams picked out ghostly shapes all around them. They moved down the tunnel in a ragged group, firing at anything that moved. This was what the ground war had been like, Jack realized. Chaos, noise, and death, and the enemy that got you was the one you never even saw. He preferred his war in the air.

The tunnel opened into a large storage space with empty barrels stacked against the walls. Jack saw more smoking corpses of Silver Star fighters and a maze of tunnels and ramps.

Across the chamber, a large group of Silver Star men were gathered behind a pile of barrels, trading fire with Madden's men. Then the first team poured in from a side tunnel, firing on the Silver Star defenders from their flank. Jack saw Duke charge in, firing in short, controlled bursts. Duke spotted Jack and gave him a wave, and then shot down a Silver Star soldier coming up from a lower level.

Madden had the battle itself well in hand. Jack realized they were doing little good here. It was more important that he and Doc find wherever the Silver Star was keeping their supply of poison. Jack looked around and saw a white lab coat on the floor with a cloud of smoke still rising from it. Nearby was a ramp leading down.

Jack grabbed Doc and led her that way. They made their way down, into a narrow corridor strung with lights and electrical wire. Someone popped out of a doorway and fired at them, but missed. Jack fired back and the man fell. Jack edged up to the doorway and then swept around the corner, leading with his pistols. The place was a storage room, full of crates whose labels said they held dried beef.

Farther down the passage, Jack spotted a sign painted on the wall. In German, it read, "Off limits. Chemical team only." He pointed it out to Doc, and she nodded.

There was one more opening near the end of the corridor. Doc hurried to the doorway with her Tommy Gun leveled. Jack saw her open fire, then charge into the room. He followed with both his pistols ready.

The room was large and well-lit by electric bulbs strung along the ceiling. It was spotless, full of gleaming steel tables lined with complex networks of glass tubes and vessels on metal frames. Jack spotted a Silver Star scientist in a rubber apron, gloves, and mask swinging a crowbar. He smashed a complicated arrangement of glassware, spraying glittering fragments and colored liquid across the chamber.

Then a commando popped up from behind a table and leveled his gun at Doc. Jack opened up with both .45s, firing through the glassware. The commando fell back and began to smoke. Another scientist charged with a vial of liquid and was about to throw it when Doc cut him down.

That left one standing. Jack whirled back to stop the man with the crowbar from destroying the chemical setup. But he realized it wasn't necessary. The man had sprayed himself with liquid from the tubing as he wrecked the setup. Now he had collapsed on the floor and was screaming as his skin turned black. Jack watched in horror as the man writhed and twitched. It was a horrible fate, even for one of the Silver Star.

Doc shot him with the Tommy Gun. The man lapsed into stillness for a moment and seemed at peace until his body began to smoke and hiss.

They looked around the chamber, but nobody was left.

"Don't let anybody in here," Doc shouted. "I'll get some samples."

Doc put on protective gear she found hanging nearby while Jack guarded the doorway. The shooting was fading, he realized. It was nearly over. He hoped their side had won. Then he heard Deadeye calling, "Jack! Doc!"

"Down here," Jack shouted.

Deadeye ran down the corridor. "You guys okay?"

Jack nodded.

"They're finished," said Deadeye. "They gave as good as they got, though. Bunch of our side killed. Madden's not happy. Says he's going to blow the place so nobody else can use it."

"That's probably not a bad idea," said Jack. "Everything okay, Doc?"

Doc was carefully pouring liquids into vials and putting them into a padded leather carrying case she'd found. "They burned their notes," she said in annoyance. "Tossed a flare into the filing cabinet, probably as soon as the shooting started. But they didn't get everything."

She closed the case and slung it over her shoulder. "Hopefully I can learn something from this."

They headed back out to the main chamber. Madden wasn't wasting any time on his vow to blow the place up. The Silver Star had apparently left behind a significant cache of explosives, and Madden's men were already setting them and running wires out the tunnel.

Madden stood near the middle of the chamber, surrounded by empty Silver Star uniforms and piles of bones. "Who the hell were these guys?" Madden snapped when he saw Jack and Doc. "Nobody just...melts when you waste them!"

"They do," said Doc. "We think it's Crowley absorbing their life force."

"Yeah, you didn't mention they were goddamn *magic*, did you?" Madden kicked a pile of bones. "All I need. But you got what you wanted, right? That's all that matters."

"If we can identify their poison, we're going to save a lot of lives," said Doc. "You did a good thing tonight."

"Yeah, don't let that get around," said Madden. "Folks will think I'm a soft touch or something. Now get out of Hell's Kitchen. And don't come back."

℘

His number was M-115. He had a normal name, but that didn't matter anymore. His name was of no use to the Silver Star. He was their tool, and he was dying.

He stumbled through the door of a tenement basement a few blocks from the former base. He staggered inside and pushed the door shut with one hand. His other hand was clutched against his midsection, and blood pulsed between his splayed fingertips. He was cold, and he hurt. He knew his time was short. But he had one more duty to fulfill before he passed into the next world.

He stumbled to a carefully arranged pile of wooden crates and moved them aside to reveal a portable radio set. It was wired into the wall for power and to an antenna on the roof. The controls were simple; it could transmit on only one frequency. He thumbed a switch and leaned close to the microphone.

"M-115 to mothership," he gasped. "M-115 to mothership. Come in mothership."

There was only static in reply, for so long he wondered if the radio was broken. But then a woman's voice came back, a voice he would know anywhere. A voice that terrified him even in his dreams. The voice of Maria Blutig.

"M-115?" she snapped. "What are you doing on the emergency channel? Why you?"

"Hell's Kitchen base is wiped out," he said through clenched teeth. "I'm the last, escaped to warn you."

She swore, then said, "Who was it? AEGIS?"

"AEGIS," he gasped, feeling himself sinking toward the floor. "With...gangsters to fight. But it was AEGIS. They were after the DL-26."

"Was it destroyed or did it fall into their hands?"

"Don't know," he said faintly. "Maybe captured. What if they...trace it...find..."

"Hah, let them come," Blutig said through the radio's static hiss. "If they find their way here, so much the better. We'll destroy them."

But M-115 didn't hear this last threat. He was a smoking pile of bones on the floor beside the radio.

- CHAPTER 7 -

Jack and the others were picked up by BOI agents three blocks outside Hell's Kitchen. They found themselves back at the BOI offices being debriefed until well past dawn. They decided not to conceal anything but answered the increasingly detailed questions honestly and completely. To Jack's surprise, the agents didn't react, either to their descriptions of supernatural events or to their report of what amounted to a major military action in the middle of New York City. They simply took careful notes, occasionally asked for clarification, then thanked the crew for their help and released them.

By the time they returned to the AEGIS facility in New Jersey, it was mid-morning. Several highly placed AEGIS officials, and Edison himself, were waiting to congratulate them on smashing the Silver Star cell in Hell's Kitchen.

"A lot of people are going to breathe easier because of what you've done," Edison told them.

But Doc pointed out that their victory was only temporary. "They were running experiments on the poison," she said, "refining it, making it more dangerous. There's no reason to think that lab was the only one. And we still don't know where it came from. As long as the source is out there, there's nothing stopping them from regrouping and trying again. If we want to stop this for good, we need to know what this stuff is, how it works, where they found it. We've got a long way to go."

Then she took her collection of samples and disappeared into the facility's lab.

Before he left, Edison took Jack aside.

"Dorothy's worn out," he said. "She needs to get some sleep."

"Yes, sir," Jack agreed. "We all do after last night. But I don't think there's much we can do about that. You know how she is about things like this."

Edison's thoughts went elsewhere for a moment. Jack remembered that he'd been a good friend of Colonel Starr, Doc's late husband.

"I do indeed," Edison said at last. "But she's no good to anybody if she runs herself into the ground. Keep an eye on her, Captain. Because of what happened to her, she's not going to think about what she's doing. She'll push herself too hard. She'll take chances. She'll be so focused on pushing ahead that she'll miss things coming at her from the sides. She'll need you and the others to watch out for her."

"We'll do that, sir," Jack reassured him.

As Edison's car pulled away, Jack stood watching it. The old man was right, he thought. But Doc's lab was her domain. Nothing would happen there that wasn't under her control, and he was of little use to her there. The best way to protect her was to keep watch over the rest of the facility. They'd bloodied the Silver Star's nose, and Crowley would be looking for revenge.

He walked back to the enormous hangar, eyes glancing up at the sky.

They didn't see much of Doc for the next few days. She had a cot brought into the lab and started taking short naps there while waiting for results from one experiment or another. She emerged a couple times to grab something to eat and answer questions about her progress in muttered scientific language

that nobody else understood. Then she'd vanish back into the lab again.

Jack and the others did what they could.
They supported Doc when she let them. Mostly, they worked on getting the *Daedalus* refit-
ted and ready for action.

It was another two days later, after a full
night spent locked in the lab, that Doc
emerged. Jack and the rest of the crew were
having breakfast. They looked up and realized
she was standing in the kitchen doorway. She
was obviously exhausted, but there was no
mistaking her expression. Jack knew she had
it before she spoke.

"Do we have an airship?" she asked.

"Oh, we've got a crackerjack of an airship,"
Rivets said with a grin. "Do we have someplace to go?"

"I think so," said Doc. "Someone call Edison and tell him we'll be out to talk. After I've
had breakfast. Good lord, I'm starving."

◌⳩

Once again they met with Edison and a
handful of other AEGIS people in Edison's
conservatory. Doc had center stage. Jack and
the rest stood back near the windows. Jack

glanced out across the lawn where a squirrel capered in the sunlight.

"It's not like anything I've ever seen," Doc was saying. "It's naturally in liquid form, not a solid dissolved in a carrier for dosing. And it doesn't produce any harmful vapors, thankfully. So the gas masks weren't necessary. Simple protective clothing is enough. As long as you don't get the liquid on your skin, you can work with it."

If you did get it on your skin, though... Jack remembered the Silver Star scientist who'd smashed the refining apparatus. The man Doc had shot as a mercy. It had been hard to watch anyone, even one of the Silver Star, go through that.

"What have you learned about the actual mechanism?" one of the AEGIS men asked. "How does it kill?" Jack hadn't met the man, but he gave off a medical air.

Doc shook her head. "All I know is what I've seen in the field. I was trying to isolate the chemicals, not test it on living tissue. I do know it has several alkaloids and proteins associated with plant-based cardio toxins. We know it sets off a cascade effect that drastically alters pH and body chemistry in general. It interrupts nervous system signaling throughout the body—though perversely enough, apparently not pain transmission to the brain. It's hideous."

The doctor was about to press her for more detail, but Edison broke in. "Thank you, Dorothy. I think the important question is, where does it come from? We need to trace this thing back to its source. Wherever that is, we'll find a significant Silver Star presence, and we have to crush them there if we want to stop this thing."

Doc nodded. "I said it's not like anything I've ever seen. That's not entirely true. This is many, many times stronger, but there are plant toxins that have some of these effects in very reduced form, that are used in folk medicine in northern India."

"India?" Edison looked surprised.

"There are medical traditions there going back thousands of years," Doc explained. "They're based on Buddhist or Hindu writings mainly. And on folk knowledge of local plants and medicinal herbs."

"Are you saying that's where this came from?" Edison pressed.

"That's my best guess, though I'm not very confident about it. But I've been reading copies of some old medical texts from the region. They describe substances that do things similar to what our toxin does being used to re-balance humors in the body. Some of the methods are almost alchemical in nature. The healers combine herbs with metals and various calcinates. It's really quite fascinating. In one process copper is beaten into thin sheets, then heated and repeatedly plunged into cow urine..."

Doc stopped suddenly, realizing she was getting carried away with her subject.

"Well, it's very complicated. I know that's not a lot to go on, but it's the only lead I've been able to find."

"We do know the Silver Star's done a lot of research into Indian and Tibetan magics," said Jack. "If they picked up on these medicines, they might have found a way to refine them, distill them down into something much more deadly."

"And that's a frightening prospect," Edison agreed. "I think it's worth investigating at any rate. Do we have any resources in Northern India at the moment?"

The AEGIS men around him shook their heads. "There's a field team in Egypt," one of them said, exasperation in his voice. "That's as close as we get. I've been saying we need to be recruiting outside just the States and Europe."

"All right, Edward," said Edison. "Your point's taken. What can we do now?"

"I know someone on the ground there," said Doc. "Dr. Christopher Rhys. He runs a field station in the Uttarakhand region. He's the one who got me those books I mentioned. He's the authority on the *sowa-rigpa* and *rasa shastra* traditions. The only westerner who's seen some of these things being done. I think he can help us."

"Well then I suppose it's settled," said Edison. "*Daedalus* will deploy to northern India, to this..."

"Uttarakhand," Doc finished. "It's a district in the foothills of the Himalayas. It's very remote country."

"And you'll be on your own," said Edison. "AEGIS doesn't have anyone in the area to help you if you run into difficulty."

"That's what the *Daedalus* is for," Jack reminded them. "To get us to places where nobody else can go."

"That, she is," Edison said with a smile. "How are the upgrades going, Mr. Holloway? Is *Daedalus* ready to fly?"

Jack noticed Rivets puff out his chest and stand up a little straighter. "Damn right, she's ready. She'll take you anywhere in the world you want to be," he said. "Faster than anybody else can get you there too."

"Very well, then," said Edison. "Start drawing up a supply manifest. You can depart for India as soon as you're prepared."

❧

It was three days later when Jack was satisfied that the ship was ready and the last of the stores had been loaded aboard. They moved the *Daedalus* out of the hangar, and into a bright and clear summer morning. It was a perfect day for flying, Jack thought. The ship seemed to sense that it was time to leave the dark hangar behind and get back into the sky where she belonged. She gleamed in the morning sun. The sound of the engines had an eagerness to it.

A few last minute supplies were still being loaded. The basics were simple enough: food and water, ammunition for the guns, spare parts, and the basics they would take anywhere. In addition to that, Doc had set up a small laboratory in the ship's unclaimed passenger cabin. Specialized equipment for that was still arriving via delivery trucks and motorcycle couriers carrying boxes plastered with RUSH stickers.

Finally, one last delivery truck drove away. Doc approached, holding a small wooden box under her arm, and declared that she was ready to go.

"About time," Jack said in mock irritation. "We should be halfway across the Atlantic by now."

Doc snorted at him. "As if you'd leave before every last strut was double-checked, every prop blade was reseated, every control cable was—"

"Okay! Uncle!" Jack said, laughing. "But let's get moving. We've got a long way to go."

They boarded the *Daedalus* and found Duke in the cockpit going over the charts. He reported that Deadeye and Rivets were in the engine room doing something to the motor linkages. Jack called them forward, and they met in the main saloon to review the flight plan. The first leg would take them across the Atlantic to Madrid, a journey that would take the *Daedalus* almost exactly two days at cruising speed. There they would drop off some special packages intended for AEGIS agents operating in Europe. They'd take on more food and water, and then set off again. They would cross over Italy and the Balkans, then skirt the Black Sea and fly over Turkey and Persia, finally crossing the Indian frontier south of Afghanistan. From there they would follow the line of the Himalayas to a remote town called Almora, where Doc's local contact was based.

In all, Duke explained, the trip would take six days, including their short stopover in Spain.

Six days to get from New York City to a remote village on the other side of the world. Across thousands of miles of oceans, mountains, and desert. Before the *Daedalus*, it would have been an epic journey by sailing ship, train, and probably weeks of dangerous overland travel to get there. They would fly there in perfect comfort in less than a week! The 20th century was shaping up to be a time of wonders, he thought. What else did science have in store for the future?

They climbed down the stairs to the tarmac and went as a group to bid goodbye to Edison. Jack noticed Doc kept glancing over to the approach road. On the way back, he fell in beside her and asked her why.

"I sent Doctor Rhys a telegram saying we were coming," she answered. "I was hoping to get a reply before we left." She sighed. "He's got a radio at the field station. I'll try to contact him from the ship."

Then the last pre-flight checklist was completed, and the last hatches were closed. Jack, Doc, and Duke took their seats in the cockpit.

"Engines to station-keeping," said Jack. "Clear ground crew."

The ship's electric engines spun up the ducted propellers and Jack could feel that he had control of the ship now. The ground crew-men released the lines holding the ship in place and withdrew. Jack saw Edison looking on with pride as Jack pulled back on the yoke and the *Daedalus* soared into the morning sun.

CR

For two days, *Daedalus* flew over the Atlantic. The winds and the weather were with them and the trip was smooth and uneventful. The only concern came from Doc, who repeatedly tried to raise her friend Dr. Rhys on the wireless, but got only static in return.

They were on the ground in Madrid for just six hours, long enough to drop off their delivery packages and top off their supplies of food and water. Deadeye wandered off into town and returned a couple hours later with an odd looking pistol. It lacked a trigger guard and had a strange lever mounted alongside the frame.

"Been wanting one of these," he said to Jack. "JoLoAr in .45 ACP. Look at that."

Deadeye explained that the gun was meant to be carried with the chamber empty—which Jack thought was probably a good idea given the lack of a trigger guard. Then the lever on the right side of the frame let the user cock and fire the pistol quickly with one hand.

"Good for when you've got the other hand full," Deadeye said with a grin. "With reins, handlebars, another gun, whatever."

Jack admitted he could think of times when the feature would have come in handy, and Deadeye went aboard to examine his new plaything.

That left Doc. She'd gone to the nearby telegraph office to try and get some word from the mysterious Dr. Rhys. But when she finally came back, Jack could tell from the way she carried herself that she hadn't had any better luck than she'd had on the way over.

"I'm starting to get worried," she confided to Jack as they checked over the ship. "It's not like Christopher to just go silent like this."

"Well, keep trying," said Jack. "Maybe it's something simple. If it isn't, we'll be there in a few days. We'll find out what's going on when we get to Almora.

They launched and set out again, across the Mediterranean and the Italian peninsula.

The next day, *Daedalus* was over the Balkans. Duke had the controls and Jack was getting a cup of coffee in the galley when Doc came back from the cockpit. Immediately, he could tell something was wrong.

"Trouble?" he asked.

"I finally raised the field station," she said.

"So he's okay, at least?"

"It wasn't Christopher. I gather it was an assistant who finally noticed someone trying to raise them and answered me. Christopher isn't there. He went out hiking in the back country. He does a lot of that. Wandering around the foothills looking for plant samples. Except this time he didn't come back. It's been more than a week and there's no sign of him, Jack. He's gone missing."

- CHAPTER 8 -

It was mid-morning when the *Daedalus* arrived in Almora in the Himalayan foothills. It was a small town, a few hundred brightly painted homes clustered around the arc of a hillside. It gave Jack the impression of a place that had been built and patched and rebuilt over and over again, going back longer than anyone could remember.

Behind the town were the Himalayas themselves. An enormous curtain of snow-capped peaks. Even the *Daedalus* couldn't make it over that range. Jack wasn't surprised the local people had always assumed the gods lived in those mountains.

They came in low across Almora and made for the airstrip. It was a half mile or so outside the town, on one of the few pieces of flat ground in the area. Jack noticed they were making quite a stir below. People emerged from their houses to stare up and point at the gleaming airship gliding by overhead. Excited crowds ran along the road toward the airstrip to meet them as they landed.

"There's the field station," Doc said, pointing out a walled compound to the north of town.

"Maybe we'll find some answers there," he said. He hoped so. He knew Doc was concerned for her friend.

He brought *Daedalus* in low over the airfield and looked for a place to moor the ship that would leave the runway clear. It hadn't been designed with airships in mind, but he found a gentle slope descending away from the far end of the airstrip. It would do.

Jack throttled the engines back to station keeping and let the *Daedalus* settle until the rear cargo ramp was on the ground. Then Deadeye and Rivets jumped out with field mooring equipment. They fired stakes into the earth from AEGIS-designed compressed air guns and moored the ship to them. Finally, Jack shut the engines down. They had arrived.

Jack and the crew spent a few minutes greeting excited townspeople and standing beside someone Jack took to be the mayor as he made a speech. As soon as they could, they left Duke to handle the diplomatic affairs, and Rivets and Deadeye to make sure no one got overly eager with the ship. Then Jack and Doc slipped away and set off for the field station.

They found it at the end of a narrow track leading uphill from the village. The station looked like it had been a fortress before Dr. Rhys took it over. Crenelated walls stood ten feet high, and Jack could make out weathered bullet marks in spots. The old place had seen war at one time or another.

There was an open gate with a sign that identified the station. They walked inside and found neatly tended gardens surrounding a sprawling, two-story brick structure. Jack noted that the gardens weren't designed for beauty. Different flowers were arranged in blocks beside leafy vines with colored stripes, or what looked like weeds with heavy seedpods hanging down. It was a collection of samples, Jack realized, no doubt arranged with scientific pursuits in mind, like a living card catalog.

"Christopher?" Doc called. "It's Dorothy Starr. Is anybody here?"

There was no answer, but Jack was sure he heard a shuffling sound inside. He glanced over to Doc and saw that she'd heard it too. He kept a hand on the butt of one of his .45s as they went inside.

The interior was furnished with paintings of ancient kings and displays of weapons alongside bookshelves and collections of carefully preserved insects. Nothing was out of place. It was as if the inhabitants had just stepped out.

They passed through a sitting room with a harpsichord in one corner, then a small hallway. Again, Jack thought he heard the creak of a wooden floor somewhere. Through a pair of double doors they found an impressive library, but Doc paid little attention.

"Aren't we looking for books?" Jack asked softly.

"This is the main library," she said. "The field notes and journals will be in his study. He keeps that door locked."

But the small door, hidden away behind a folding screen in a back corner of the library, wasn't locked after all. "It's been forced," Jack said. He pointed out the broken wood around the latch. It creaked as Jack gently pushed it open.

"Christopher?" Doc said once more. There was only silence.

This room had more of a personal feel. There was a large glass and bronze hookah beside an overstuffed armchair. The ottoman was stacked with hand-drawn maps and papers and a huge wooden desk sat in one corner. Above the desk was a portrait of an Englishman in a bright red army uniform. It looked too old to be Dr. Rhys.

"His grandfather," Doc said. "He looks just like him though. Oh, something's wrong! There should be a lot more books here."

She studied the bookshelves built into the wall. "And the ones that are here are out of place. Someone's been through here."

Again, Jack heard something moving nearby. He homed in on a rattan panel on one wall, lined with a row of spears and polearms. Faint scratches on the floor, suggested that the panel slid to one side.

He gestured to Doc, and she moved around the armchair and readied her revolver.

"I don't see anything here," Jack said as he drew a .45 in his left hand and reached for the panel with his right. "We may as well—"

Jack yanked the panel aside. Behind it, a short, wiry man in a purple kurta screamed and hid his face in his arms. He stumbled back into the corner of the small storage closet and cried "I know nothing!"

Jack gestured with his pistol. "Come out of there! Who are you?"

"I am Adesh! I clean the house!" The man obeyed Jack, but kept his back pressed tight against the wall.

"It's okay," Doc said. She nodded to Jack and put away her pistol. Jack lowered his, but kept it out. "We're friends of Doctor Rhys," Doc said. "We're looking for him."

The man called Adesh suddenly lowered his hands and leaned forward to peer into Doc's face.

"I know you!" he said at last. "You came here. Three summers ago, yes?"

"That's right," said Doc.

"You are a Doctor too!" Adesh said. "You came to ask Doctor Rhys about the ancient healers! I remember how happy he was to speak to you of his work! Yes! Thank God you've come!"

Doc managed to calm him down, and then they asked him what had happened. He explained that Rhys had left to go hiking in the foothills. It wasn't unusual for him to be gone for a week or more, sketching and collecting specimens. But this time he hadn't returned. Townspeople had gone out to search for him, but they found nothing.

"What happened to the rest of the staff?" Doc asked. "Someone answered the radio a few days ago."

"Strangers came," said Adesh. "Dangerous men. The others ran away, one by one. Only I am left."

"What strangers?" Jack asked.

Adesh looked around the small study, and Jack saw he was trembling with fear. "Servants of the Nine," he whispered. But then he would say no more about them.

"What happened to the books that should be here?" Doc finally asked, when it became clear they were getting nowhere asking about the mysterious Servants of the Nine. At this Adesh smiled.

"Before the Doctor went away, other men came," he explained. "Westerners. To talk about the ancient healers, just as you did. But these were not good men. When they left, Doctor Rhys brought his notebooks to me and told me to hide them. Strangers come now and look through the house for them, but they do not find them!"

"Will you take us to them?" Doc asked.

Adesh nodded. "I think Doctor Rhys would want me to do so."

He led them outside. The grounds behind the house were extensive, with a grove of trees and a pond. Beside the pond was a gazebo in the English style with a chair and small table from which Rhys could presumably sit and enjoy a cool drink while looking out over the water.

Adesh led them into the gazebo and pulled aside a few of the floorboards to reveal a wooden trunk. "The Doctor's field work," he said, proudly. "I have kept it safe for him."

"Well done, Adesh," said Doc.

Doc opened the trunk and started sorting through the battered notebooks inside. "This may take me a while," she said.

Jack took the hint. He and Adesh withdrew and explored the grounds while Doc got to work.

⚭

It was almost sunset before Doc left the gazebo. Adesh had long since gone inside to resume his duties. When she emerged, Jack joined her. She clutched a small notebook of her own and walked quietly beside him, lost in her thoughts.

"Did you find anything?" Jack finally asked.

"Sorry," she said with a smile. "Yes. Maybe. I hope so. All there was to find anyway. He talks about something called the Mother of Medicines. He was excited about it when I was here before, but it was just something he was tracking down. Now it's all he writes about. Supposedly it cures, well, everything."

"Including poisoning?" asked Jack.

"Maybe. I need to find someone who knows more. Christopher hints about a source who was teaching him the old arts. But it's hard to make sense of his notes."

They stopped off at the house long enough to reassure Adesh that they'd carefully hidden the trunk. Then they walked back toward the airfield.

Again, Doc was lost in her thoughts. If he wasn't there, Jack wouldn't have trusted her not to tumble down the hillside.

"But how would they do it?" she murmured at one point. "You'd kill yourself before you ever got down to a safe concentration."

Jack didn't ask. He'd learned to just let her mind work at times like this. When she had something, she'd let him know.

They were almost back when Jack heard an engine overhead. A biplane was approaching the airstrip. As it came closer, he recognized the model. He broke out into a grin.

"Well now, that brings back memories!"

"Huh?" Doc looked up suddenly as the sound broke her concentration. "Is that a Biff?"

"That it is," said Jack. "Let's go see who's flying her!"

The Bristol F.2 "Biff" was a British two-seat fighter. Jack had had occasion to fly one a couple times during the war, and he knew Duke had done most of his flying in one. She was an agile thing, able to carry a pilot and a rear gunner and still keep up with single seat fighters. A rear-mounted Lewis machine gun in addition to her normal forward-facing Vickers guns gave the Biff quite a bite. They gave at least as good as they got from the German Fokkers. Jack still harbored a fondness for the airplane, and was well-disposed toward anybody with the good sense to fly one.

By the time they reached the airfield, the Bristol had landed and was taxiing back toward them. Duke, Rivets, and Deadeye joined them and watched as the pilot rolled off the runway onto the grass and cut his engine.

"How about that?" Duke said as he clapped Jack on the shoulder. "Haven't seen one of those in a while."

The plane had obviously once been Royal Air Force. The colors and numbers were still faintly visible on the rudder and fuselage. But now she bore the name, "Padgham Air Service."

The pilot jumped down to the ground. He was a stocky fellow in a long leather flying coat. He pulled off his helmet and goggles to reveal a flushed red face and a bushy mustache.

"That's a fine looking airplane," Jack said, striding forward and offering the pilot his hand. "Which engine you got in her?"

The pilot's brows furrowed a bit. "Sunbeam Arab," he said as he shook Jack's hand. "Just like it says on the surplus papers."

Jack and Duke traded a look.

"Not flying that smooth you don't," said Duke. "That piece of junk would have shaken her to pieces by now. You managed to sneak a Falcon engine out of the RAF, didn't you?"

"Certainly not," the pilot said with a wink. "You lot know your airplanes though, don't you? Gordon Padgham, Royal Flying Corps, later Royal Air Force, currently Padgham Air Service. Call me Padger."

They made the introductions all around, and Padger couldn't keep his eyes off the *Daedalus*.

"Enough about my old girl," he said. "What in the world is that?"

"That's the *Daedalus*," said Jack. "Birds like yours will always be my first love, but for a dirigible, she's a heck of a flyer."

"She looks it," said Padger. "What kind of props are those anyway?"

"Come on," said Jack with a grin. They gave Padger a tour of the ship, and he was clearly delighted by it, peppering them with questions about every mechanical detail and expressing polite disbelief about the *Daedalus'* range, speed, and ceiling.

Jack managed to direct enough questions back at Padger to satisfy his own suspicious nature. Padger had flown in the war, then come over to India with the RAF's No. 20 Squadron and flown patrols along the North-west Frontier. Eventually he'd mustered out, bought his Bristol as surplus, and had been making a meager living ever since flying mail, cargo, and the occasional passenger among the region's hill stations. Jack decided he liked him.

After the tour, they ended up at a bar Padger recommended, enjoying an excellent meal of curried chicken and talking shop. Eventually, the subject of why they'd come to Almora came up. Apparently, Doc and the others had decided they could trust Padger as well. Doc told him about the Silver Star, the poison that they were searching for, and about the missing Dr. Rhys.

"Well that's a hell of a story," Padger said when she was finished. "I met your friend Rhys a couple times. Brought in some packages for him. Seemed a good bloke. This Silver Star lot, though, they sound like trouble."

"That they are," Jack agreed. "Not people to be trusted with a deadly poison, to say the least."

"You said they're about magic and spirits and all that mumbo-jumbo, eh." They were drinking ale from large earthenware mugs. Padger tipped his back and soaked his mustache with foam. "Now, did you say that fellow up at the station mentioned the Servants of the Nine?" he asked.

"That's right," said Doc. "You've heard of them?"

He grinned at her over his ale. Jack had noticed Padger couldn't seem to resist flirting with Doc. "You fly around these hills long enough, my dear, and you hear a little of everything. There's hardly a village around these parts doesn't have a couple yobbos puffing themselves up claiming they're connected to the nine unknown men somehow."

"Nine unknown men?" Doc asked.

"Old legend. Goes way, way back."

Jack could see Padger relishing his role as the center of attention.

"Started with old Emperor Ashoka, they say. He's sort of India's King Arthur. Unified the land and ruled a golden age long ago, that kind of thing. The story goes that he collected philosophers and scientists at his palace, and they discovered all kinds of things. Ashoka figured a lot of it was stuff the world just wasn't ready for. Way beyond even modern science. Real Frankenstein stuff."

Jack and the others traded looks around the table.

"So he appointed nine wise men to guard the secret knowledge," Padger continued. "And to develop it for a time when the rest of us were ready. And as time went on, they chose successors and followers, and the traditions got handed down. Eventually it turned into a kind of secret society. Like I said, these days, somebody wants to sound bigger than he is, he starts hinting how he's tied to the nine men. Fairy stories, all of it. But even if it's nonsense, sounds like something that would catch the attention of your Silver Star fellows, doesn't it?"

The rest of the table agreed it did. It was the first thought that had occurred to Jack as well. Legends of an ancient secret society guarding mysterious knowledge would be like catnip to Crowley and his followers. And if the Silver Star was sniffing around these mountains, who knew what they might have found?

"You know the local stories and customs, Padger," Doc was saying. "Doctor Rhys's notes claim he got a sample of the medicine we're looking for from a healer and mystic of the Bhotiya people. Do you know anything about them?"

"Ah, he probably means the Long Walker," said Padger as he scooped up another serving of rice and curry. "The Bhotiya are hill nomads. A little more settled these days, but still doesn't take much to shake them loose, send them roaming back through the mountains. The Long Walker's one they still tell stories about. Old fellow. Supposedly been places no other man's ever seen. Has magic of his own, some say." Padger laughed. "If you had to pick someone to be one of old Ashoka's nine wise men, he'd make the list for sure."

"Do you know how to find him?" Jack asked.

Padger shrugged. "Never met him myself, but there's a village way back in the high valleys. He lives on a hilltop near there, unless he's taken off again. The locals bring him food and the like. There's no landing a plane anywhere near, and it's a rough journey by land.

Now with something like your airship though…"

Jack grinned. "If you wanted a ride, Padger, all you had to do was say so."

"Wouldn't mind it at that," Padger said happily.

- CHAPTER 9 -

The following morning, Padger joined them at the airstrip with a battered leather bag slung over his shoulder. The *Daedalus* took off into a clear blue sky and flew north, higher into the mountains. Padger paced the command deck behind Jack, looking over the comms and navigation stations, or simply gazing out the panoramic windows. Jack could tell he was delighted by the airship, though he tried to hide it as he teased Jack about his "flying parlor" and joked about "real piloting" in his Biff.

Jack noticed the ship becoming less responsive as they rose, an effect of the thinner air. But they were still well within the *Daedalus'* operating envelope. He marveled at the landscape they passed over. The land was folded into one steep ridge after another like a sheet of paper. At first these were steeply terraced, with narrow strips of cultivated land in rows all the way to the top. But soon the terraces were gone and there was nothing below but ridge after ridge of thick forest.

Padger guided them seemingly by instinct, with occasional direction to turn more to the east. But after an hour or so of climbing into higher elevations, Jack spotted a cleared area ahead with a small village along a ridge.

"Right, that's the place," said Padger.

Jack brought the *Daedalus* in low over the village. It was a maze of narrow paths lined by high stone walls. Buildings crowded on top of each other on the few pieces of flat land. From the looks of it, the locals had laboriously built even those flat spaces by packing earth behind thick retaining walls.

The most likely landing spot was a packed dirt clearing a few hundred yards outside the village. Jack brought the ship in and set her down. After Duke and Rivets moored the *Daedalus*, they got out and looked around. There was no sign of the excited crowds that had welcomed them in Almora. They left Rivets to watch the ship while Padger and the rest of the crew headed into the village.

"This far back, they likely don't speak English," said Padger. "But I can get by in the local lingo."

"I speak a smidgen of Hindi, as it happens," said Duke. "Enough to get myself in trouble at least."

"Might help," said Padger.

They entered the village by a winding path between two high walls leaning outward from the path itself. Multi-storied stone dwellings loomed over them, dotted with windows and connected by ropes flying brightly colored pennants. Jack spotted someone looking down on them from an open window high above. He waved, but the face vanished, and the window quickly shut.

The path brought them to a small central plaza crowded around with more tall stone houses. There was a fount of fresh water at the center of the plaza, but the place was deserted.

They spread out, studying the buildings and examining the well. Jack tried knocking on a door, but the only answer was the sound of shuffling footsteps inside.

"Shy, are you?" Padger muttered. "Well, we'll see about that."

He sat on the stone shelf at the lip of the fount and rooted around in his bag, coming out with a glass jar sealed with a rubber strip.

Inside was a milky white liquid. He tossed the jar to Jack.

"What's this?" Jack asked.

"Chhaang," said Padger. "The local beer. They claim it's a cure-all, but they say that about everything around here. Drink up, and I'll get them out to chat."

Jack opened the jar as Padger shouted something at him in the local language. Doc and the others looked on curiously.

The *chhaang* had an unusual taste, but Jack felt a rush of warmth through his extremities. It must get cold up here in the winters. He could see how this would be a popular drink.

"What are you saying?" he asked Padger.

"Apologized to you," Padger said as he opened a second jar. "Told you I'd heard they made really good *chhaang* here, but I guessed it wasn't true after all, and that out of town stuff I gave you must be the best there is. They won't stand for that, I wager."

Jack grinned as a door creaked open and a bald, middle-aged man poked his head out. The man studied Padger for a moment, then shouted something at him.

Padger shouted back and brandished his jar of *chhaang* at him. A moment later, the man emerged with an earthenware jug and crossed to the well. Jack looked on in amusement as they argued in the local dialect, then traded vessels and drank. Within a few minutes they were fast friends, sitting side by side, drinking and laughing.

Gradually, other faces appeared at windows. Doors opened. Jack waved at a little boy in a doorway and got a shy smile in return. A few more people stepped out into the plaza with jars of their own. Apparently a consensus had been reached that, if the strangers were starting a drinking party, they must not be all bad.

"Village healer lives over there," Padger announced, gesturing toward a wooden door at the far end of the plaza. "My mate here says he'll introduce us."

He led Jack, Doc, and Padger to the door, where he knocked loudly and called out. The door opened slightly, and there was a quick round of discussion through the crack. Eventually, the healer silently welcomed them inside and led them into a small room lined with wooden cabinets and shelves, studded with tarnished brass fittings. The varnished black wood looked ancient, long since rubbed smooth by countless hands over the years. Dusty jars were stacked in every open cubbyhole and atop the shelves, almost as high as the rough-hewn roof beams. Sunlight filtered through a window and fell on a low, round table in the center of the floor. They sat around this on cushions and their host brought tea in a polished brass pot.

Padger translated as Doc thanked him for seeing them. She told him she was a healer from America. There was a strange poison killing people there, she explained, and she had heard of something called the Mother of Medicines that might protect people and save many lives.

The healer's expression grew grim as Padger translated, then he spoke, gesturing to his cabinets.

"He says the Mother of Medicines would have helped, sure enough," Padger translated. "Deadly poison itself in its pure form. But the old healers knew how to combine it with herbs or treat it with metals, make different medicines for just about anything."

"You said 'would have helped?'"

Padger and the healer conversed quietly for another minute. "He says it's gone now," Padger explained. Says it was hard to grow around here. Needed the help of the spirits, and the spirits don't talk to man anymore. Everything's about spirits up here. They just used it all up if you ask me. Anyway, he says there was still some about in his father's day, but even then it was hard to find. Now," Padger shook his head. "No more."

Doc took this in and nodded. Jack understood her concern. Whatever the Silver Star was using to make their poison, they didn't seem to have any shortage of it.

"Does he know where we can find the Long Walker?" Doc asked finally.

Padger asked. "Half hour up the trail to the west. He says the old fellow has a hut on a hillside up there. If we see him, we can't miss it."

Something about the phrasing bothered Jack. "Is that how he said it? If we see him?"

Padger turned back to the healer and confirmed it. "He says not everybody can find him. But he's very wise. If we see him, he can help us."

Jack wanted to ask what that meant, but the healer was rising, as were Padger and Doc. The interview was over.

They thanked the healer, and Doc gave him a set of steel forceps and a bottle of sterile alcohol from her kit. Then he showed them out again.

The party in the plaza was in full swing as they emerged. The villagers' former reserve had vanished, and Jack realized they were teaching Duke and Deadeye the local drinking songs and laughing uproariously at their efforts to keep up.

Jack nudged Padger. "You're a useful fellow to have around," he said.

Padger grinned back. "Kind of you to say so. You'd be amazed how many doors you can open with a handy bottle of hooch. Worked pretty much the same way with officers back in the Flying Corps too."

They headed out of the village along a narrow trail. Steep slopes rose to their right. Jack was amazed by the deep green of the foliage. Beyond that lay the imposing mountains, a jagged wall of gray stone and snow. Gradually they fell silent and listened to the cries of distant birds echoing across the hills. Doc was the first to spot the sturdy wooden hut perched on an outcrop high above. They'd seen no signs of human habitation since they left the village; this had to be the place. Jack wasn't sure how it avoided sliding down the hill in the first strong wind, but it looked homey enough.

Then he heard a thin, reedy voice calling from the distance.

"Hello!" It called in English. "Come and sit. I brought *khaja*. There's plenty to share."

They all looked around, but it was several seconds before Jack made out a tiny figure sitting atop a flat rock by the side of the trail. The figure waved, so Jack waved back.

"You think that's him?" Doc asked.

Padger shrugged. "If he isn't, he probably knows him."

"What's khaja?" asked Doc.

"Means eat and run," Padger answered. "Snacks. Could be most anything. Let's find out!"

The speaker was a wizened old man, Jack saw as they came closer. He wore tan trousers and a tunic with a heavy mantle draped over his shoulders the color of the mountains. A white skullcap was perched on his shaved head. He grinned and beckoned them over.

"Come and sit with me. Have some tea and tell me about your travels."

"You speak English!" said Doc. They stepped up onto the smooth, worn stone and settled down in a circle.

"A wanderer taught me, long ago," the old man said.

"Are you the one they call the Long Walker?" Doc asked.

He grinned and opened the flap on his leather bag. He pulled out a ceramic jug and unstopped it. A tuft of steam drifted out with the smell of tea.

"They've called me all kinds of things," he said. "I used to wander myself when I was younger."

"And you're just sitting here waiting for us with tea and khaja?" Padger asked.

The old man produced a stack of small, engraved brass cups—four of them, Jack noted—and poured them each some tea.

"Lucky for you I am," he said with a smile. He tossed his head in the direction of the hut. "Otherwise you'd have to climb all the way up there."

Padger nodded and accepted his cup of tea.

Over tea and a tasty mixture of roasted beans and dried fruit, they answered the old man's many questions about the places they'd been and their adventures. Jack noticed Padger was taken aback by their stories of clashes with the Silver Star. He could see him wondering whether he should believe them or not.

"Such busy lives," the old man said, refilling their cups. "We've nothing so interesting here. Whatever brings you to such a quiet place?"

Doc once more told the story of the poison, and how they'd heard it might have something to do with the Mother of Medicines.

He looked them over for more than a minute, studying each of their faces in turn and saying nothing. "We are each made of flesh and spirit," the old man said at last. "Both must be in balance for us to live and be well. Flesh and spirit too, are made up of different elements. Different tissues form the body; different energies form the spirit. All must be in balance or we grow ill in body or spirit. A healer's art is to sense imbalance and correct it. If an energy is too weak, stimulate it with medicines. If it is too strong, stimulate its opposite until balance is restored. You are a healer. You have seen this too, yes?"

Doc nodded politely over her tea.

"That is what the Mother of Medicines was for. It comes from a plant that once grew here. It was hard to grow. Harder still to use properly. In its pure form, it stimulates all the energies, all the tissues. It's too much. The patient is overwhelmed and the result is only death. So the medicine must be tamed, its strength channeled so it stimulates only what is weak and restores the patient's health."

"But it doesn't grow here any longer?" Doc said.

"It does not," said the old man. "But it was never the true medicine."

Jack and Doc traded a look. "What do you mean?" Doc asked.

"What grew here was only a shadow of the true medicine," the old man said. "It only comes into its full strength when grown in the eye of the world."

Doc leaned forward, fascinated. "Eye of the world?"

"Where this world and the spirit world overlap. That is where the true medicine was found."

Jack set down his cup. "This world...and the spirit world?"

"There must be such a place," the old man said. "How else could the spirits reach our world? Many things are possible there. The true medicine could do even more. But even it is just a shadow. The ancient scholars spoke of a way to temper the pure medicine so it fuels all the energies in balance, yielding bodily perfection and spiritual enlightenment. Beside that, what is curing sleeplessness or gallstones? Trivial."

"So people sought this place out," said Doc, "and brought the medicine back."

"But it grew poorly away from the spirit world, and its medicine was weak. Eventually it died out and was gone."

"You went there, didn't you?" Doc said, fixing him with her eyes. "You brought it back."

"I wandered many places when I was young," he said. "I saw many things. I'm old now. Now I stay here and tend my chickens. It's nice to have visitors."

Doc persisted. "What if someone else found the eye of the world?" she said. "What if they used the true medicine to kill instead of heal?"

He nodded sadly. "Killing is always easier."

"How do we find it?" Jack asked.

"I would stay away, if I were you," he said. "It's very dangerous there."

"We have to try," said Jack.

The old man smiled. "I suppose you do." He pointed off into the deep mountains. "Look for the twin pillars. They mark the path."

Jack started to push for more detail, but the old man rose suddenly. "And now, I must say goodbye. Chickens are impatient creatures. Short-lived, and they know nothing of the troubles that drive us."

They rose and thanked the old man for his hospitality.

"No, no, thank you," he said. Then, as he was turning to the steep, narrow path up the hillside, he turned back. "I almost forgot," he said.

From a pocket inside his mantle, he produced a stoppered ceramic vial and offered it to Doc. "For brightening an old man's day with your company," he said.

Then he turned and started up the path muttering about his chickens.

They walked back down the path toward the village, and it wasn't until the old man's hut had disappeared around a curve that Padger finally broke the silence.

"Well that was quite a fairy tale."

Doc fumbled through her kit and came out with a paper test strip. She opened the vial the old man had given her and dipped it into the liquid inside.

"You're not buying it?" said Jack.

"And neither should you," said Padger. "There's nothing growing back in those mountains. It's too high, too cold. There isn't even any dirt. Nothing but ice and bare rock from here to bloody Burma!"

Jack glanced up into the high peaks. He had to admit it seemed unlikely that there was a place back there full of unknown plants. And a place where the real world and the spirit world overlapped seemed even less likely. "Still, quite a story," he said.

Doc gasped and stood still in the middle of the trail.

"What's wrong?" Jack asked in concern.

She showed them the paper test strip. The bottom half had turned a deep black. "This contains the same plant alkaloids as the poison samples from New York. I don't think the true medicine's a fairy tale. I think this is it!"

- CHAPTER 10 -

A storm system moved in from the mountains as the *Daedalus* flew back to Almora. By the time they landed, the sky had grown dark and restive, and the first brief, sudden bursts of rain had begun to spatter against the airship's skin. Padger said he knew a good inn for dinner, and they hurried there as the winds intensified and the first rumbles of thunder rolled across the hills.

They reached the inn and made it inside just as the rain began in earnest. They found themselves in a comfortable looking room paneled in dark wood with a long dining table at one end and armchairs and side tables at the other. A door in a far corner presumably led to the kitchen, and stairs led up to a second floor balcony lined with guest rooms. It was small, but homey and welcoming.

"Auntie!" Padger shouted. "I brought company! Six for dinner tonight."

The kitchen door opened and an old woman entered, muttering to herself. She looked up at the crew and shook her head, then put on a wide smile and greeted them with a bow. "Welcome to Almora Summer House," she said. "Please be at home."

Then her smile vanished as she turned to Padger and scolded him in stage whispered Hindi.

"Well, hire one of the local boys to play waiter for the night," Padger said, and he embraced the old woman as she pretended to protest.

"More trouble than I'm worth?" Padger fished a few rupee notes from his pocket and thrust them into her hand. "Pff. Place would go bust if I didn't go out and drum up business. Get one of Choudhury's boys. They're always looking to make a few coins. More trouble than..." He shook his head and raised his voice at her back as she headed back to the kitchen. "Nonsense! Balderdash! And put on some tea!"

The old woman made an annoyed sound as she vanished through the door. Jack gathered that mutual mock irritation was how they chose to express a long and affectionate friendship.

They took seats in the lounge at one end of the room and a few minutes later the old woman reappeared with tea. Jack and Doc had filled in the rest of the crew on their encounter with the enigmatic Long Walker. None of them seemed quite sure what to make of it. Padger was the only one with a firm opinion.

"It's just not possible!" he maintained.

Outside, the storm had picked up. The wind howled around the eaves and rattled the windows. Rain hit the side of the building in wind-whipped sheets.

"I don't know," Jack said. "That poison, or true medicine if you take his name for it, it had to come from somewhere."

"Doesn't have to be here, does it?" said Rivets. "Could have come from the other side of the world for all we know. No offense, Doc."

Doc smiled at him. "None taken. I was wondering myself. I thought the poison from New York looked a bit like Himalayan plant toxins, but maybe I just convinced myself because I wanted an answer so badly. Maybe I sent us on a wild goose chase halfway around the world. But when I tested that sample today, I knew. We're in the right place."

"But the plant's gone extinct," said Duke. "Where's the Silver Star getting theirs? Unless you're willing to buy that 'sacred valley in the mountains' story. What did he call it?"

"The Eye of the World," Doc answered.

Padger snorted. "Believe me, there's no such place. I spent most of a year looking for a route through the mountains to China. Flew all through those mountains. High as the air would hold me anyway. If there was a chunk of the spirit world up there, I'd have found it. Where the devil's our dinner anyway?"

The kitchen door opened and a young Indian man in a linen tunic and pants emerged carrying a tray with more tea.

"Ah," said Padger, "there you are. How's the food looking?"

The young man simply nodded and said, "Tea, sir." He took the tray to Deadeye, who was sitting closest to him in a thick, stuffed armchair, and repeated "Tea, sir?" Deadeye hadn't finished his cup yet. He said "no, thank you," and waved the boy away.

"I'll find out what's keeping her," said Padger. "Man could starve around here," he added more loudly, in a voice meant to carry into the next room.

As Padger disappeared into the kitchen, the waiter turned to Jack and refilled his cup. Jack smelled the warm, flowery scent of the tea as he raised the cup.

Then there was a deep, anguished wail from the kitchen. Jack froze. Around him the others turned in surprise. The waiter remained in place, leaning over to refill Doc's cup.

Then the door burst open once more and Padger strode through it, a heavy Webley pistol in his outstretched hand. Padger fired and the waiter spun away, struck in the chest. Jack and the rest of the crew sprang to their feet as the brass teapot fell to the floor and hot tea soaked into the rug.

Padger strode forward and fired again, then a third time. At last he raised the Webley and held it against his chest. "The bastards murdered her!" he said, and his voice was strained with anguish. "I wouldn't touch that," he added as Doc bent down toward the overturned teapot.

And then the room seemed to explode. The front door was kicked open with a loud crash. Figures smashed through the windows. Jack caught a glimpse of someone charging out of the kitchen toward Padger, but Padger whirled and fired point blank into his attacker's face.

A man in a kurta shirt and tight churidar trousers charged through the doorway, framed for a moment by the storm outside. He had a long, curved blade in one hand and a black hood. Jack was closest to the door, and before he could draw his pistols, the man was on him with a high-pitched scream. Jack caught his arm as the knife plunged toward his heart, but their momentum carried them backward, and they tumbled over Jack's chair to the floor. Jack struggled to hold the knife at bay. Around him he caught glimpses of motion, heard shouting and gunshots.

He slammed his attacker's wrist against the edge of the low coffee table, then again, until he lost the knife. The hooded man punched him and they rolled against the table. Jack felt himself rolling over the dropped knife. He managed to wrench his right arm free and throw a devastating cross to the man's jaw. That dazed him long enough for Jack to throw the man off him, and follow up with another punch that put him out.

Jack drew his twin .45s as he sat up and his eyes quickly took in the situation. Doc had taken cover behind a chair and had her pistol out. He saw her drop another hooded attacker. Deadeye was firing the strange pistol he'd picked up in Madrid up into the balcony. There must be more of them up there. Another one came at Deadeye from his side and Jack opened up on him. The .45s roared and the man fell. Jack and Deadeye traded a brief glance of acknowledgment, then Deadeye sidestepped as a heavy knife thudded into the wall where he'd been standing. He fired back into the balcony again, and Jack heard the railing give way. A body fell beside him and smashed the coffee table.

There was no time to organize a defense, or even count their attackers. They were each in a desperate battle for their own lives, reacting on instinct as new attackers seemed to spring out of nowhere each time they took one down.

Jack fired at another one coming in through the doorway. Then he heard a clash of metal and turned to the sound. It was Rivets. He'd gotten his hands on a metal serving tray and was using it as a shield. He blocked a slashing blow with a knife then drew back and slammed his attacker in the head with it. The man staggered back, and Rivets finished him off with another fierce blow.

"Rivets, look right!" Jack shouted, and tossed him one of his .45s. Rivets caught it and quickly shot another hooded figure coming in through one of the shattered windows.

They aren't Silver Star. The thought flashed through Jack's mind as he realized the bodies were simply lying on the floor instead of dissolving into smoke. He didn't have time to wonder who they were before someone leapt onto his back from the balcony above, and he crumpled to the floor. The impact dazed him. He saw the hooded face over him, the arm preparing to plunge its long blade into his chest.

He willed his body to move, to fight back, but he knew he would be too late.

Then the man jerked back with a grimace. The knife tumbled free of his fingers, and he fell across Jack's chest. Behind him, Doc looked down with concern. He nodded

to show her he was okay, and she turned and fired her revolver again at someone he couldn't see.

As he lay there, clearing his head, Jack saw a pair of high leather boots stride across the floor. He looked up and saw a long, black coat and a trench-modified pump shotgun with a short barrel and an attached bayonet. Jack didn't know who he was; he hoped the stranger was on their side.

He heard the shotgun roar as he was climbing to his feet. Then he scanned the room and saw Doc crouched behind her chair, reloading her pistol. Deadeye had gone to a window and was firing out into the night. And Rivets was grappling with one of the hooded men. He still clutched Jack's .45, but the slide was locked back, empty. Jack strode quickly over and clubbed the attacker in the back of the head with the butt of his pistol. He fell, and Jack quickly scanned the room for another enemy but saw none.

Then there was a shotgun blast from the kitchen. Jack hurried that way. As he approached the door, something caught his eye and he turned. Padger lay in the corner behind the dining table in a pool of blood.

"Doc!" he shouted. "Padger!" Then he hit the kitchen door hard with his shoulder and crashed through it.

The first thing he saw was the man with the trench gun, standing with his back to him. As Jack came through the door he pumped the gun and raised it to fire again. Jack's eye followed the line of his aim—to Duke, bloody but still in the fight. Duke had apparently just plunged an assassin's own blade into his chest. He turned to see the shotgun pointed at him and his eyes widened. Jack dove for the man in the dark coat.

He hit him in the left side, just below the shoulder, as the trench gun roared. The gun flew up and the blast went wide and high, but the man in the coat instinctively thrust the butt back and hit Jack in the chest. Then he whirled and pumped the gun. Jack caught the gun's receiver, and they each struggled to control it for a moment. The man was strong, too strong to be natural, Jack realized.

Then he saw Duke in the corner of his eye, steadying the wavering aim of his Luger. Duke's pistol cracked, and the shot winged the man in the coat. It was enough for Jack to wrench the shotgun out of his hands, spin it, and thrust the bayonet into the man's chest.

The man crumpled to the floor and tendrils of smoke rose from him. Within moments he had dissolved into a pile of bones inside the long, black coat.

"You okay?" Jack asked Duke.

Duke nodded. "Just a scratch. Or two."

The old woman lay dead near the back door. Three of the hooded attackers were scattered around the room. And of course the Silver Star operative. Jack picked up the trench gun and the black coat.

Back in the main room, Doc was working feverishly on Padger, her arms and torso covered in blood. Deadeye and Rivets had taken up positions at the door and a window, but it seemed the attack was over, if only because there was no one left to attack them. Jack counted more than a dozen of the hooded men strewn around the room, or on the balcony above or the stairs. Jack remembered that Adesh, the servant they'd found at Dr. Rhys's house, had spoken of a secret society called the Servants of the Nine. Could these be them, working with the Silver Star? The idea was a worrying one. The Silver Star were trouble enough without allies.

"We have to move him," Doc announced from the other end of the room. "He needs a hospital."

"Can you stabilize him?" Jack asked.

"For a while. But I can't save him with what we've got here."

"Nearest hospital would be in Delhi," said Duke. "Make that in a couple hours."

"It's not exactly flying weather out there," Deadeye added from the door.

"We get him there now, or he dies," said Doc, and that was the end of it. They carried Padger out into the drenching rain and hurried through the narrow, windswept alleys to the *Daedalus*.

As Deadeye had noted, it was not good flying weather. The wind buffeted the ship from the moment Jack took her up. He tried to get above the storm, but that wasn't working. If anything the air higher up was more chaotic. So he took the ship back down to a thousand feet and pushed her south, toward Delhi.

In the main saloon, Padger lay on blankets on the deck as Doc worked to keep him alive.

"Can you keep this thing more steady?" she shouted forward in frustration after an especially rough patch of turbulence.

"Do you want steady, or do you want fast?" Jack called back.

There was a moment of silence, then, "fast."

As they neared Delhi, they finally came out of the storm into clear sky. The stars blazed above, and they saw the city lights in the distance. Duke radioed ahead and sent a message to a British military hospital to expect them. He checked the ship's charts and found the closest open landing area and asked that an ambulance be sent there.

As Duke guided him into what turned out to be a polo ground, Jack could see the ambulance waiting at the edge of the field. He set the ship down and Doc immediately had the hatch open. She and Rivets lowered Padger down to the waiting corpsmen. Doc, Duke, and Deadeye went with them, while Jack and Rivets stayed with the ship.

While they waited, Jack stayed in the cockpit, nervously checking the ship's systems and making sure the radio was working properly. He hadn't known Padger long, but he'd taken a liking to him. He hated to think they'd gotten him killed.

Rivets passed the time in the saloon. "Hey, who was the guy with this coat back here?" Rivets called out finally. "And the trench gun."

"Silver Star," said Jack.

"Great."

Then the call came in on the radio. It was Doc.

"He's going to make it," Doc said as Rivets came into the cockpit. Jack let out a sigh of relief and Rivets clapped Jack on the back.

"It was pretty close," Doc continued. "If we hadn't had the *Daedalus*..."

"How's Duke?" Jack asked.

"Couple shallow knife wounds," said Doc. "They're stitching him up now. He'll be okay. But Padger lost a lot of blood, and they had to do some major surgery. He's going to be here a while."

Rivets leaned over and clicked the mic. "Doc, it's Rivets. When Duke's cleared to travel, you should get back to the ship. I was going through the Silver Star's coat. Came up with something you want to see."

- CHAPTER 11 -

It was almost dawn by the time Doc, Dead-eye, and Duke returned. Duke assured them he was all right.

"Just a few cuts," he said. "Worst part of it was losing that shirt. I rather liked it."

Doc was able to give them a more detailed report on Padger. He'd taken the bigger part of a blast from the trench gun to his midsection. He'd lost a great deal of blood, obviously, and it had taken surgery to repair damage to his intestines and to remove a portion of his liver. He would be in the hospital for some time, but he would eventually recover.

"Now what have you got for us?" Doc asked when she'd finished her briefing.

They gathered in the main saloon and Rivets took the floor.

"While we were waiting for you, I started wondering if that Silver Star boyo had anything interesting in his coat pockets," said Rivets. He produced a folded sheet of paper and opened it.

"Cable with his orders," said Rivets. "Looked like that code thingy you found on that diner menu back in New York, Jack. So I figured I'd try and decode it the way Duke did with that."

Duke's brow furrowed. "What? That was a top secret German High Command code! I only know it because—"

Rivets waved him down. "Yeah, yeah, I watched you do it. Not that hard. Just because I'm good with an engine, people think I'm some kind of yokel right off the turnip truck."

"What does it say, Rivets?" Doc reminded him gently.

Rivets cast one last irritated glance at Duke, then he read from the page. "To number 713, from...M. Blutig."

A quick wave of consternation swept through the group.

Maria Blutig was a high ranking commander in the Silver Star who ran her operations from the bridge of her personal airship, the *Luftpanzer*. They'd crossed paths many times in the past, and she held a particular hatred for Jack ever since he shot down her fiancée during the war. That hatred extended to the rest of the crew, and AEGIS as a whole. In a plot to undermine AEGIS, it wasn't much of a surprise that Maria Blutig would turn up sooner or later, although Jack could have sworn he'd seen her perish in a fiery impact deep in the Amazon jungle just last year. He should have known a mere plane crash wouldn't do her in. She was a relentless and dangerous enemy.

"So Maria's still with us," Deadeye said at last, expressing what they were all thinking.

"Looks that way," said Jack. "And it makes sense she'd be tied up in this."

"Find crew AEGIS airship *Daedalus* in Almora," Rivets went on. "Secure cooperation of local disposable assets. Kill all members of *Daedalus* crew. Secure airship *Daedalus* only if crew already neutralized. Destroy airship if necessary to achieve primary goal. If possible, determine source of *Daedalus* crew's apparent knowledge of Shambala. Transmission ends."

There was another silence while they all looked at each other, searching for some sign of recognition.

"Shambala?" Duke said at last. "Maria's barking up the wrong tree this time. We don't know anything about a 'Shambala.' Do we?"

"I've heard of it," Doc said quietly. "It shows up in various occult sources, mostly derived from Madame Blavatsky and the Theosophists."

"What is it?" Jack asked.

Doc gave him a smile. "You'll like this. It's a secret kingdom, deep in the Himalayas, run by a group of immortal wise men called the Masters of the Hidden Brotherhood. Blavatsky claimed she was in contact with them. They guard secret knowledge and pass it on to select people they find worthy."

"That sounds a lot like the old King's nine unknown men," Jack observed.

Doc agreed. "It does, doesn't it? If you want another connection, Crowley's claimed he's been contacted by them as well."

"And supposedly they live in this place in the mountains called Shambala," said Duke, "full of ancient secret wisdom. That sounds like just the thing the Silver Star would go looking for."

"Sounds like they found it," Deadeye added.

"They found something anyway," said Jack.

Duke stood up and stretched his bandaged arm with a grimace. "So what do we do about it?"

"We know we're on the right track," said Doc. "Everything lines up. The poison sample in New York. The Long Walker, and now Maria being worried enough to send people after us. Jack, you have to see this all adds up to something at least."

Jack smiled. "Calm down, Doc," he said. "I'm convinced. I don't know what this Shambala really is, but I'm convinced the Silver Star found something back in the mountains, and that's where they came up with their poison. So that's where we're going."

&

The next morning, they flew the *Daedalus* back up to Almora. The hospital had reported that Padger was still unconscious after coming out of surgery shortly after dawn. He was getting the best care possible. There was nothing more they could do for him in Delhi.

The storm had cleared, and the flight back to Almora was considerably calmer than the previous night's frantic journey. They made Almora in a bit less than two hours, then headed higher and deeper into the mountains.

The air grew even thinner as they climbed up through the lower peaks, and cold winds whipped the ship. The cabin was heated so the cold wasn't an issue. But Jack noticed his breaths were coming short and shallow. He glanced over and saw that Doc was experiencing the same thing. At the comms station, Duke was listening to the tones of the radio detector through headphones, but Jack saw that his breathing was shallow and rapid as well. They were approaching the limits of altitude. If they went too high, the air would be too thin to sustain them. Worse, even with her new lighter frame, the ship would eventually reach its flight ceiling. The *Daedalus* flew because the gas in her cells made her lighter than the air. As the air grew thinner, the ship's density would eventually match that of the surrounding atmosphere. Then she would go no higher, no matter what they tried.

Jack wasn't sure which limit they would reach first, the ship's or their own. Both offered serious danger, and flying through the treacherous air currents around the high peaks was dangerous enough to begin with. Late in the war, he knew, the Germans had flown their airships much higher, and they'd had to give the crews oxygen tanks to breathe from. If they planned to keep operating this far back in the mountains, they'd need something similar.

Duke coughed and rubbed his temples.

"You okay?" Jack asked.

Duke nodded. "Just a headache," he said. "This air."

"Me too. Anything on the radio detector?"

"Who knows?" Duke answered in frustration. "So many echoes off all these mountains, I can't make out a thing."

For the rest of the day, they flew around the high peaks, but found nothing. For Jack, it was at least useful practice in controlling the *Daedalus* in the unusual conditions. The controls were sluggish this high. The engines ran perfectly, but the propellers generated less thrust and the rudders and control planes seemed muted as well. She was slow to steer.

Eventually, Jack turned and took the ship back down toward Almora before they lost the light. If nothing else, they had been able to map a section of the mountains that was simply a blank space on the official charts they carried.

The next day, they went searching again, and again found nothing but snow-covered mountain peaks and dangerous flying conditions. At least they seemed to be getting better acclimated to the low air pressure. Duke reported that he was getting better at interpreting the chaos of echoes the mountains generated on the radio detector as well. And Rivets spent the day climbing around inside the *Daedalus'* hull, making adjustments to the controls and the engines to try and improve her performance at the very top of her flight envelope.

Even with Rivets' adjustments, though, Jack found it difficult to control the ship with any precision. Even when he released the ship's full capacity of lifting gas into the envelope, she climbed with a sluggishness that worried him. Lateral turns were more responsive, but only slightly, and so close to neutral buoyancy, the ship tended to be tossed off course by every gust of wind. And the wind conditions were like nothing Jack had ever flown in before. He felt as if the *Daedalus* was as short of breath as he was, simply wallowing in the air, carried around on the currents.

Before taking off on the third day, they removed some gear from the ship and stowed it in Almora to reduce her weight. They weren't going to be using the ship's life raft or electric motorcycle deep in the mountains. Rivets broached the idea of removing the guns. The two forward-facing Lewis guns and the two Hotchkiss guns mounted in the top turret, along with their combined ammo load, accounted for a lot of extra weight. But Rivets seemed relieved when Jack rejected the idea. Jack was nervous enough about the handling of the ship at altitude. He wasn't going to make the *Daedalus* an unarmed sitting duck when he knew the Silver Star was around.

The third and fourth days were as unproductive as the first two. They mapped more of the range but saw nothing that suggested the "twin pillars" the Long Walker had spoken of.

By the fifth day, Jack was becoming disenchanted with the whole operation. The weather was even more turbulent than usual, and the ship fought him as he tried to steer around sheer mountain faces. The *Daedalus* bobbed like a cork in a storm, with barely any buoyancy to work with.

Perhaps Padger was right, Jack thought, adjusting the ship's forward trim for the hundredth time to adjust for a new air current coming off the mountains to his right. They'd covered hundreds of square miles of untracked, mountainous terrain and they'd seen nothing that suggested a place that could sustain human life, much less rare poisonous plants or a spot where someone might land to collect them. He had no idea where the Silver Star was finding its poison, but he didn't see how it could be here.

They passed through a small band of cloud and the sun glittered off the canopy as they rounded a mountain spire on their right. Before them were two long, nearly parallel ranges of peaks stretching away to the east. Jack aimed the *Daedalus* down the gap between them to give Doc a clear view. She sat behind him, sketching the mountains and recording their altitude to help fill in the blank spaces in their charts.

At the radio console Duke suddenly started. Then he turned back to the controls and listened closely.

"Got something?" Jack asked.

Duke held up a hand for quiet. Then a moment later he shouted, "Contact! Something moving. Dead ahead and below us! It's big."

Jack scanned the sky ahead of them but saw nothing. Long walls of sheer stone and ice flanked them, and a rolling deck of gray cloud formed the floor of the corridor they flew down.

Then something roiled the top of the cloud before breaking through into the sun. A long, dark shape emerged from the cloud bank like a U-boat surfacing from dark water. It broke through into the bright sun and angled upward to climb. There was no mistaking it. It was the *Luftpanzer*.

"Deadeye!" Jack shouted, "Man the guns!"

"Aye, aye," Deadeye shouted from behind him, and Jack heard him clambering up the ladder to the top gunnery position.

"Guns hot!" Deadeye shouted down from the turret.

Jack flipped the cover off the switch that activated the forward-facing Lewis guns and pressed it. "Forward guns hot," he called back.

"How many times do we have to do this?" Doc asked, and Jack could hear her worry beneath the irritation in her voice.

It was a fair question. They'd already destroyed the *Luftpanzer* once. A year ago, they'd caught the ship on the ground in the Amazon jungle and had blown it to pieces. They knew Maria Blutig had survived that encounter. But Jack had hoped they'd dealt Silver Star a more serious blow. He'd hoped they didn't have the resources to simply build another *Luftpanzer* and carry on with their plans. But apparently they did.

But if their luck held, perhaps they could take out the second *Luftpanzer* much more easily than the first. The *Luftpanzer* was much larger than the *Daedalus*, she was better armed, and she carried deployable fighter biplanes that multiplied the damage she could inflict. But on the other hand, they were positioned almost ideally, above and behind the larger ship. With a quick run at them from behind, they might be able to take down the enormous Silver Star airship before she could deploy the fighters or bring most of her heavy guns to bear.

Jack throttled the engines to full and tried to estimate the *Luftpanzer*'s rate of climb. A long strafing pass straight down her back was the goal, unloading all the guns as they passed.

"Ready?" he called to Deadeye.

"On your mark!" Deadeye shouted back. Jack knew he would have the twin Hotchkiss guns aimed where they would do the most damage. They closed the gap. Jack watched the Lewis guns' aiming point slide closer and closer to the *Luftpanzer*'s stern.

"Fire!" Jack shouted, and he jammed his thumbs down on the twin triggers. The forward guns opened up with a chatter, and he heard the roar of Deadeye's twin Hotchkiss guns join in an instant later. Machine gun rounds began chewing up the Silver Star ship's stern, shredding rudder panels and puncturing the rear gas cells.

Then the wind changed, and Jack felt the ship fall away to the left and the forward trim go out again. The nose pitched up and the ship came almost to a dead stop, then was carried off to the left, toward the mountains. Jack's line of fire whipped up, and the rest of his bullets streaked harmlessly over the top of the enemy ship.

Jack swore loudly and released the triggers to save his ammunition. With the swivel mount in the top gunner's position, Deadeye was able to keep his guns trained on the *Luftpanzer* for a few more seconds, but then the Hotchkiss guns fell silent as well.

"Starboard, Jack! Starboard!" Deadeye shouted down from above. "And bring the damn nose down!"

"I know that," Jack muttered to himself. He adjusted the trim to drop the nose and threw the rudders hard over to slew the ship back out toward the center of the corridor.

But the element of surprise was obviously lost. The *Luftpanzer* was climbing fast now, and turning toward them. Jack saw the other ship's forward gondola swing into view and knew that Maria Blutig was standing on that deck, preparing to take her turn.

The corridor narrowed ahead of them. The *Luftpanzer* had little clearance to do a full turn. That was something. But her port side guns began to fire and Jack saw tracers sweeping the air in front of them.

"Incoming!" he shouted, and dove the ship downward. The sound of bullets slamming into the ship's skin echoed across the deck. Then Deadeye's Hotchkiss guns opened up again.

"Ballonets one and three," Rivets shouted from the rear intercom. "Losing pressure, but I can keep her steady if you can."

That was easier said than done. Jack wasn't sure if he could regain the lost altitude, especially with the ship leaking gas. She was fighting his efforts to steer too. The winds wanted to carry her closer to the mountainside, and the nose kept trying to pitch to port so that he had to steer starboard just to keep her even. It wasn't worth trying to aim the fixed Lewis guns like this. Deadeye seemed to be having better luck with his swivel mounted guns, so Jack decided to dive beneath the *Luftpanzer*. That would give Deadeye a chance to do what damage he could, and at the moment Jack was willing to trade altitude for speed and control.

The *Luftpanzer* kept raking *Daedalus* with fire as they passed beneath her, but Deadeye was returning fire. Jack heard him whoop in triumph and knew what that meant—he'd hit something important on the Silver Star ship.

They passed beneath the *Luftpanzer* and both ships' guns went silent for a moment. Jack turned again, trying to get farther from the mountains and give Deadeye a firing angle. The Hotchkiss guns chattered again. Then they slid out from beneath the ship, and the *Luftpanzer*'s starboard machine guns came to bear. More bullets slashed through the gas cells.

Instead of falling, however, the ship began to swiftly rise. They'd hit an updraft, Jack realized. He slowed the engines and let it carry them higher, even as it pulled them relentlessly closer to the mountains.

"Getting a little tight out there," Doc observed nervously.

"I know that," Jack replied. "She'll hold."

"Contact!" Duke announced. "One, no two. Small planes! I've got radio chatter."

Jack scanned the sky for what could only be a pair of *Luftpanzer*'s biplanes, but he saw nothing.

He had lost sight of the *Luftpanzer* herself, but neither her guns or Deadeye's were firing at the moment. Rivets made a report about patching cell three, which Jack took to be good news, but he had other things to worry about now.

"It's *Luftpanzer*'s planes all right," said Duke. "She wants them to attack us, but they say they don't have fuel. They need to dock immediately."

"Oh, my god," said Doc, "Look!"

She pointed out the main canopy, and Jack followed her direction. On the other side of the corridor, just visible through the cloud cover below, he saw a pair of enormous rock spires at the top of a mountain. They reached up into the sky like talons ready to grab them out of the air.

"The twin pillars," Jack said in amazement. He couldn't believe it. But there they were, just as the Long Walker had promised.

"Lock down our position!" he snapped. "Mark that spot!"

"Already on it!" Doc said behind him.

"Got them!" Duke added, pointing out the canopy himself.

Jack saw the small black shapes of two bi-planes emerge from the cloud deck below the twin stone spires and break away down the corridor to his right. He turned the ship to follow them and caught sight of the *Luftpanzer* herself once more. She'd aborted her turn after *Daedalus* passed beneath her and was now turning back. She was flying a steady course down the corridor so her airplanes could dock with the landing hooks that were even now extending down from their hangar.

"Have you got our position fixed?" he asked.

"Got it," said Doc. She stepped around him and leaned close to the canopy with the Leica camera she'd picked up on their last mission and snapped several shots of the spires jutting out through the clouds.

Jack thumbed the intercom so everyone could hear him. "We're breaking off," he announced. "Deadeye, Doc, go aft and help Rivets patch the ship. We need all the gas pressure we can get."

Then he hit the throttles to break the ship out of the updraft and took her down and away from the *Luftpanzer*. This wasn't a fight they could win. They'd take on Maria Blutig's new toy another day.

Besides, he thought as he rounded the end of the corridor and the giant Silver Star airship disappeared around the mountain face, they'd found what they were looking for.

- CHAPTER 12 -

They landed at the airfield in Almora and inspected the ship to assess the battle damage. Thankfully it was minor. There were punctures in several gas cells, and patching them and checking for hull integrity took the rest of the available daylight and then lasted well into the night. But the mechanical systems—controls, power, the steering gear and engine housings—were mostly undamaged. There was nothing that called for replacement parts they didn't have on hand. By morning, the ship was in prime flying condition once more.

The next morning dawned behind high layers of scattered cloud, but the weather didn't suggest rain. Rivets led one more sweep of the ship looking for damage before he finally declared her ready to fly. Deadeye reported that he'd fired a little more than half the ammunition for the Hotchkiss guns. Because of the control difficulties, Jack had barely fired the Lewis guns. Their magazines were almost full. They could fight if they had to.

Duke returned from a trip into town and reported that nobody in Almora had seen the *Luftpanzer*. The airship was able to remain aloft for weeks at a time, limited primarily by food and water for the crew. They knew Silver Star tactical doctrine encouraged keeping away from towns and cities when possible to avoid being observed and tracked. That suggested that Maria might not pursue them here and try to destroy them on the ground. On the other hand, Jack thought, now that she knew they were in the area, she might well suspend normal tactics in her zeal to destroy the *Daedalus*. They would need to be ready to take off at the first sight of anything in the air.

By midday, there was nothing left to do, and Jack had had time to consider their next move. He called the crew together in the ship's main saloon. They gathered around and the jokes and banter faded. They looked to Jack for leadership, and this was a situation that called for it.

"So, it looks like the Twin Pillars are real," he began. "Maria Blutig's in the neighborhood, and the Silver Star is conducting operations. I wasn't easy to convince, but it all adds up. I think we have to accept that there really is a place the locals call the Eye of the World back there in the mountains. The Silver Star found it, and they found at least one very dangerous thing there. There may well be more. Now it's our job to stop them. Doc, have you got a solid map of the region we flew over yesterday?"

Doc nodded. "As good as we can get from sketches and photographs. I wouldn't stake out building plots quite yet, but I can get us back to the Twin Pillars again." Then she added, "As for what's beyond them, well, take a look at this."

Doc had brought a folder with her. She opened it up and took out a half dozen photographs. "I took a few shots with the Leica before we hightailed it out of there."

"Tactical withdrawal," Jack said with a grin.

"Call it what you like," she said, then winked at him. "I made some enlargements. Take a look."

They all crowded around to study the photos. There were the pillars, two gnarled, weather-beaten hooks of stone. They looked even more ominous closer up. Below them were sheer rock cliffs plummeting down into the clouds, cracked and crumbling stone plates that overlapped to create a maze of crags and seams. And off to one side was a shadowed gap. It was hard to make out, but Jack could tell it was the mouth of a canyon. At some point, probably millions of years ago, the mountain had strained under the impact of the collision between Eurasia and the Indian subcontinent. The bedrock had folded, and finally it had split, pulled apart by the patient forces of gravity and erosion. Those forces had created a rift that led into the mountainside.

Duke let out a low whistle. "Will you look at that?"

"Can't tell how far back it goes," said Deadeye, rather dubiously.

That was true enough, but Jack knew the canyon wasn't just a dead end. It led to something. "Those Silver Star pilots flew it," he said.

"Well bully for them," Duke shot back. "But I don't see how it matters. We're stuck. There's no way the *Daedalus* is going to make it into that. Even if we could keep her steady at that height. And you saw how hard she is to handle up there."

"You're right," Jack admitted. "We can't take the ship in there. But a small plane could do it. The Silver Star's proved that."

"But we don't have a small plane," Deadeye protested.

This was the part they weren't going to like, but there was nothing else for it. Jack took a deep breath and plunged in.

"Actually, we do," he said. "Padger's Bristol."

For a moment, they all looked at him as if they didn't quite believe what they'd heard. Then there was a chorus of protests—from everyone but Doc, Jack noted.

"No! Absolutely not!" Duke nearly shouted. "You are not going in there in a two-seater and leaving the rest of us behind! That's not how we work."

Rivets and Deadeye chimed in agreement behind him.

"It's the only way," said Jack. "You said yourself the ship can't make it."

"That doesn't mean you two go flying off on your own," said Rivets. "What if you get in trouble in there? We won't be able to help you."

"I don't like it either," said Jack. "But it's a chance we've got to take. Somebody's got to go in and find whatever's back there. It's the only way to stop the Silver Star."

"No, it isn't," said Duke. "If we need planes, then we go back and get planes."

"No time. Maria Blutig's troops are back there now. By the time we get back with a full expedition…"

"Then we hunt down the *Luftpanzer* in the mountains and shoot it down," Duke replied, his voice taking on a hint of desperation. "We did it before. We can do it again."

"This isn't the Amazon," said Jack. "We're not going to catch her on the ground. She's got an advantage over us in the mountains. She's big and heavy, so she's more stable. They can fly their ship. Best we can do is keep from flying into a mountainside."

Duke had run out of objections. As he searched for another, Jack turned to Doc.

"You haven't had much to say. You're the poisons expert. You'd be the one to go with me. What do you think?"

Doc looked up at him, and her voice was clear and confident. "You're right," she said. "We have to stop the Silver Star, and that's the only way to do it. And if anybody can fly through that canyon and make it out again, it's you. I'll go with you."

She smiled at him. "Besides, don't think you're going in there without me, Jack."

❧

Once it was settled there was nothing else to argue. They did what they could to prepare. Rivets checked over Padger's Bristol from the propeller bolts to the tail flaps and announced he was satisfied with the way Padger had maintained the airplane.

"And if that engine's a Sunbeam Arab, I'll eat it," he added. "You called it, Duke. He's got a Rolls engine in there. Looks like he's jury rigged the air intakes and the carburetors for this altitude too. She'll get you where you're going, if you don't come to your senses before then."

Jack and Doc spent the time thinking through what supplies they would need and assembling portable kit bags that would fit into the airplane. Doc's was mostly taken up with scientific equipment. If they found the source of the poison where they were going, she first had to be able to handle it safely. Then she would have to identify it, analyze it, and search for an antidote. Jack worried about more mundane survival needs. He loaded a few days' worth of food and water, cold weather gear, a small canvas tent. He was endlessly weighing things and trying to decide if they were important enough to add that much more weight to the airplane. The Bristol should be able to operate at the altitude where they'd found the Twin Pillars, especially if Padger had modified it to breathe the thinner air. But Jack didn't know what he'd find past the pillars, or how challenging the flight would be. Overloading the plane could prove fatal.

On the second morning, Duke left on the ship's electric motorcycle and headed off down the road that led south out of Almora toward the lowlands. He returned near sunset with the sidecar loaded with oxygen cylinders and gear.

"Personal breathing apparatus," he said as the others looked over his haul. "Or at least they will be when I'm done. Oxygen tank, breathing mask, flow regulator. They'll keep you from blacking out up there."

"You know how to make something like that?" Doc asked in surprise.

"Germans used them during the war," Duke said. "We started shooting down the Zeppelins they sent over to bomb London, so they started flying higher. So high the crews needed these to keep conscious and working. I might have seen the plans at one point."

"Stolen the plans, more like," Rivets said with a grin. Duke only spoke about his wartime experiences in broad hints, and then only rarely. Jack assumed it was because he was still bound by the Official Secrets Act. But they all knew he had worked for British Intelligence in an extremely covert capacity for much of the war.

"Let's just say I know how they work," Duke replied, and winked at Doc. "The tricky bit was finding the right parts out here."

"Thanks, Duke," Jack said, and put a hand on his shoulder.

"Don't mention it," Duke said quietly. Then he went off with his parts and got to work. Jack knew it was his way of saying he was on board with the plan. Even if he disagreed, he'd do everything he could to keep his friends safe.

Finally, after four days of preparation, they couldn't think of anything else to do. Rivets had rigged an external drop tank to let the Bristol carry extra fuel. Their kits were optimized and measured down to the ounce and stowed aboard the plane. And Duke had completed his breathing kits, one for each of them.

The weather was clear and bright. It looked like a perfect day for flying. They gathered on the airstrip with the Bristol and the *Daedalus* lined up behind them.

"You be careful," Deadeye said, giving Doc a hug. "Jack," he added. "I know you'll take care of the both of you. Just keep an eye on your back. There's bad guys up there."

"Watch your fuel mix," Rivets said in a conspiratorial voice. "Padger's done a good job juicing up that engine, but the air's awful thin up there."

Jack promised that he would.

Duke hugged Doc as well and made her promise to be careful. Then he turned to Jack. "Hey Jack," he said. "What's the best thing about having a wooden leg?"

Jack smiled. It was a ritual they'd begun in the war and kept up until now.

"I don't know, Duke. What?"

"I'll tell you when you get back."

They grinned and shook hands, then Jack helped Doc into the Bristol as the others un-moored the *Daedalus* and prepared her to fly.

As the Bristol's engine sputtered to life, Jack hoped Padger wouldn't be too upset that they were flying his beloved Biff into danger. He suspected Padger would mainly be disappointed that he couldn't come along.

Then the *Daedalus* lifted off and rose into the morning sky. A moment later, Jack taxied the Bristol down the runway and took off himself. The two aircraft headed north, up into the high mountains.

Jack realized he'd missed flying this way as he put the Bristol through its paces and got accustomed to how she handled and how she responded to wind conditions. He loved the roar of the engine and the wind over his face in the open cockpit. The *Daedalus* had the edge in stability, in cargo capacity, in safety;

obviously the future belonged to the airship. But Jack would miss this experience when the airships had driven the fixed wing plane from the sky.

"You all right?" he called back to Doc in the observer's position.

She gave him a thumbs up. She was practicing putting on the breathing mask Duke had made for her. Jack's was in his lap in case he needed it. He hoped they'd acclimated somewhat to the high altitude by now. The headaches they'd suffered in the first few days seemed to have faded. But Jack knew he would need to be razor sharp once they flew into the canyon. Every reflex had to be honed to perfection. There would be no room for a second run at something. He checked the gas gauge and studied the Biff's controls to make sure his vision remained clear. At the first sign of haziness or confusion, he'd put on the mask.

The trip was uneventful as they flew high into the previously uncharted mountains once more. They saw no sign of the *Luftpanzer* or her flock of small planes. The green slopes gave way to bare earth as they climbed, then quickly to rock and ice. Jack breathed carefully, and checked the gauges again. The lines all appeared straight and clear. There was no blurring. He seemed to be getting enough oxygen. But there was no reason to risk it, he decided, since Duke had gone to the trouble of providing an oxygen supply.

"Masks on," he called back to Doc as they turned into the long, straight corridor where they'd spotted the Twin Pillars on their last flight.

"Roger that," she shouted back.

Jack got his mask on and started oxygen flow through the regulator. He did feel the effect, like drinking really strong coffee, except it hit him all at once. He looked back to confirm that Doc had her mask on.

She pointed over his shoulder, and Jack looked ahead to see the Twin Pillars looming above them. It was time.

The *Daedalus* was off to Jack's left, the midday sun gleaming off her silver skin. Ahead he could make out the canyon entrance, a sudden slash in the jagged line of the mountaintops. He checked the fuel and dropped the external tank. It had gotten them this far and left them with a full fuel load. Jack hoped that would be enough.

He waved to the *Daedalus* and waggled the Bristol's wings. He thought he could make out Deadeye in the upper gun position waving back at him. Then he pushed the throttles open all the way and flew straight into the mouth of the canyon.

- CHAPTER 13 -

As soon as the Bristol entered the canyon, Jack felt the stick steady itself in his hand, and the plane settled into a smooth course down the long rift in the mountainside. He'd stopped noticing the winds and turbulence around the high mountain peaks. Countering the buffeting of the Bristol had become a matter of simple, instinctive reactions. But here the winds were suddenly absent, and the air was calm. He glanced up and saw a wisp of high cirrus cloud whip across the canyon and vanish beyond its lip. The winds were still just as brutal up there, but the canyon's interior was shielded from them.

That would make it easier to fly here, Jack thought. But it also left him no option to pop up out of the canyon if he found himself boxed in. Go too high, and the winds would seize the small plane and batter it against the cliffs. No matter what he encountered here, his only choice was to stay low and thread his way through the canyon. It was all right, he reminded himself. The Silver Star pilots had managed it, so he could do it. But his maneuvering room was considerably tighter in here than he would have liked. He throttled back his speed, took another breath from the oxygen bottle, and focused on the feel of the Bristol and the slope of the cliffs around him.

The first turn was easy enough, a gentle bend to the left that revealed another long, straight gallery. This one was pierced by several tall fingers of stone that rose nearly to the top of the canyon. It looked too tight to try and go over them without catching the wind. He picked the widest spot he could see and aimed the Bristol into it. He would be about eighty feet above the canyon floor, he estimated. And there was room to clear the Biff's wingspan if he rolled her slightly.

"Jack, what are you doing?" Doc shouted as he dove into the maneuver. He could hear her voice rising.

"I've got it," he called back. Then he rolled the plane up to the left and slipped through the spires in a moment. Within a few seconds he'd settled the wings back to level, and the spires fell away behind them.

"Is there going to be a lot of that?" Doc asked.

Jack just shrugged. He was already looking ahead to the next maneuver, but he couldn't see it. The canyon appeared to simply end in a blank wall of rock. That wall came closer with each second, and Jack still couldn't see a way forward. He scanned the sides and floor of the canyon but saw only jagged rock. He glanced up and saw nothing else above but the lip of the canyon, where the winds waited to slam them into the mountain. He slowed the plane as much as he dared, but they still swept relentlessly toward destruction. There had to be something else here!

Jack was on the verge of yanking back on the stick and taking his chances with the winds when he saw it. On his right was an outcrop of rock that hid a sharp twist in the canyon as it curved almost completely back on itself and went into a steep downward grade. On pure instinct, Jack dove toward the canyon floor to regain speed that he knew he would need in a moment.

"Jack!" Doc screamed.

He ignored her. Every fiber of his being was focused on the plane, its speed, its lift, the drag of gravity. He couldn't have done the math, but he knew he could make this turn. He dove almost directly into the stone wall, then pulled back hard and cut the throttle. The Bristol pointed up to the sky with its wheels only feet from the sheer wall it was now climbing.

His airspeed fell away precipitously. Not yet, he told himself, not yet. The airspeed indicator was sliding toward stall speed. Jack could feel the plane beginning to lose its grip on the air. Now!

He rolled off to the right, and the plane tumbled away from the cliff face, slewing to the side and falling back into a sort of loop. Doc had gone silent behind him, and he wondered if that was good or bad.

Then he looked up over the wing and saw the canyon floor coming up fast. The Bristol was upside down and plunging toward the ground. But he wanted to go down to keep inside the canyon. Jack knew he had made it, and suddenly he was laughing with the sheer joy of it. He slammed the throttle open. The V12 Rolls Falcon engine roared in defiance, and Jack roared with it. The plane surged forward, and Jack rolled it back upright and leveled out. He was almost perfectly on line with this new descending leg of the route. A minor yaw correction and they headed down the clear center of the canyon.

A long scar in the stone caught Jack's eye. Beneath it, a streak of debris lay scattered down the canyon floor, twisted fuselage and shattered wings in Silver Star colors. Down there somewhere was whatever remained of a pilot who wasn't as good as he was, Jack thought. Or one whose instincts betrayed him just once. It was a horrible way to die, even for an enemy. The Silver Star might have found a way through, but they'd paid a steep price for it. The first pilots must have been incredibly brave, he thought. They flew in here not knowing if they had a chance of coming out the other side or if they'd been dead the moment they flew into the canyon.

Then Doc was pounding on his shoulder. "Damn it, Jack!" she yelled over the engine. "Don't you ever do that to me again! I swear I'll —"

"Trust me, Doc!" he interrupted. "I won't let you down."

"I know that! You think I don't know that? But, damn it, Jack!"

Jack grinned to himself.

"All right," she said after a moment. "I'm okay now."

"Good," he answered. "Because you're not going to like this either."

Then he hit the rudder hard, and Doc screamed again as he slewed the Biff into another hairpin turn barely an arm's reach from the stone side of the canyon.

They made that one, and the next two, though the second was a tricky maneuver over a rockslide that squeezed the Bristol up against the top of the canyon with its treacherous winds. Jack saw that he was right to fear those winds. Again he saw the wreckage of a Silver Star plane. It looked like it had been caught in the winds, smashed against the rim of the canyon, and then rained down in pieces.

Jack's heart was pounding, and he could feel himself tingling with nervous energy. This was the hardest flying he'd ever done. He was making blind turns, trusting his instincts and hoping for the best. If he didn't know the Silver Star had succeeded at this, he would have doubted it was possible. He still feared that the canyon would simply dead end somewhere, and there'd be no place for them to go.

One more sharp turn and Jack thought he'd found it. Ahead of him, the canyon ended in a jumble of stone blocks the size of skyscrapers that had separated from the walls and fallen. He couldn't see daylight through them, but there had to be a way. Again he slowed the plane to buy time. He knew the Silver Star pilots had figured this out. How? Where had they flown through?

There was only one choice, he realized. A gap between the huge stone masses at the very bottom. Inside was darkness, but it had to pass through. The Silver Star had done it. He took the plane lower, toward what amounted to a cave mouth. It'll work, he told himself. There's a path through.

Behind him Doc put a hand on his shoulder. "Jack..."

"I know. Trust me. We'll make it through."

She said nothing, but she left her hand on his shoulder.

Jack dove and flew into the hole. They were instantly plunged into blackness, but Jack saw light ahead. A small patch in the distance, not quite square. He aimed the nose straight for the center of it and hung on, holding his breath.

Suddenly the left lower wingtip scraped stone. The plane shuddered violently, and the wingtip threw back a trail of sparks. Doc jumped and screamed in surprise. Jack edged to the right as much as he dared. There was rock all around them, but he couldn't see it. He just aimed the plane for the growing square of light.

And then they were through it. The Bristol sprang out the other side of the huge stone wall, and Jack climbed a bit. He glanced to his left and saw that a bit of the lower wingtip had been ground away. Broken spars and torn fabric whipped in the wind, but the damage was minor. The Biff would still fly.

"Jack! Look!" Doc shouted over the noise. But this time there wasn't fear in her voice but wonder. Jack looked ahead. The canyon opened out ahead of them and beyond it he saw…green.

The Bristol shot out of the canyon, and Jack was stunned by what he saw. They had flown into a lush valley that stretched out in front of them as far as Jack could see. The bare rock gave way to nearly flat grassland. There were thick stands of trees in the distance. The air felt warmer here. He didn't feel the need for the breathing mask; he could breathe normally. A waterfall tumbled down the valley slopes to his right. How could any of this be here? It was incredible, impossible!

Behind him Doc shouted, "Animals! I see a herd of something! Look!"

But Jack wasn't looking at the herd. He was looking down, at a small base. There were at least two dozen large tents arranged in neat rows. He saw a couple larger and sturdier buildings and watch towers, obviously made from the local wood. There was a radio mast and an airstrip carved into the grassland, complete with two small biplanes. All of it bore the colors and insignia Jack knew all too well.

The Silver Star. Already, Jack could see figures sprinting toward the waiting planes. This was going to get hairy.

They shot over the Silver Star camp and Jack opened up the throttle. They sped away down the valley. Perhaps a mile from the camp at the valley mouth, the grassland gave way to thick forest and the Bristol flew over a dense canopy. He glanced over his shoulder to see Doc snapping photos with her Leica.

"What kind of trees are those?" she shouted.

Jack had no idea. He glanced back and the Silver Star planes were small dots in the air far behind them. But they were in pursuit, and they were armed while the Bristol no longer was. Jack looked around for a place to run. The valley was huge, but on all sides it was fenced in by sheer slopes that rose until the plant life once more gave way to bare stone and ice. And presumably the fierce winds. The canyon appeared to be the only way in or out.

"Jack, we've got company!"

Doc had finally stopped gawking at the flora and fauna long enough to spot the Silver Star planes.

"I know," he shouted back. "I'm going to try and outmaneuver them."

He veered right and headed toward the edge of the valley. Ahead of them he saw a plume of steam escaping from a vent in the rock, like a boiling teakettle. That must be what made this place possible, he realized. Volcanic steam vents kept it warm, and apparently released more moisture and oxygen from underground. Perhaps the warmth created some kind of permanent temperature inversion layer over the valley that kept the thicker air here from dissipating. Jack didn't know; it wasn't his field, and he had bigger things to worry about right now.

One of the Silver Star planes fired a burst at them. The enemy was still too far back; his rounds fell harmlessly behind the Bristol. They were just making sure Jack knew they were there and were prepared to shoot the Bristol down. Jack wasn't sure what to do about that. All he had was his .45s. It wasn't beyond possibility for a pilot to outmaneuver another plane and get close enough to fire on its pilot with a handgun. He'd heard of pilots being killed that way in the war. But that had mainly been early in the war, before everyone had synchronized machine guns. Besides, there were two of them. He didn't like the odds, but that was the hand he'd been dealt.

He dove toward the forest canopy to pick up speed, and the two biplanes followed. Jack went into a wide turn and studied them. They were small, smaller than the war surplus Fokkers the *Luftpanzer* used to carry. It looked like the Silver Star had designed their own planes now, allowing the *Luftpanzer* to carry a larger complement. He'd never seen these planes in combat before, and didn't know how the Bristol would stack up against them.

She had been a fine fighter during the war, strong and agile, even though she was a two-seater. But a lot of her success against single seat fighters had been due to the rear mounted Lewis gun the observer could use to protect the rear—a weapon that Padger's surplus Bristol no longer had.

Behind him, Doc was still taking pictures of the ground features. He didn't like the idea of bringing her into a dogfight, especially one so one-sided.

If there were only one of them, he could try leading it into a Lufberry circle, always turning to force the other plane to follow to line up a shot. The result was two planes chasing each other around in a tight circle, gradually losing altitude until one pilot or the other had no choice but to break away. But if he tried that, the second plane could simply stand off and bring him down. The more Jack looked for options, the fewer he saw, and time was running out.

As if to emphasize that thought, the nearer pilot opened up on him again. This time the rounds passed just to the right of the Bristol as Jack slid away from the line of fire.

"Hang on!" he shouted to Doc, then pulled up and rolled away to the left. The second plane moved in at an angle and fired as well. This time bullets tore through the upper wing.

He wasn't going to fly his way out of this, Jack realized. He started looking for a place to put the plane down in an at least partially controlled landing. There were occasional openings in the canopy, but there was no telling what was down there. He flew over one as he dodged incoming fire and saw a rocky stream channel that offered him nothing.

He took the Bristol higher, to get a better view of the ground. The breaks in the forest canopy were small and scattered, but he saw something perhaps a couple miles down the valley that looked like a larger break.

He dove again as both fighters fired at him. A couple rounds punched through the tail, but that was minor. Jack accelerated and leveled out just a few feet above the treetops, racing over the forest. He thought he'd seen open water in the distance, a pond or a small lake. At least there was a break in the forest. He was hoping he'd find a stretch of beach, or some open grassland where he could put the plane down. But he didn't know. He wasn't even certain the bright glint he'd glimpsed was really water.

"What do we do, Jack?" Doc shouted.

"Put the camera away," Jack called back. "We're going down hard. Nothing loose."

He jinked right as a burst of fire slashed into the nose. A moment later the Rolls engine started to smoke and rattle. The airspeed indicator began to drop. The throttles were fully open and he was on the deck. There was no way to pick up more speed. The only maneuvers available to him would just bleed off speed faster. He glanced over his shoulder and saw one of the Silver Star planes pull in above to keep him pinned down while the second slid into place on their tail. They were out of time.

Out of the corner of his eye he caught a glimpse of an open slash in the forest. Without even taking time to think, he slewed left, closed the throttle, and threw the elevators to full down. He saw the two Silver Star planes shoot past. Their pilots turned sharply to get him back in their sights, but Jack knew they were no longer a factor. Now it was just a question of surviving the crash.

"Brace!" he shouted, and then the right wingtip caught a tree top. The plane jerked hard, and he heard Doc scream. Then the

Bristol was ripping through a tangle of leafy vines. The engine snarled and stopped, Jack was thrown hard against his harness, and everything was green.

- CHAPTER 14 -

Jack came to with Doc shaking him and shouting directly into his face.

"Jack, wake up!"

He was still in the cockpit of the smashed Bristol. Oh, Padger was not going to be happy about this. He hurt, but he hurt everywhere more or less equally so he assumed he didn't have any critical injuries. And Doc seemed to be okay, but he should make sure of that.

"Are you okay?" he asked. That was just the right question, he realized. It focused right in on exactly what he wanted to know, and didn't take them off on any irrelevant tangents. So it seemed like his mind was working. All things considered, he decided, it could have been a lot worse.

"Damn it, Jack, move! NOW!"

He shook it off and unsnapped his harness. Overhead he heard the Silver Star planes coming closer. Doc was hauling him out over the edge of the cockpit, and he managed to help push himself clear. He tumbled out of the smashed plane, hit the dirt, and quickly got to his feet. He recognized the sound of an airplane going into a dive. He grabbed Doc's arm and pulled her with him.

"Come on! We need to move!" he snapped.

"Oh, do you think?" said Doc, and they sprinted for the cover of the jungle.

They made it the few feet to the trees and dove under the thick foliage as machine gun bullets strafed the wreck behind them. The Silver Star plane pulled up, and its partner came in for a pass of its own. More bullets ripped up the deep green leaves and fronds and stitched across the ruins of Padger's Bristol.

"Keep your head down," Jack said.

Doc sighed. "You are just full of good ideas today. Yes, by the way."

"Yes, what?"

"In answer to your question, I'm okay. In better shape than you, I think."

"I'm okay," said Jack. "Just shook me up. Not used to being the one that gets shot down."

"Well, I think we made it out of this one okay," she said. "But let's not make a habit of it."

One of the planes made a final pass over the site, and a smoke grenade tumbled down to the ground alongside the wreck, sending up a thick plume of bright red smoke. Then they heard the engines recede into the distance.

"Well, here we are," said Doc. "And I don't think we're flying out in that."

Jack gave her a confident smile. "Oh no, not nearly enough runway to get her up to takeoff speed."

"Oh, poor Padger," said Doc. "We didn't even ask. We kind of stole his airplane, didn't we?"

"Kind of," said Jack. "All right, let's see how much of our gear made it. They marked the crash so their ground troops can find it. We need to be far away by the time they get here."

They hurried back to the wreckage and managed to dig their kit bags out of the rear compartment. Doc's bag hadn't taken any damage from enemy fire, though it remained to be seen how much damage the crash itself had done to the scientific gear she'd packed.

Jack's bag had taken a couple bullets, but a quick check showed that they'd mainly shredded the top layer of cold weather gear. It looked like that would be unnecessary here anyway.

They shouldered the bags and set off. The valley appeared to run mainly along an east/west axis, with the canyon mouth and the Silver Star camp at the west end. So they headed east. Jack estimated that the valley was five to six miles wide at its widest point and ran for a good twenty miles. That meant about a hundred square miles of territory to hide in. It would be difficult for the Silver Star to track them down. Of course they might discover that the Silver Star was the least of their worries.

"Don't eat anything," Doc said as she took a photo of a strange plant with clusters of juicy looking purple berries concealed beneath its striped leaves. "Remember, there's at least one plant here that will drop you in your tracks."

"And one that will make us immortal and enlightened, if you believe the Long Walker," Jack said.

"Well, I don't like those odds," said Doc. "We've got a couple days' worth of food and water, right? Hopefully by then I'll have some idea of what's safe to eat and what isn't."

They made slow progress through thick undergrowth for perhaps a quarter mile. Then the thick jungle gave way to less dense trees without so much ground cover or the thick, parasitic vines that hung from the branches like Spanish Moss. They soon found a small river that flowed east, deeper into the valley, and they made better time moving along the bank. Jack had to hurry Doc along more than once as she kept stopping to photograph some new plant species or collect something in one of her seemingly endless supply of small, glass vials.

"This is astonishing! We're going to rewrite the botany texts!" Doc exclaimed after collecting specimens of yet another new plant. "I've discovered more new species in the last hour than were reported in the last ten years! And not just new species. I think some of these represent whole new families! I don't know how, but we've got to get a real scientific expedition in here."

Jack congratulated her, but he couldn't stop thinking that none of that was going to happen if they didn't find a way to survive here, evade the Silver Star, and somehow make it back to civilization. He didn't have a very good plan for doing any of those at the moment.

"It's not just plants," he said quietly as they headed off downstream again. They were following a dirt game trail that ran parallel to the river bank and connected various small watering holes. Jack wasn't much of a hunter, but he could definitely make out tracks near the water's edge. Some were small, but some suggested a large enough animal to possibly be dangerous. He kept the holsters of his .45s unsnapped and scanned the wilderness around them, looking for movement.

They found their first animals as they rounded a bend in the river. The channel widened into a broad, shallow pool—an ideal place to drink. A group of animals started and took off through the pool when Jack and Doc appeared.

Doc gasped and whipped her camera up, managing to get a shot just as they cleared the water and crashed through the underbrush on the far side. Jack counted perhaps a dozen of them. They were about the size of a pony, but looked more like antelope, or perhaps goats. Jack couldn't decide. They had long, deep gray hair and a blunt face that suggested a capybara more than anything else. The males had two long, spiraling horns like corkscrews that extended back over their shoulders.

Then they were gone. Jack listened to them crashing away through the foliage, then even that sound was gone. It was as if they'd never been there.

"Caprids!" said Doc. "Family Bovidae, Tribe Caprini. Beyond that, I don't know."

"They looked like a cross between a goat and a sheep," Jack offered.

"Yeah," Doc said cheerily. "Like I said, Caprids."

"Okay. As long as we're on the same page here."

"Sorry," said Doc with a grin. "I'm all splifficated on science."

"Perfectly okay," Jack said. "Shall we? I'm sure there's plenty more science up ahead."

They set off again, Jack in front and Doc happy to follow wherever he led. He should let her enjoy it, Jack thought as they moved farther down the trail. If she was all giddy with the thrill of new discoveries, she wouldn't be worrying about how precarious their situation was. Right now, he was worried enough for both of them.

Jack didn't know what time it was; his watch had apparently smashed against the Biff's control panel during the crash and was out of action. But the flight up from Almora had taken a good part of the day, and they'd been hiking for at least an hour now. He glanced over his shoulder and saw the sun already nearing the edge of the cliffs behind him. The days would be short here between the valley's high cliffs, he realized, and twilight would come on suddenly. He started looking for a place to shelter for the night.

Not far past the watering hole, the river narrowed again and tumbled through channels it had carved through upthrust fingers of rock. About twenty yards from the bank, Jack found an overhanging precipice that would hide them from the air. He stopped and let Doc inventory the small flowers along the riverbank while he checked it out. There was a flat space beneath the rock that they could clear easily enough. The stone overhang would be a low ceiling, but there was enough space for their tent with enough room left over to build a small fire. Best of all, Jack thought, they could build a lean-to from branches and vines that would hide them from outside. It would do, he decided.

"Okay, we camp here," he announced when he came back.

Doc was kneeling beside a small flowering plant, taking notes. But now she put her notebook away. "All right, I'm back," she said. "I can discover more things tomorrow. What do we need to do?"

He explained his plan, where he wanted to set up the tent, where the lean-to would go.

"Sounds good," she said. She helped him clear the brush from beneath the overhang, revealing a hard packed earth surface with a fringe of grass at the edges. Once she decided it was time to put her toys away and get serious about helping them survive here, she had shifted gears completely. Jack asked her about it as they worked.

"I knew you had my back," she said. "You were keeping us on course and watching for anything important. I knew while you were doing that, I didn't have anything to worry about. I could afford to look for new plants and make sketches. You'd make sure I was safe. It's just what you do."

Jack stepped back and watched her as she unfolded their small tent and laid out stakes where it would go. She stretched the canvas shape up, checked the clearance beneath the stone roof, and decided she could move it back another foot or so.

She trusted him, he thought. Even in a place like this, where she had no idea what dangers they might face, she trusted him to keep her safe. She was right, he thought. No matter what happened, he knew he would protect her and their daughter to the end. It was a strange feeling. He'd always done his best to protect the men who fought alongside him in the war, and the crew of the *Daedalus*—including Doc—as they fought against the Silver Star. That was his responsibility. But this was more than that.

"What are you looking at?" Doc asked, looking up at him from the half-assembled tent. The look in her eye told him that she understood completely.

"Nothing," he said. "I just like watching you put up tents. I just realized that."

"Well, you'd be amazed at the things I can do," she said with a grin. "Go get some branches and you can watch me build a lean-to. If you're really good, I'll let you help."

"Yes, ma'am," Jack said. He threw her a playful salute and headed out into the forest.

He moved quietly along the game trail, listening for movement as he collected sticks. He heard only the cries of distant birds. Even those sounded strange, different from the bird calls he knew in some way he couldn't put his finger on. It was all so unreal. How could a place like this exist? How had the various plants and animals gotten here in the first place?

He'd spotted steam vents from the air. The warmth had to be the result of volcanic activity. But the air pressure felt like normal sea level. If anything the air was richer in oxygen than what he was used to. He felt energized here. Could the volcanic vents be putting out oxygen? He had no idea. Perhaps Doc knew something about that.

But at any rate, the place was astonishing in every way. No wonder the Long Walker had decided this place overlapped with the spirit world.

He stopped suddenly, listening intently, his nerves singing as a rush of adrenaline hit him. It took him a second to realize what had caught his attention. There. A boot print in the soft earth at the edge of the trail. Definitely not his.

He listened, but still heard nothing. He studied the print. It looked fresh. The tread was obviously of modern industrial manufacture. The print's edges were well defined and a twig lay snapped across its edge. Whoever made it had been here recently, no more than a day ago, he thought.

Jack quietly drew one of his .45s and looked for more prints. He found another one perhaps twenty feet down the trail. And then something else. A sapling just off the trail that had been bent over and tied down. He edged closer and glimpsed something metallic. Someone had built a snare trap along what looked like a small game run through the underbrush. He knelt down and carefully examined it. They'd bent over the sapling and fastened a wire loop to the end, then fashioned a simple trigger out of scrap metal. But not just any metal, Jack realized. They'd used tin snips to cut the pieces out of a cheap cooking pot. Jack felt his unease growing. He'd seen pots like that before. There was the particular curve of a lid that was meant to double as a dish once the meal was ready. He moved carefully around the trap, looking for the stamped inventory number he suspected would be there. And there it was.

The pieces had come from a Silver Star field mess kit.

Jack edged away from the trap, his mind racing. He'd been thinking of large search parties, awkward groups crashing through the undergrowth, making plenty of noise. Something they would hear coming and could easily avoid. But the real danger might be something else entirely. He quickly finished gathering branches and vines and headed back to their small camp.

As Jack expected, darkness came quickly. The sun fell behind the cliffs while he was still on the trail, and by the time he made it back to the tent, it was almost too dark to see where he was going. But the tent was set up and Doc had a small lantern lit. She was inside, laying out bedding and organizing their supplies. Jack dropped the sticks outside and joined her. He turned down the lantern's wick to dim the light, and sat cross-legged with his back to the flaps so his body blocked most of the light from outside. Doc's tone changed in an instant.

"What's the matter?" she said, and Jack could hear concern in her voice. He quickly told her what he'd found.

"We already knew the Silver Star was here," she said after a moment's thought. That was true of course. But still there was something unsettling about the improvised trap.

"Why so far from their camp?" Jack mused.

"They're not trapping small game for food," said Doc. "I got a good look at that camp as we flew over. They must have a good fifty men there."

Jack nodded. "They won't feed all those mouths trapping a few rabbits, especially all the way out here. More likely they're sending out hunting parties to shoot those things we saw before. The um..."

"Caprids?"

"Caprids. Yeah." Then a thought occurred to him. "Do you think they could be trapping specimens for research?"

She shook her head. "They could do that closer to home. And if the Silver Star wanted to trap animals, they wouldn't jerry rig something out of old pots. They'd show up with the best traps money can buy."

Jack sighed. He'd reached the same conclusion. "They've got scouts out here," he said with a resigned nod. It was the only thing that made sense. One or more experienced wilderness hands detached from the main camp and sent out to explore the valley, gather information, and draw maps. They'd travel light, moving around and living off the land. They'd be used to improvising with what they had. A Silver Star scout was who would have one of their mess kits out here. And that was who would cut it up to make a crude snare trap.

"You said the prints were recent?" Doc asked.

"No more than a day. And no reason for him to go off and abandon his trap. No, he's still around here somewhere. And if I can find his trail, any half decent scout should have no trouble spotting ours. We've been gallivanting around like tourists all day."

"We have to be more careful," said Doc quietly. "Keep our eyes open out there."

"Yeah," Jack agreed. "I don't know what else we can do though. We can't just hunker down here and wait for them to find us. I guess just keep in mind that someone's out there and be alert."

Soon after that, they put out the lantern and Doc went to sleep. Jack sat up with one of his .45s, gazing out into the night and going over the list of things out there that might kill them.

It was a list that kept getting longer all the time.

- CHAPTER 15 -

The night was chill, and a cool breeze picked up from the south, coming down across the valley from the mountain peaks above. Jack and Doc were happy to be well-protected beneath their rock overhang. Jack got little sleep. He stayed up well into the night, keeping watch while Doc slept, and the wind rustled the crude lean-to that hid them. Someone was out there, and Jack didn't know when they might appear.

But the night passed uneventfully. It rained at some point, but by dawn it had cleared, and the morning was clear and warm. Doc got to work with the test equipment she'd brought with her. It wasn't much, but she was able to do some basic tests. She quickly determined that the river water at least was safe, and sent Jack off with a folding canvas bucket to retrieve some.

Then she started preparing samples. All morning she crushed leaves with a small mortar and pestle. She spread stains on slides and left them out in the sun. She painted plant resins on test strips and muttered to herself. Jack spent the morning working on the shelter. He strengthened the shield of branches and vines that hid them from outside view and extended it farther around the rock overhang. The problem with that was that it blocked too much of the daylight from outside, so Jack worked on a way to move the walls farther out from the rock and create a kind of skylight in the gap. That proved more difficult than he anticipated. It would have worked better with actual lumber, but he didn't have the tools for serious woodworking. Besides, he concluded, that would make the shelter fairly obvious to anyone passing by.

By noon, it seemed that they were treating being marooned as some particularly exotic form of camping. Jack noticed that he kept planning new and elaborate conveniences for their campsite, and Doc was happily humming a Gershwin tune as she tested her specimens. It was almost as if this had somehow become their vacation, and when they were finished they would simply go home.

That changed after they ate lunch from their rapidly dwindling food supply. They both heard the steady drone of distant airplane engines.

"Southwest," Jack announced after they listened in silence for nearly a minute. "Maybe five miles. Long way from here anyway, and they're not coming any closer."

After a few moments, the wind shifted, and the sound faded away.

Doc let out a sigh of relief. "It's a big valley, but it doesn't go on forever. You think they'll keep looking for us until they find us?"

"Oh, yes," Jack admitted. "They'll have reached the crash by now, so they know we got out. And there's no other way out of the valley, so they know we're still back here somewhere. They can't leave us running around loose behind their lines."

Jack went outside and checked the lean-to again, adding more leaves and vines to conceal the underlying branches. Then he heard Doc call his name.

"This is it!" she said as Jack came back inside the shelter. She showed him a series of darkened test strips and a petri dish full of a yellow waxy substance lined with dark streaks.

"Some things the Long Walker said," Doc said quietly. "I thought it might be this one."

She showed him a vial containing a sprig of something. The plant had lacy white flowers with pinkish stems emerging from a wooden twig.

"Take a good look, and keep away from it," Doc said. "It's all over the place out there. Whole meadows of the stuff."

"This can do what we saw to a person?"

"Not like this," Doc said. "The Silver Star version is an awful lot stronger. They must have found some way to refine it, amplify the effect. But it's the same active substances. A lot like cicutoxin. That's a central nervous system stimulant. Scopolamine. Some very complex plant alkaloids and other things I can't even begin to identify. But this has everything I found in the poison samples we got from New York. Trust me, this will kill you dead enough on its own."

"What about the other plants? Are they poisonous too?"

"Some of them," said Doc. "Not all of them, and nothing like this. There's got to be something we can eat around here. Those caprids we saw yesterday are herbivores. Hey, maybe we can watch them and see what they eat. That'll give us a starting point for figuring out what's safe. And I'll keep testing."

"All right," said Jack. "You do that. I'm going to take a look around outside. See if there's anything nearby we can use. Or something we should move away from."

"Can you use my camera?" Doc asked. She collected it from a pile of gear next to the tent and offered it to him. "If you find something interesting, I'd appreciate some pictures. They could help."

Jack nodded and slung the camera strap around his neck. Then he gathered a couple spare magazines for his .45s and a folding machete for cutting through brush, and set off.

They'd followed the river most of the way here, so Jack started out at a right angle to it, moving up a gentle slope and then down the far side of a ridge. In places the jungle was thick, and he had to cut his way through the underbrush. But he found clear areas that let him move more quickly and let those guide his path since he didn't have any particular reason to choose one direction over another. He could still see the mountains on either side of the valley, so all he had to do to get back was head toward the northern edge of the valley until he hit the river. Then he could follow it back to camp.

As he wandered, noting landforms, plant life, and the occasional distant animal, he considered their longer term strategy. They couldn't stay here forever. The Silver Star had plenty of men in the valley, and all the time they needed to mark the terrain off into grid squares and tear each one apart until they found them. Besides, Jack and Doc had a daughter waiting for them, and a life outside this place.

Their reason for coming here was to identify the poison, and Doc had done that with remarkable speed. She would find an antidote soon enough, if there was one to be found. And then they'd have no reason to stay beyond scientific curiosity. The place certainly deserved a real scientific expedition. But the two of them gathering samples and taking pictures while they dodged the Silver Star hardly qualified.

So they had to leave, and pretty soon, Jack guessed. And there was only one way to do that. Well, two actually, he corrected himself. It apparently was possible to get in and out of the valley on foot. The Long Walker had done it, and he seemed to think others had as well. But Jack had no idea how. The thin air outside the valley alone would make the trip next to impossible. Even without that, it would take world-class mountaineering skills to make it back to civilization over land.

No, the only way out for them was the way they'd come in. Which meant they needed an airplane. And of course there was only one place in the valley to find one of those.

He hadn't gotten a very good look at the Silver Star planes; he'd been too busy dodging their machine guns. But they were pretty small. Still, they had to be able to carry at least one passenger. How else would the Silver Star have gotten their soldiers into the valley? Not to mention all the equipment and supplies to support them. So Jack was confident he could fly one of the small planes, and confident that Doc and their gear would fit inside somehow.

He was crossing a relatively open field now, in an area where the jungle had thinned out. He noticed that the valley shifted from one type of environment to another with surprising speed. Thick jungle gave way scrub brush and stunted trees, then to open grassland, and back to jungle again, all within a couple of miles. Doc would probably have some explanation for it, but it put Jack's teeth on edge. The place just didn't feel real somehow. Again, he thought of the Long Walker's claim that this place touched the spirit world.

The ground was rocky where he was walking. It looked almost paved, with flat stones scattered across the grassy landscape like cobblestones. Other rocks thrust up from the earth, looking like small huts. He rounded one of these latter, and stopped short. The ground here had been ripped apart. Several of the heavy, flat stones had been levered out of the ground, rolled aside, and left where they fell. Scattered piles of dirt surrounded a rough hole. The rains had rounded the edges and filled the bottom with muck. The hole had been here a while, and he couldn't detect any signs of human presence. But someone must have been here. It would have taken several men most of a day to do this with shovels, rope, and heavy tools. Was the Silver Star digging for something? Perhaps there were valuable minerals here, or perhaps they were digging for some buried occult artifact. Jack unsnapped the case of Doc's Leica and took some pictures of it.

When he'd done that, he glanced up at the sun. It was getting toward late afternoon and the night came quickly here. He decided he'd better start back.

He retraced his steps back to the north, letting himself take a different course. Once he spotted a hillside covered in the white flowers Doc had shown him and gave them a wide berth. There didn't seem to be any other plants competing for the land and sunlight there, he noticed. Perhaps the plant's poison leached into the ground and killed anything else that tried to take root.

But something wasn't afraid of the poison, he realized to his surprise. There were animals on the hillside. They were small, four-legged mammals with brown fur and bushy tails. They looked like weasels, or maybe some kind of wild cat, but they were neither. Jack had no idea what they were. But they were eating the exact plants that Doc claimed were the source of the poison. He took several photos of them, and considered shooting one to take back to Doc. But he didn't relish the idea of wading into the flowers to recover the body. In the end, he left them in peace, happily nibbling at the poisonous flowers.

Soon he was back in the heavy jungle and could hear the river somewhere ahead of him. He recognized landmarks now, and knew he was close to their camp. While he walked, he considered how to steal an airplane from the Silver Star camp and escape.

They'd have to do it during the day; it would be suicide to try and make the flight through the canyon in the dark. But in the early morning the sun would be low behind them and not in his eyes as he flew. That would work, he decided. They could approach the camp during the night. That was the best choice since the valley mouth was mostly open grassland that offered little cover. Then, when dawn came, they could go for one of the planes. He'd have to disable the other one, he realized. The last thing he needed while threading his way through the canyon in an unfamiliar airplane was another plane on his tail, spraying them with machine gun bullets.

He froze suddenly. Had he heard something moving? A moment later he heard it again. A faint tearing sound. Some of the parasitic vines clung to the tree trunks through thousands of tiny fibers. As he'd moved through the forest he'd yanked handfuls of the vines aside to clear his path, and they made that sound as they ripped away from the nearby trees. He recognized the top of the rock overhang where they'd built their camp off in the distance. It might be Doc, but Jack knew it wasn't when he heard the sound once more. Whoever it was was moving slowly, with a caution Doc didn't need.

Jack edged closer, careful to avoid the vines. He kept low, angling toward a smaller clutch of rocks that would hide him. When he reached them, he put down the Leica and crept up the slanted top of one of the larger boulders.

There. A figure moved between the trees. Jack could see the lean-to a few dozen yards to his left. The figure was creeping slowly in that direction. He was shielded by a tangle of undergrowth now, but he would have to cross into the clear to reach the shelter.

Jack unsnapped one of his holsters, but then thought better of shooting. He didn't know if the man was alone. If he was an advance scout for a Silver Star search party—or even if he wasn't—a shot would alert any others nearby.

A moment later the figure emerged into view, and Jack held his breath. He recognized the dark field jacket and pants of the Silver Star field uniform, as well as the matching boots. Those boots would have been perfect for making the prints he'd found earlier. But the most worrying thing about him was the spear he gripped. It had a bamboo shaft perhaps six feet long, and he'd thrust a bayonet handle into one end and wrapped it tightly with leather thongs. It was obviously improvised, an unusual weapon for a Silver Star soldier.

His unkempt blonde hair and several days' worth of beard was unusual for the Silver Star as well, as was the ratty condition of his uniform. He looked like he'd been out here for some time. This had to be the scout who'd made the snare trap.

He was edging closer to the shelter where Doc was busy and distracted with her plant samples. Jack plotted his slow course across the open ground between them and the lean-to. He waited for the man to take a few more cautious, silent steps forward, until he was in the perfect position. Jack moved into a low crouch on top of the stone, like a sprinter getting into position. One more step...

Jack unleashed all his strength. He powered through the few steps to the edge of the boulder and then leapt into the air. The man caught sight of Jack as he hurtled toward him, but too late. Jack slammed into him. The impact ripped the spear from his grasp, and it flew across the clearing as they both fell in a heap.

The man whipped a second bayonet from his belt, and Jack jerked his head back as the blade flashed an inch in front of his eyes. Then he sank a knee into the man's side and struck the inside of his elbow. The bayonet flew away into the brush, and Jack rolled on top of him. He grabbed the man's throat with his left hand and slammed his head back against the ground. He drew back his right hand in a fist and was about to unleash a devastating cross when suddenly Doc screamed.

"Jack! No!"

They both froze, Jack on top of the other man with his arm cocked to finish him off. The blonde man looked up at Jack in confusion.

"Wait, you're not..." Then he looked over at Doc. "Dorothy?" Now he sounded even more mystified.

Doc nodded. "It's okay. Jack, for God's sake, put your arm down. You look ridiculous."

Jack unclenched his fist and slowly lowered his arm. Now he was just as confused as the man he was still pinning down by the throat.

"You two know each other?"

"That we do," said Doc. "Jack, allow me to introduce you to Dr. Christopher Rhys."

- CHAPTER 16 -

"You're Rhys?" Jack said in disbelief. He noticed his hand was still on Rhys' throat and hastily removed it.

"At your service," said Rhys.

"Boy, when you go missing, you don't do it halfway!" said Jack. He got off Rhys and extended a hand to help him up. "Jack McGraw. Sorry about that. I thought you were Silver Star."

Rhys looked down at his scratched and stained uniform. "What else would you think? When I saw your camp, I assumed you must be Silver Star too. I mean who else is here? How are you here anyway? Did you come looking for me?"

"Sort of," said Doc. "We have a problem we hoped you could help us with, but we couldn't reach you. When we got here, your man Adesh told us you'd disappeared in the hills. But I never dreamed we'd find you here."

"This problem," Rhys said, brushing off his jacket, "it wouldn't have anything to do with poison, by any chance?"

"Maybe you should start at the beginning," said Jack. They walked back to the lean-to that hid the shelter—not well enough apparently, Jack told himself. Rhys retrieved his spear and sat down on a rock.

"It started several months ago," he said. "I was visited by a young German mountaineer. He was full of questions about ancient alchemy and the lost kingdom of Shambala. Nonsense, I thought, and I sent him on his way. You see it from time to time. Westerners come to India and get caught up in the ancient mysticism of the East. I thought no more of it. But then I set out on a walking tour through the hills. Looking for examples of *pandanus furcatus* mainly. Local subspecies of screw pine. Say, you wouldn't have some cigarettes with you?"

Doc smiled and shook her head. "Sorry," said Jack.

"Oh well," Rhys said without obvious disappointment. "Anyway, I was two days out when along comes a whole troop of very heavily armed Germans on motorcycles. They hauled me off to the top of a nearby hill. A few minutes later the biggest bloody airship I've ever seen in my life settled right down, as pretty as you please. They bundled me aboard, and a few days later, here I was. And that was my introduction to the Silver Star."

"Some people have had worse," Jack observed.

"I believe it," said Rhys. "Nasty bunch. I got off light because they wanted my expertise in the local botany and folk medicines."

"I can guess why," Doc said. She quickly filled Rhys in on the poisonings in America and how they'd followed the trail here. Rhys looked pale when she was finished.

"Knew they were up to no good, of course," he said. "But they didn't give me much choice. I helped them. Have you found the white flower? Yes, good, you know to stay clear of it then. Well, they found it too. They call it *totenspitze*, Death Lace. The substances they were able to isolate from it are...very troubling."

Rhys was silent for a moment, then he shook it off. "Eventually I managed to escape, and I've been out here playing hide and seek with them ever since. So you must have been the cause of that commotion yesterday. I thought they were looking for me. You've got an airplane, then?"

"We've got a pile of junk that used to be an airplane, I'm afraid," said Jack. "We went down in the jungle a few miles from here."

"Ah, the red smoke," Rhys said. "Of course. Too bad, that. An airplane would come in handy right now."

"I'm working on a plan," said Jack.

"Well, in the meantime, this is where you're setting up camp? This won't do at all. If the Silver Star doesn't find you, the Tarasques will."

"The what?" Doc asked.

Rhys grinned. "I named them *Amphicyon Rhysi*," he said, "though I'm just guessing about the genus really. More commonly, Tarasque, after a monster from an old French legend. You'll have noticed the animal life here is rather different from what we're used to."

There was a bit of the professor in this man, Jack thought to himself. Still, he found himself liking Rhys. He might have been forced to help the Silver Star, but he'd found a way to escape and deny them his knowledge. Perhaps he'd slowed their research down a little in the process.

"Apex predators," Rhys was saying. "Huge blighters, ugly as sin. Not picky about what they eat. Can't afford to be, I expect. But it turns out they're especially fond of a large worm that lives under rocks. They're very well adapted to digging them out."

"I found a hole like that today," Jack said. "Rocks and dirt thrown everywhere. I thought the Silver Star had been digging."

"No, that's the Tarasques' work all right. They go about eating anything that crosses their path and devastating the countryside. Thus the name. But you can see why this place just won't do. I've got a base of my own up in the cliffs across the river. Well concealed from the air, and much less trouble with the wildlife. I'll take you there. Plenty of room. It'll be nice to have houseguests!"

Doc and Jack traded a questioning look. Jack thought for a moment. Doc apparently trusted this man, and Jack remembered the hole he found. If that was the work of an animal, he didn't want to tangle with it.

"Thank you, Doctor," he said after a moment. "We appreciate the warning. And the hospitality."

They packed up their gear. While they were working, Rhys broke down the lean-to and scattered the branches so there would be less for Silver Star search parties to find if they came this way.

Then he led them down the river with his spear over his shoulder. He had snares and other traps for small game scattered about and veered off from time to time to check one. Doc confirmed that Rhys had found quite a few plants and species of small game that were safe to eat.

"I'm mainly after the civets, though," he said as he reset a snare that had tripped but failed to hold its prey. "They're for research."

"Civets?" said Jack.

"*Paguma Rhysi*," Rhys answered with a sheepish grin.

"I'm noticing a trend," said Doc.

"All I wanted was a nice hike through the foothills and to draw some trees," said Rhys. "If I'm to be subjected to this kind of adventure against my will, I don't think a touch of scientific immortality is too much to ask in return. Don't worry, there's plenty left to name after you two. But the civets are important. They actually eat the Death Lace. It ought to drop them in their tracks, but they adore the stuff. Something protects them. If there's an antidote, that's where we'll find it."

They headed back to the river and Rhys led the way downstream. The river channel grew narrower, and boulders lay strewn across the stream bed. Then they lost sight of the river as the trail veered away into deep forest, and they descended a steep slope. Jack could hear the river roaring to his left. When the slope leveled off again, the trail turned back toward the river.

"Want to see something impressive?" Rhys shouted back.

They broke through the trees and stopped, stunned. Doc gasped. "Caroline Falls!" Rhys announced proudly. "After my mother. It's something, isn't it?"

Jack had to admit it was. The land fell sharply away to a deep gorge. They'd followed the slope down perhaps halfway, Jack realized. But the river had carved the land farther back to create a sheer lip a couple hundred feet above them. The water fell past them and plummeted down into the gorge where it vanished into a cloud of mist.

"What's down there?" Doc shouted.

"No idea!" Rhys answered. "Not keen to find out, really. This way!"

They followed him down a path along the edge of the gorge. On the other side were jagged cliff walls with scattered ledges and a few hardy trees in those rare places where the ground was flat enough to hold soil.

A few hundred yards farther down, a huge tree had fallen across the gorge. It formed a natural bridge to a wide ledge on the other side. Rhys hopped onto the massive trunk and started across. Doc glanced back at Jack, and then followed. Jack let them get a few feet farther ahead, then followed them. He could feel the faint touch of spray from the falls against his skin and realized the smooth worn wood of the trunk was damp and more slick than he liked.

When they reached the other side, Rhys turned and led them along the grassy ledge until it gradually narrowed to a bare stone shelf a few feet wide winding along the cliff face.

Rhys walked along it with confidence, looking over his shoulder and conversing with Doc about the local plants as he walked on the very edge of oblivion. The man certainly didn't lack courage. Jack brought up the rear, watching where he stepped.

"Almost there," Rhys announced cheerily. "Home sweet home."

He stepped around a blind turn in the path and then into a wide crack in the cliff face. They followed and found themselves in a surprisingly comfortable space. Rhys had lanterns for light, a bedroll on what looked like a very comfortable pad of local vines and tree fronds. He even had some simple furniture lashed together from what looked like bamboo.

"Well this is impressive," said Doc.

"No reason to give up civilized comforts," said Rhys. "We'll get you set up soon enough. Tomorrow we'll get you some of these *Drynaria* fronds to put your sleeping bags on. In the meantime, come see the lab!"

"Lab?" Doc said. They followed Rhys into a side chamber. Here, on a long table made from roughly hewn logs, was an impressive collection of scientific equipment. Some of it was improvised from local materials, but there was a surprising amount of glassware, metal frames, and rubber tubing. Jack noted bottles of various chemical reagents, boxes labeled in German, and a thick notebook.

"I raid the Silver Star camp for what I need," said Rhys.

"What in the world are you working on?" said Doc.

"Oh, just studying the native biology. Have to occupy myself somehow. Take a look at this!"

He turned to the far wall, and Jack realized the place was naturally lit. Rhys had punched through the stone face of the cliff with a hammer and chisel to create two windows that let in the afternoon sun.

"And here's the water supply," he was saying, pointing out a crack in the back wall of the lab chamber. A spring trickled water into a natural stone basin until it overflowed and disappeared through another crack in the floor.

Jack was impressed, but he recognized that nagging feeling in the back of his mind that something wasn't right. He looked over the lab equipment, the dozens of stolen glass bottles lined up and neatly labeled. He flipped through the notebook. The pages were filled with chemical diagrams and lined with dates and symbols. Along the right edge of each page was a column listing a number of milligrams, and always a final entry, "no effect." These continued until Rhys had started simply jotting "NE."

Rhys returned with Doc and noticed Jack looking over his notes. "We'll get you set up, don't you worry," he said, and he subtly but firmly put a hand on Jack's shoulder and guided him away from the table and back out of the lab. "My word, it's good to have someone to talk to. So much you have to tell me."

They filled Rhys in on AEGIS and their long battle against the Silver Star while Rhys prepared dinner. He cut some meat off a dried hind quarter of what Jack realized was one of the caprids they'd seen at the water hole. He added some roots and vegetables, and soon had a hearty stew bubbling over a fire pit.

"Home cooking," Doc said softly.

"I'm glad your friend's okay," Jack murmured back.

Doc nodded. "I know. But he's lying to us."

"To carry all this stuff back here by himself? That's got to be six trips at least."

"Just for the lab gear alone," Doc agreed.

"Sneaking into a Silver Star camp like that's a heck of a risk. Nobody does that a half dozen times without a real good reason."

Then they fell silent as Rhys returned with the stew pot. "Dinner is served!" he said cheerily. "So good to have company. I know I'm repeating myself, but it's just wonderful you're here. Well, not for you, I suppose. But it's good to have visitors. Especially one who can fly an airplane, right?"

He ladled the stew out into metal bowls from a Silver Star field kit. Over dinner, Jack laid out his plan to steal an airplane and escape the valley. "We won't be able to take much," he said, "but we can make it. And we're leaving soon. We've identified the poison. As soon as you two can get a working antidote, we need to get back to the outside world with it, before the Silver Star kills more people."

"An antidote may be trickier than you think," said Rhys, and Jack could sense the meaning behind his words. For some reason, the man was reluctant to leave.

☙

After Dorothy and her friend had gone to sleep, Dr. Rhys slipped up from his bedroll and made his way into the lab. Outside was darkness and a few scattered stars, so he turned up one of the lanterns until it cast a faint glow over his experiments.

He opened a stolen box of hypodermics and took out a needle. He'd sterilized this one yesterday, but all his instruments were so crude. It was a miracle he'd survived at all, and now to actually have a way out of this cursed place...

He filled the syringe from a glass jar of a clear liquid and rolled up his sleeve. He tapped the needle to clear air and was clenching his arm to bring up a vein when he realized he wasn't alone.

"We need to talk, Christopher," said Dorothy.

He looked up and saw her standing in the rough doorway.

"Whatever's happening, we can help, but you have to tell me the truth. What is this?"

He sighed. He had no choice, really. If anyone could help him, it would be Dorothy Starr.

"I can't leave with you," he said. "I'd be dead within a couple of days."

"What are you saying?"

"The Silver Star already had the Death Lace extract when they took me, and they'd already refined it. They didn't need my help for that. They wanted my help to make it more controllable."

"What do you mean?"

"The Science Leader of their expedition is a Dr. Mencken. There's a military commander too, Captain Ardinger, though they have a difference of opinion over who's actually in charge. Mencken's a madman. A sadist. Ardinger tries to keep him in check, but their leaders place a high value on Mencken's work."

He closed his eyes for a moment, then he plunged ahead.

"They'd figured out the civets are immune. They didn't want an antidote, but they wanted to slow the poison down so it wouldn't kill the victim outright. They wanted a serum that would keep a poisoned victim alive as long as they kept taking it."

"My god," Dorothy whispered. "That's horrible. They'd be dependent on the Silver Star for their lives."

He nodded.

"By then I'd already tried to escape once. Dr. Mencken was furious."

Realization broke across Dorothy's face. "Oh no, Christopher!"

"He used me as a test subject. They injected me, used me to test the dosage of their control serum. Mencken figured that would keep me from trying to escape again."

"But you..."

"I've got a trick or two up my sleeve still. The serum's an extract from the livers of the civets. I figured out how to make my own. But if I'm away from the civets..."

"There's got to be a way to stop it!"

"I'm trying. I've found some promising avenues. But I live in a cave!" He felt the frustration boiling up inside him and forced it back down. "It's not the best laboratory, to be honest."

Dorothy stepped forward and placed a hand on his forearm. "We'll find an answer, Christopher. We won't just abandon you here."

But after she returned to the main chamber and left him alone, he realized that eventually she would do exactly that. She wouldn't want to. But he was one man, and the Silver Star threatened the whole world. The way to stop this was to escape, to warn the world, and then to come back with a fleet of airships from their secret army and burn this valley until not a twig remained. No, they'd leave, and if he wasn't able to leave with them, he'd be trapped here until his luck ran out.

Fate had nothing good in store for him. Unless he made his own fate. Rhys flipped through the notebook, then closed it. What he was considering now was less science than raw superstition. There was a formula in ancient books, passed down from healer to healer for centuries. Many alchemists had tried to recreate it and failed. They didn't have the right ingredients; they weren't here. They'd corrupted the formula by trying to substitute what was available to them. But here, seeing the plants, watching the behavior of the animals, it was obvious to him what the original had been.

He took another small case from deep within a box. Inside was another hypodermic and a small glass vial sealed with wax. It held a pale yellow substance. Rhys stared at the vial for a long time. If he was wrong, this would kill him. The records of failed experiments suggested it wouldn't be an easy death.

But what choice did he have now?

Rhys glanced at the opening to the main chamber. Then he filled the syringe and stopped thinking. Conscious thought had taken him as far as it could. What was called for was raw instinct.

He slid the needle into his arm and slid the plunger home.

For a moment, nothing happened. Rhys withdrew the syringe and placed it on the table. Then he felt it hit, and the pain was intense, like his skull being torn open. He fell to the floor and writhed in silent agony, unable to cry out.

There was a great rushing sound and a pale glow that seemed to emanate from everywhere. Then, even though he could still see the stars through the windows and feel the cold stone at his back, he felt himself falling. The stars were different somehow. Everything was different. He felt energy coursing through him and it terrified him because he knew it could tear him apart.

The energy was everywhere. In the rock as a stolid, heavy force. He could see it in the sky, burning in the stars. He saw the spiraling forms of Dorothy and Jack, side by side in the next room. He saw everything. And still he fell.

Dr. Christopher Rhys lay on the stone floor, twitching and shaking. Around him, the universe opened up, and he fell all the way to its very center. And the heart of the universe received him and took him in.

- CHAPTER 17 -

The next morning dawned clear and bright, and Jack awoke to the sound of Dr. Rhys softly whistling a tune as he prepared breakfast for them in the back of the cave.

"Sorry I kept my situation from you," he said as they ate. "It seemed the thing to do at the time. Now I'm not sure why, really."

The man's mood had changed from yesterday, Jack noted. There was still a cheery friendliness about him, but now it felt more natural, less forced. It made sense that the secret he'd kept had weighed on him. With that out in the open, he could be himself, and he seemed a truly open and likable person. He'd been through a lot, Jack knew. But he seemed to be dealing with it well. Jack found himself gaining a new respect for the doctor's resiliency. Escaping from the Silver Star, especially under the circumstances, and achieving what he had here in the wilderness was truly impressive.

Over breakfast, they discussed the situation they faced. The Silver Star now had two poisons to work with. One they'd already seen. The other came with a serum that inhibited its action, but only as long as the victim kept taking it. Once it was withdrawn, the victim would die as horribly as Cobb, Ponderby, and the others. Jack wasn't sure how that was possible. Doc was the poison expert, and she was amazed as well.

But that didn't really matter. Their job was to stop it. Rhys had done some of the work for them. He could produce the serum, though whether it could be synthesized in a lab outside this valley remained to be seen. But what they really needed was a true antidote, something that would free a victim from the need for a serum entirely, as well as protect against the original, immediately fatal poison.

Rhys was convinced the civets held the key. So after breakfast, they decided to go hunting.

"We don't want to go wading into fields of Death Lace for them," Rhys said. "But there's a watering hole upriver. They'll show up there when the sun's high. We can get there before them and prepare if we don't dally."

He brought out several crude nets he'd woven from dried vines and they helped him pack them into a canvas backpack. "Tried this when I first got out here," he explained. "But it was like trying to herd cats. By myself, best I could manage was trapping them one at a time with the snares. I've been catching maybe a couple a day if I'm lucky. Barely enough to keep myself going. But with the three of us working together, I think we might have better luck."

They left the cave and walked carefully along the ledge until it widened out. Then they once more crossed the gorge on the fallen tree trunk. The waterfall roared behind them and threw off small rainbows in the bright morning sun.

They made their way back upstream, past the rock overhang where they'd built their first camp. Rhys stopped from time to time to check his traps, and found that one had caught a civet. He stuffed it into a sack he slung over his shoulder.

"Shame to kill them," he said as he reset the snare. "They're harmless creatures. Charming to watch them play without a care in a meadow full of Death Lace. But we all have to eat. And without the extract from their livers, well, one does what one must."

Jack understood. They couldn't afford sentimentality. The Silver Star certainly had no time for it. They would wipe out their enemies efficiently and ruthlessly unless he and Doc and Rhys could find a way to stop it. If they failed here, if they were captured by the Silver Star, many people would die.

When they reached the watering hole, Rhys walked carefully around the bank, studying tracks in the soft earth. Then he stood on a rock near the shore and surveyed the area.

"Over there," he said, pointing across the river. There was a line of bushes and undergrowth a few yards from the river's edge. "When we flush them, they'll run for the nearest ground cover."

They waded through the shallow water to the far bank, carefully unfurled Rhys' nets, and laid them out along the brush. Rhys had a few stakes in his pack, and Jack gathered branches from the woods nearby to make more. They hammered them into the earth and hung the nets. The dried vines were roughly the same dull color as the brush. When they were done, Jack could barely make them out from twenty feet away. He decided it would do.

"They come here to drink every day?" Doc asked.

"As far as I can tell," Rhys answered. "The predators mostly hunt by night, so they give the morning some time to get going right and proper. Then they'll show up. We just need to move away and let our scent clear."

Rhys led them up into the higher ground and onto a small promontory that offered a clear view along both banks of the river as well as the approaches to the watering hole and the line of nets they'd strung against the brush. There, they sat down on the grassy shelf, and Rhys stretched in the sun. "Time to relax," he said. "Can't get over how warm it is here. Volcanic steam vents, you know. Outside this valley it's freezing. In here, practically tropical. You have to tell me how you two met, by the way."

Rhys lay back on the grass, and Jack and Doc sat down to wait with him. Rhys chatted with Doc mainly, as she told him about how she and Jack had met and the odd paths their lives had taken before they found each other again. Jack contributed to the conversation from time to time, but mostly he scanned the land and the air with the binoculars in his kit bag. This was a place where it didn't pay to drop your guard. Once, he spotted two black spots in the air in the distance. At first he took them for birds, but his binoculars revealed the shapes of the two Silver Star fighters. Their enemies were still searching for them. He was about to point them out to Doc and Rhys when he thought better of it. They were far off, so far that he couldn't hear their engines. He decided to let Doc and Rhys enjoy a moment of peace.

"Well of course you have a little girl," Rhys was saying. "Look at the two of you! It's obvious! You're meant to be happy together."

The phrasing was odd, Jack thought, but he certainly appreciated the sentiment. He smiled and met Rhys' eyes. His happiness for them was clear.

"The people here," said Rhys, then he laughed, "well, not exactly here, but, well you know, they say nothing's all good or all bad. Nothing's that simple. All things contain their opposites. They present different facets to the light. Even the war. How many people found each other in the middle of that hell who otherwise never would have met? Or perhaps met but never found the courage to reach out to one another?"

He glanced away for a moment, suddenly wistful. "The war stripped away our armor, and we stood naked before each other. We could no longer hide who we truly were."

And just as suddenly he was back. "You two found each other, and you truly saw each other. You can run from that if it frightens you, but you can't deny it."

Doc was embarrassed, Jack realized. "What's gotten into you today, Christopher?" she said a bit suddenly. "You're coming down with philosophy!"

Rhys just smiled and placed a hand on hers. "It's okay," was all he said.

Doc didn't seem to know how to respond. There was an uncomfortable feeling now, not because Rhys was hostile, or evasive as he'd been the previous day. Just the opposite, in fact. Jack still wasn't sure what to make of the man. But a change of subject might be wise at the moment.

"What about yourself, Doctor Rhys?" he asked. "Did you find someone?"

Jack realized immediately it had been a mistake. He was never good at this social stuff. That was Doc's strength. Rhys sat up and was suddenly distant again. "I did, in fact," he said. "But you know. The war."

They fell silent as the cries of birds drifted over the jungle. Jack decided to call it a draw. They sat for a time, feeling the warmth of the sun and the gentle breeze and listening to the sounds of the water. Rhys sat with his arms around his knees and his eyes closed. His spear lay on the ground beside him. He was breathing slowly and regularly and seemed to be looking around despite his closed eyes.

"Hear that?" he said quietly. "They're coming."

Jack didn't hear anything, but he scanned the edge of the jungle with his binoculars and soon spotted a small troupe of animals edging out of cover. They cautiously sniffed the air and looked around. Then the bravest of them hurried down to the water's edge. Soon more and more emerged, singly or in small groups, and scuttled down to the water.

"What do we do?" Doc whispered.

"Let's give them a few minutes," Rhys whispered back. "Then we go down the other side of the promontory here, approach from upstream. We charge them in a line, through the water. If we're lucky, they'll head out the other side and into the nets."

They waited perhaps another ten minutes. No more civets had appeared, and the ones here were drinking and playing in the water. Then they crept down off the promontory and slowly made their way toward the water.

When they were in position, they waited for Rhys to give the signal. Jack felt his heart racing. In this primitive place, he realized, the civilized world might as well not exist. They'd been returned to the world of their uncivilized ancestors. Then Rhys waved his arm and they did what those early ancestors had done to survive for thousands of years. They roared, and they charged.

CR

The sun was still high as Jack, Doc, and Rhys walked back down the game trail along the river. Rhys carried his spear in one hand, and a sack over his shoulder with nearly two dozen civets inside. By Rhys' estimate, it would have taken him nearly two weeks to trap that many in his snares or by taking them one at a time with his spear. With this many livers to process, they would be able to isolate a significant amount of the fluid that seemed to give the civets their immunity to the poison. Perhaps if they got this much of it to a real laboratory in the outside world, they might even be able to synthesize more. That would give them a serum that would counter the slower version of the poison. From there, it would hopefully be a short step to a full antidote that would render the poison useless.

Jack didn't really know that, of course. The chemistry and biology he left to Doc and Doctor Rhys, and even they were working blind at the moment. But he hoped so. With an antidote they could stop the Silver Star in their tracks, and save who knew how many lives in the process.

They'd find out when they got to the cave. Rhys and Doc would run their experiments. They'd know if they had enough civet livers, or if they needed more. If this was enough, then it would be time to go. From Rhys' description, he had an idea how much cargo space was available in the fuselage of the single seat Silver Star fighters. It wasn't much. He wasn't sure the plane could carry both Rhys and Doc. Even if it could, they'd be able to bring very little with them.

They passed the overhang where they'd sheltered when they first arrived and headed downstream toward the waterfall. Rhys was in the lead with Doc in the middle and Jack bringing up the rear. Rhys was the first to realize something was wrong. He stopped and listened to the sounds of the jungle. Then he dropped the sack and clutched his spear with both hands.

"Run!" he shouted, but it was too late. A shape exploded out of the trees, bounding across the narrow strip of open space that separated them. It was an animal—a huge quadruped. It charged with a snarl. Jack caught a glimpse of gray fur and a long, muscled tail.

Rhys sprang away from the sack of dead civets and the creature ran between the group and the sack. Then, with amazing agility, it whirled on them with the sack at its back.

Jack was drawing his .45s but never managed to fire. The creature swatted him with a paw the size of a dinner plate and sent him flying a good ten feet into a tree. Jack lost both his guns and slumped to the ground, dazed.

He heard Doc scream as the creature charged after him. It scrabbled for traction on the ground with long claws adapted for digging. They were like a badger's claws if a badger was the size of a grizzly bear. The head was vaguely canine, but stretched out of proportion for a dog's head. It moved on thickly muscled legs, and it displayed dagger-sized fangs as it came at him. This had to be one of the creatures Rhys had warned them about, the ones that tore open the earth and scattered boulders like toys.

Jack reached for the nearer of his guns, but his vision was doubled. His fingers scratched against bare earth. Too late. It was going to kill him, Jack realized with a strange certainty. There was nothing he could do. This was how he died. Here, with Doc watching.

Then Rhys gave a feral roar, and Jack saw him plunge his spear into the creature's flank.

It wheeled and reared, and Rhys stabbed it again. Then he fell back to the sack, thick with the smell of blood and prey. That was what had drawn it, Jack realized. Rhys kept his eyes on the creature and the spear pointed at its chest as he bent down to grab the sack.

"Hah!" he yelled. "Come get it!" Then he turned and sprinted away down the trail. The creature roared and gave chase.

Jack was trying to struggle to his feet when Doc reached him.

"You're bleeding!" she gasped.

"I'm all right." He stumbled while reaching down to retrieve his guns. Then he staggered off after Rhys and the creature with Doc beside him.

His side hurt like hell, and he could see bloody gashes in his shirt. But he could tell the wounds were shallow. He'd be fine as long as they didn't become infected, and Doc would see to that. But they had to help Rhys. He'd stabbed the thing twice with his bayonet-tipped spear and done little more than make it angry.

Doc drew her revolver as they ran down the slope past the waterfall. They saw huge slashes in the soft earth where the creature had passed, and once they saw a spatter of blood on a fallen frond.

They heard the creature's roar even over the sound of the waterfall. Then they rounded a curve in the trail and saw them through the foliage. Rhys was at the near end of the log bridge over the canyon. He leapt up onto the trunk, still holding the sack with the civets they'd killed in one hand and his spear in the other. He ran partway across the log, apparently thinking the creature couldn't follow him. But then it slapped the trunk with one huge, clawed paw and shifted it. Rhys stumbled and nearly fell, but he caught himself and set the sack down on the trunk. He turned and brandished the spear as the enraged creature leaped onto the fallen trunk. With a deep, angry growl, it moved carefully toward him. Rhys yelled and taunted it, and thrust the spear at it.

Jack and Doc had been running down the trail as Rhys and the creature faced off. Now they were finally in range, but Jack couldn't see a clear shot with Rhys so close to the creature.

"Christopher, get down!" Doc shouted as she tried to position herself for a shot.

Rhys saw them at the edge of the canyon. He met their eyes and smiled. He mouthed something Jack couldn't make out. Then he swung the spear behind himself to point at the sack with its precious load of civet livers.

The creature took the chance to spring forward, and Rhys blocked it with the shaft of his spear. They grappled there for a moment, and the Silver Star plane came out of nowhere. Jack hadn't heard its approach over the roar of the waterfall. It was just suddenly there, a dark shape falling from the sky, so close he could almost make out the pilot's face.

The machine guns opened up and the creature screamed in agony and rage. There was a spray of blood, and then the plane shot past the crude bridge, already starting to pull up from its strafing run. Jack turned and followed the plane with his .45s, firing both until the magazines were empty and the slides locked back. Then he heard Doc scream.

Like one being, Doctor Rhys and the creature he had been battling toppled off the tree trunk and plummeted down, down into the gorge until they vanished into the mists and were gone.

"Christopher!" Doc screamed again and ran toward the bridge. Jack followed, grabbed her arm and pulled her back. She fought him, yelling, "Let me go!"

"We can't help him!" Jack shouted. Over her shoulder, he saw the Silver Star plane climb straight up, then fall over into a hammerhead turn as it came back for another pass at them. He shook Doc by her shoulders.

"We have to go! Now!"

She was trembling, but she met his eyes and nodded. "I know," she said faintly.

They turned and ran.

- CHAPTER 18 -

"I think it's gone," said Doc.

They were crouched in the gully dug by a small stream. They'd been there for almost twenty minutes, breathing hard and feeling their hearts pound in their chests as the cold water flowed around their ankles. The drone of the Silver Star fighter's engine had faded, but Jack knew that was just temporary. The other one would tag in soon enough.

They'd run away from the river, toward the center of the valley, into unfamiliar terrain. They'd managed to keep under the tree canopy so the pilot couldn't get a clear shot. He'd hoped that they could lose the plane by evading it until it ran low on fuel. But soon they'd heard the sounds of men shouting and moving through the jungle, and they realized that the plane was the least of their worries. It was directing search parties on the ground. The soldiers were scattered along a long line sweeping through the bottom of the valley.

He and Doc had managed to keep ahead of them so far. But they couldn't keep up this pace forever. Even if they could, there was only so far for them to run. They were being herded against the far side of the valley, where the land rose sharply into icy cliffs, and the winds waited to freeze them. This side of the valley was steeper than the other. The air was cooler, and the foliage was different. They'd gone from jungle to more temperate woodland with fewer trees and less of a solid canopy. Here they had to wait and move from cover to cover when the plane was searching somewhere else. The farther they went, the less cover there would be. The plane would pinpoint them, and that would let the commander on the ground deploy his troops more effectively, over a smaller area. The net would tighten. Jack wasn't sure how they were going to get out of this one.

"Can you keep going?" he asked.

Doc looked at him in dismay. "I don't hear anything."

He put a hand on her shoulder. "I'm sorry," he said. "But they've got two planes. They can spell each other. The other one will be here in a few minutes. They can keep one on us as long as it takes."

He saw her take it in, realize the implication. She reached up and squeezed his hand on her shoulder.

"Let's do all we can," she said.

Their eyes met and Jack nodded. If this was going to be the end, he'd meet it with her, and they'd make sure the Silver Star paid a high price for their lives.

They climbed up out of the gully and ran toward the distant cliffs. Jack set a pace he felt they could maintain for a while. They found another stream that ran cool and clear from the mountains ahead of them. It was flanked by a stand of pines that would provide some cover from the air, so they followed it. As Jack feared, the other plane appeared a few minutes later, buzzing the forest canopy over their heads.

From time to time, they heard shouting or gunshots in the distance. Somehow the soldiers had managed to get around them and were closing from the east. They made a point of making noise from that direction to make sure Jack and Doc knew they were there, to steer them back toward the south.

They followed the stream for a mile or more, up into the hills. The current grew more energetic and larger rocks lay strewn in the stream bed, water splashing and gurgling over them. The airplane was a near constant drone now, passing back and forth overhead. Jack assumed the pilot had figured out that they must be somewhere in this particular stand of trees.

Eventually even the pines gave out. The forest thinned, and the trees grew shorter and less straight where the cold winds had twisted them. Jack and Doc stopped at the edge of the reliable cover. Ahead of them was just open slope covered in thick grass tufts and strewn with lichen-spotted boulders.

Jack pulled out his binoculars and swept the landscape ahead of them. They were nearly to the cliffs now. He looked for some place they could hole up and defend but saw nothing.

He swore as the Silver Star airplane buzzed low over them and pulled up sharply. A few moments later puffs of colored smoke erupted in the distance to his right. The ground troops were signaling their location. Why would they do that, Jack wondered.

He checked that direction with his binoculars. There was something about the contour of the cliffs there. He thought for a moment, then made his decision. If he was wrong, he'd take the blame for it. They didn't have much time left anyway.

"That way," he said, pointing toward the dissipating smoke. We're going to make a run for it."

"That's toward them."

"They're trying to drive us the other way," Jack said. "So we're going where they don't want us going. I think there's a canyon mouth. We just need to reach it before they cut us off. Can you run?"

Doc let out a dismayed sigh, but then she nodded. "I'll keep up. But the pilot will see us. We'll be in the open."

"No choice," said Jack, putting his binoculars away and checking the straps of his pack. He turned Doc around and adjusted hers so she could run more easily. "We're out of cover. I'm betting they want us alive. He won't just strafe us."

"Hope you're right," Doc said with a lightness that he knew cost her some effort.

He squeezed her hand. "I love you," he said.

"Bloody hell, Jack," she said, "Why'd you have to tell me that now?" As Jack looked at her in surprise, she squeezed his hand back. "I love you too," she said. "Lead the way."

Then they broke from under the trees and dashed out onto the open. The grass was thick and hummocky, and it was hard to keep up their speed over the uneven ground, but they ran for their lives. There was no sense in holding back anything now. If the canyon was really there where Jack thought it was, and if they reached it before the Silver Star, they would at least have a position they could defend. If not, there was no chance.

Barely a minute into their run, Jack heard the airplane coming in fast behind them. He ignored it and kept running, waiting for the chatter of machine guns, the impact, the blackness. But it never came. The plane shot by no more than fifty feet overhead, and Jack saw another grenade spiral down, marking their position with a corkscrew of blue smoke.

A few moments later they crested a small rise, and Jack saw that he'd been right. There was a cleft in the rugged gray cliffs, a narrow canyon leading back into the mountainside. Another stream led out of it and tumbled down the slope toward another finger of forest like the one they'd just left behind.

Then he saw shapes moving near the tree line. Silver Star soldiers were advancing up the slope toward them. But they were too far away, he realized. He and Doc would reach the cover of the canyon mouth before the soldiers could close to a realistic firing range. He glanced up and saw the biplane flying away toward the west. It had reached its fuel limit. They were going to make it, he realized. At least as far as the canyon. They'd be boxed in, but at least they'd bought some time.

"Jack!" Doc shouted. Then there was a crackle of weapons fire from his right. Jack turned toward the sound and saw a single figure perhaps fifty yards away. He wore a black Silver Star uniform and stood alone near the edge of the stream with a submachine gun.

Jack drew his pistols.

"Keep going!" he shouted at Doc. Then he veered off course and headed straight toward the scout. The man fired another short burst, and Jack heard the bullets slice through the air nearby. Jack dodged as he ran, weaving around tufts of grass. Then he dove to the ground, steadied his aim and fired both guns. The scout staggered back and fell.

In an instant, Jack was back on his feet and sprinting toward the fallen man. His comrades were firing at Jack now, but they were far away, and Jack was a moving target. He reached the body—already smoking and dissolving—and stooped to grab up his dropped weapon and his gray canvas shoulder bag.

Then Jack turned and dashed toward the canyon mouth, running uphill along the edge of the narrow, tumbling stream. Doc was well ahead of him, nearly there. It would take a very lucky shot to hit him now. He kept moving, one stride after another as his heart pounded in his chest and his lungs burned. He saw Doc clear the canyon mouth. She was safe now.

A bullet drilled past him as one of the Silver Star soldiers got too close for comfort. Jack zigged to the side and forced himself to keep moving. Just a few more paces.

Then he was there. The grass gave way to loose shale and he fell forward, banging painfully against the rock fragments. Two more bullets smacked into the stone overhead, but their pursuers didn't have a clear shot anymore.

"Come on," Doc said, leaning down to help him to his feet. "We have to move."

Jack struggled to his feet and they moved quickly up the narrow canyon. It bent gradually to the left, twisting its way back into the mountains. Jack could hear water falling somewhere up ahead. He stopped, knelt beside the stream and stuck a hand into the water. It was frigid, barely above freezing. He guessed it was coming from a melting glacier up above them. Whatever volcanic source heated the valley had just enough energy to melt the ice at the top of the cliffs and send this stream tumbling down into the valley below.

They rounded the curve and found their path blocked by a rock fall. At some point the left face of the canyon had collapsed here, sending a rain of stone down to fill most of the stream channel with boulders. The stream had widened as it worked its way around them and become more shallow. Leaping from stone to stone, they picked their way across the stream and slipped around the far side of the rock fall. The fall had made a natural dam that held back a large pool. Again, there were enough loose boulders scattered around for them to make their way back across to a tiny arc of sandy beach protected by the dam.

This might be a spot they could hold, Jack realized. The only way to reach them was to cross the stream as they'd just done, or else try to climb the dam itself. Either way, their pursuers would be sitting ducks. With luck, the two of them could hold the Silver Star off here until they ran out of bullets. Or food, he supposed, if the soldiers decided to just hang back and starve them out. But he was thinking in longer terms than before at least. They had food for several days if it came to that. Maybe they'd come up with a better idea by then.

Doc appeared to have reached the same conclusion. She looked over the spot with approval. "Well, I've stayed in worse places. There's clean water at least." Then she noticed the submachine gun and pack Jack held in one hand. "What you got there, flyboy?"

"German MP-18," he said. "I thought it might come in handy." He showed her the gun. It was an intimidating weapon. The barrel was wrapped in a perforated cooling shroud that made the gun's business end look like a cluster of a half dozen muzzles. It used a round drum magazine that stuck awkwardly off to the side on a metal feed strut. The magazine held thirty-two 9mm pistol rounds, and the gun could empty it in a couple of seconds. Jack preferred his .45s, but he had to admit this was a situation that called for the MP-18's raw firepower.

He dug through the scout's pack and found several spare drums, along with some dried ration bars, a pair of smoke grenades, and the real prize: three fragmentation grenades. He showed those off to Doc with a grin. "Can make some noise with these anyway."

Doc nodded. "You look like hell, by the way. Get that shirt off and let me take a look at those."

She carefully cleaned and bandaged Jack's wounds with antiseptic and gauze from the small first aid kit in her pack. Then, without much else to do, they took up positions along the top of the natural dam and waited for the Silver Star.

An hour went by, then another. It was cold here, Jack realized. The sun was already sinking behind the rim of the canyon. It would be dark soon. If he was the Silver Star commander, Jack decided, that's when he would make his move. If the soldiers had to approach straight up a narrow canyon, darkness would at least provide some cover.

Jack guessed he had about an hour and a half left before dark. Perhaps he could make use of that time. "I'm going to see what's behind us," he said quietly. He gave Doc the MP-18 and made sure she was familiar with it. "You see anything moving out there, you open up with this, and I'll be back in a heartbeat, okay?"

"Bet on it."

He left her the grenades as well, then moved quickly up the canyon. It looked much like what they'd already found. It was narrow, the sides were sheer, and there were patches of snow and ice scattered around. Jack wasn't sure what he was looking for. Even if he found a way to climb out of here, they'd emerge into the high mountains and fall to their deaths somewhere if they didn't freeze first.

The canyon ended suddenly in a shadowy recess and a thin spire of water tumbling from above. The canyon was very narrow here. For the last hundred yards or so, there'd been no way forward except by clambering over rocks deposited in the stream channel. Jack stood on a large boulder and looked up to see a huge overhang of granite and massive, hanging spears of ice. The water wasn't flowing over the canyon's lip, he realized. It was draining straight down from a large gap in the ceiling of the recess, as if someone had punched a hole in the bottom of a bucket. He heard a grinding sound, and chunks of ice fell into the basin at the bottom of the falls. The whole place was unstable. There would be no getting out here.

Then he heard the chatter of automatic fire behind him.

Jack turned and ran, leaping madly from boulder to boulder until he reached open ground. Single shot rifle fire was peppered among the bursts now. He rounded a bend and saw Doc standing at the top of the dam, firing bursts from the MP-18 down into the canyon below. When the ammo ran out, she tossed the empty drum aside and seated another, but the gun refused to fire. She tried to clear it, then tossed it aside with a frustrated snarl and ducked down behind the dam.

"Piece of crap gun!" she snapped at Jack as he ran up to join her. "You trying to get me killed here?"

"What's with you and the language today?" Jack answered as he drew his .45s. "You're so unladylike. You kiss your mother with that mouth?"

He peered over the edge of the rocks. Several black clad figures were running toward them. Jack's pistols barked, and one attacker fell, then a second. The charge melted as the others took cover behind the boulders.

Doc had her revolver out. She fired off a few shots as Jack tried to get the MP-18 working again. It was no good. He sighed and tossed it away.

"Oh, come on!" Doc said suddenly. "Seriously?"

She was looking over the rim of the stone dam. Jack popped up and saw it too. The Silver Star troops were setting up a heavy machine gun on a tripod mount.

"Well that's just plain poor sportsmanship," Jack observed as they dropped back behind the cover of the stone again. A few moments later the gun opened up and bullets spattered off the lip of the dam just above their heads.

That changed the situation. The gun could put down suppressive fire to keep them down while the soldiers moved up and around the dam. Not good.

"Come on," Jack said. He took Doc's hand and led her down from the top of the pile of stone. He took the two smoke grenades from the pack and tossed them into the gap at the far end of the dam. That would cover their retreat at least. Then he led the way back toward the waterfall.

When the canyon grew too narrow to walk, they leaped from boulder to boulder along the stream. Above them, the encroaching masses of ice loomed, and a cold mist chilled their skin. Jack picked out a route that led straight back to the waterfall itself, and realized there was a small space behind it. It was a cleft in the rock just big enough for the two of them. Jack leapt from a boulder and managed to catch the edge of the stone and pull himself up. He braced himself and leaned out to catch Doc's hand and pull her up alongside him.

And there they were, encased by stone with a curtain of water in front of them and heavy claws of ice hanging down at its sides. As tombs went, Jack supposed he'd seen worse.

Doc was still holding his hand, and Jack didn't want to let go. The war had taught him that the end came for everyone, whether you were ready or not. He'd been ready to die for years. But now things were different. Now there was Ellen, a little girl who would never know what became of her parents. Just when you thought you'd made your peace with the world, something always seemed to come along and throw you off.

"Ellen," he whispered.

Doc squeezed his hand. "She'll grow up strong. She'll make us proud."

He heard shouting voices. They were close now.

Jack hefted the pack with its three heavy frag grenades. "We can wait," he said, "or we can take some of those bastards with us. What do you think?"

She grinned. "You kiss your mother with that mouth?"

Then she kissed him, hard and long, clutching him to her. It was a kiss that said all the things they'd never managed to say to each other.

"Let's go," she whispered at last.

Jack reached into the pack and pulled the pins on all three grenades. He swung the pack around by its straps for momentum and hurled it high into the air. The pack arced up, toward the overhanging mass of rock and ice. He heard someone shout in alarm.

Then there was a massive roar and a crack that sounded like the earth itself being torn in two. He heard a deep rumble, and then everything was moving. He felt Doc torn away from him as a wall of freezing water hit them with a shock that ripped the breath from him.

And then there was nothing.

- CHAPTER 19 -

Jack awoke to the sound of dripping water. For a moment he assumed a faucet wasn't quite closed somewhere. Someone should fix that, he thought, whoever had left it on.

Then he sat bolt upright. "Dorothy!" he cried. There was no answer.

Jack was sitting on wet stone worn smooth to the touch. He was cold. He was alone.

He was alive.

He took a moment to check himself out and take in his surroundings. He had some bruises and minor abrasions, but somehow he appeared to be unhurt. He'd clearly been wet, but his body and his clothes had nearly dried in the morning sun. He recognized the canyon, but it was different. The stream was gone, he realized suddenly. There was no waterfall, no water tumbling over the stones as it escaped the canyon. There was only a slow drip into a small pool nearby, the sound he had heard.

The explosion had reshaped the whole end of the canyon. It had blown away ice and rock and ripped away the side of the glacial basin that had fed the stream. The entire body of water must have drained out in moments. He remembered the impact, and the shock of cold water. From the looks of the canyon, it must have carried away everything in its path. It would have scoured the canyon and left behind only scattered pools of standing water and a bare stream bed.

Jack stood up, amazed to be alive but fearful for Doc. One of his .45s was still snapped into its holster. He found the other some fifty feet down the canyon, still operable. He cleared the chamber and tested the action, then put it back in its holster.

He began walking slowly down toward the canyon mouth.

He found lost guns and ammunition bags scattered across the canyon floor. Black uniforms lay soaking wet and stretched across bare bones. Each time he saw another body, Jack felt his heart leap into his throat, thinking it was Doc. But there was no sign of her. Finally he called her name again. "Dorothy! Doc!"

But no one answered. He was alone here. Had the fury he'd unleashed killed all of the Silver Star soldiers? Or had they simply withdrawn and somehow not found him lying there? Where could Doc be? She wouldn't have simply left without him, not by choice at least.

He made his way to the canyon mouth, past more empty black uniforms and scattered rifles. Near the mouth, he found the twisted mount for the heavy machine gun, the gun itself simply missing.

Jack stopped at the mouth of the canyon and looked out over the grassy slope they'd fled across the day before. The stream channel was now just a dark, muddy slash in the land, running downhill toward the pine forest. The grass had been pressed flat and stained with mud in a fan spreading out from where he stood.

What the hell was he meant to do now? But he knew the answer before the thought formed. Living or dead, Doc had to be somewhere. He was meant to find her.

Jack set out down the slope toward the forest. Then there was a quick pneumatic hiss and something stung his neck. Jack's hand flew to the spot and he felt something foreign there. His hand came away holding a small, feathered dart.

He drew one of his .45s and whirled in the direction the dart must have come from, but he could already feel his body slipping away from him. The gun wavered in his hand and his legs wobbled. He raised his gun at the dark figure he saw silhouetted against the bright morning. But he couldn't steady it. Then his knees gave out, and he hit the ground in a heap. He had a glimpse of a man standing over him in a black uniform. Then, once more, the darkness rose up and took him.

⧼

"Jack! Damn it, Jack, will you wake up?"

She really was swearing a lot these days, Jack thought. Had she always been like that? He didn't think so. It seemed to be a pretty recent thing.

Then he worked out the implication that Doc was alive. She was okay. It followed that they were both alive, since he was hearing her. And then it occurred to him that his mind was just starting to put things together as it came out of unconsciousness. It was getting to be something of a habit.

"Well, that can't be good for me," he murmured.

"Try to make sense, Jack," Doc said. Then, "Ow! Son of a bitch!"

Jack opened his eyes. He was inside, lying on a narrow cot. There was a light directly overhead. He looked away, and there was Doc, lying on a metal table nearby. He was so happy to see her he couldn't help laughing. She didn't seem to appreciate it.

"Really? What is so damn funny?"

"Did you always curse like this?" he asked, very seriously.

"Only when it's appropriate, Jack. It's been really appropriate these last couple days."

"I don't remember you cursing a lot."

"That's because I used to mind my manners around you."

"What? I don't rate anymore?"

"At the moment, no, you do not. Maybe if you made yourself useful and tried to get out of those ropes. Because I'm not having a hell of a lot of luck with mine!"

He was tied down, Jack realized. They'd tied him to the cot by his wrists and ankles. Doc was tied to her table, he noticed, struggling to get free.

Then it dawned on him. He understood what was going on, and he was seized by the urge to explain it to Doc. If she understood, maybe she'd give him a break.

"They drugged me!" he announced. "That's why I'm like this!"

"I know," said Doc. "It's really annoying."

There was a sound nearby, a lock opening he thought.

"Play dead!" Doc hissed as a door opened. A man's shadow fell across the room.

"That's not going to work," Jack said. "It's their drug. They know how long I'll be out."

"Quite correct," said the stranger. "For an adult male, approximately six hours, which has now passed. That is followed by perhaps two hours of disorientation, which is what you are experiencing now. So perhaps we will talk more later. In the meantime, I'm told the experience is not unpleasant. So...enjoy."

His accent was German, and the voice suggested an older man. As he crossed the room to Doc's table, Jack got a look at him and decided he was perhaps sixty, tall and lean, with rapidly graying hair cropped short. He wore a dingy looking white lab coat and a tunic over black uniform pants and boots. He looked over Doc and then Jack with a hungry leer.

"I am Doctor Mencken," he said after a moment. Jack thought he'd heard the name before but he couldn't quite recall. "I am the Science Commander on this expedition, and I am very happy to meet you. Very happy indeed. I am engaged in world changing research here. Positively world changing. Very important work, under what I'm sure you realize are very trying conditions."

"We know what you're doing," Doc snapped. "You're making poisons."

Mencken stepped over to a utilitarian looking wooden workbench that ran the length of the wall. Jack saw plants growing in pots, a watering can on the floor beside them. The bench itself was strewn with glass vessels, rubber hoses, a tank of some gas. Flasks waited on metal frames. On the wall above them were row after row of glass jars with paper labels marked in thick, black lettering that Jack couldn't read from where he lay.

"Toxins are part of my work, yes," he said. "Through chemistry we manipulate the body, just as through magic we manipulate the spirit, and through both we manipulate the mind, the intersection of the two. With these tools we remake man and man remakes the world. Some minds must be trimmed away, like dead flesh. So certainly, toxins, yes. But there is so much more to be discovered here. So much more!"

He plucked a glass jar from the workbench and showed it to Doc, then briefly to Jack. "This, for example. It causes a deep sleep of indefinite duration. How long does the subject remain disconnected from external sensory stimuli, able to focus fully on the more subtle stimuli of the mind and spirit?"

He shrugged. "I don't know. Perhaps forever! But I simply cannot say. There are no test subjects here, and so I have been unable to fully explore its properties."

"You're a madman!" said Doc.

Mencken chuckled. "You're hardly the first to say so," he said. "I was offended once, but I see now how it appears to the unenlightened. Science pushes into unknown realms. From them, it brings back new ideas, often startling ideas. And so does madness, yes, yes. So what is the difference, we may ask. The only criterion I can suggest is a simple one; do these new ideas actually work? I assure you, mine do."

"You like having an audience, don't you?" said Jack.

Mencken laughed again. "It is true, I admit. From my professorial days." He turned back to his bench and started to work over a pair of dishes positioned under a light.

"I used to have a pair of assistants, you know," he said over his shoulder. "Remarkably stupid, but able to follow simple orders. And good listeners. But that has changed with your little stunt at the glacial falls. Do you know you killed more than a dozen of Captain Ardinger's soldiers?"

"And that's just the two of us," said Doc. "Wait until our reinforcements come looking for us. If you're smart you'll untie us and get us out of here. We'll put in a good word for you."

Mencken ignored her. "Now my assistants are needed elsewhere, and I must do my own chores and talk to myself. So I'm doubly glad to at least have the two of you. How much do you weigh, my dear?"

"Kiss my ass!" Doc snarled. Then she unleashed a stream of expletives, some of which Jack didn't even recognize.

Mencken looked surprised. "You are a rude one, aren't you?"

"This is pretty new, actually," Jack offered helpfully. "She used to be on her best behavior around me, but I don't rate anymore."

"How unfortunate," Mencken said, but Jack didn't think he meant it. "Fifty to fifty-five kilograms can't be too far off," he said, and turned back to his work.

As soon as Mencken's back was turned, Doc resumed worked her wrist back and forth against the ropes that bound her to the table.

"Now this that I'm working on, this is the most intriguing of all," Mencken said as he worked. "More than the poisons, or even the sleeping formula, this drug asks fundamental questions about the very nature of self. Of all of them, this is what will win me the Nobel."

Mencken turned with a glass flask, and Doc quickly let her wrist go limp. He showed her the clear liquid inside. "Essentially a surgical anesthetic," he said. "Honestly, you can't spit in this place without hitting a plant with some kind of sedative property. I've isolated several already, but they're trivial. This, though."

He took a hypodermic from the shelf, inserted it into the flask, and drew back the plunger to fill it. "It completely suppresses higher brain function, while leaving simple physical control completely intact. The subject's personality, their will, is completely removed, but they are able to carry out instructions. Spoken instructions, you understand! Their minds still decode language! But the results are simply accepted by the involuntary mind and acted on automatically, with no consciousness at all."

"That's monstrous!" Doc said, and Jack could hear the fear in her voice now.

"It's fascinating! But Captain Ardinger severely limited my tests on his men. Another reason I'm so thrilled to have actual test subjects!" Mencken tapped the hypodermic to clear any air bubbles, then leaned over Doc, who struggled in vain against the ropes.

"I wouldn't do that if I were you," said Jack.

Mencken looked up and glanced at Jack with a smile. "I don't think that's quite correct," he said. "If you were me, that implies you would think as I think, and I absolutely intend to inject your friend here. So if you were really me, you would do the same in a heartbeat. Yes?"

Jack considered it and decided that made sense, actually. He'd gotten caught up in the words without quite working out what they really meant. He should keep it simple because the raging part in the back of his mind was insistent on getting his meaning across.

"I guess so," Jack said. "I should have said, it's a very, very bad idea."

Now Mencken seemed intrigued. "And why is that?"

"Because if you hurt her, there's no power on Earth that will stop me from killing you."

There, Jack thought. That was simple and clear. That was a good sentence. He was good at this.

Dr. Mencken shook his head. "I doubt that, under the circumstances," he said. "You are just in a particularly...uncomplicated state of mind."

"That's how you know I'm telling the truth," said Jack.

Mencken raised an eyebrow, then turned back to Doc with his needle poised.

Jack heard a noise from the other side of the room. The door opened again and a shaft of afternoon sunlight shot across them. Mencken looked up again in irritation.

"Stop!" a man's voice barked. "What do you think you're doing?"

The newcomer was a short, brawny fire-plug of a man in a black uniform and cap. Jack thought it didn't have quite the look on him the designers had intended. He was flanked by two younger, taller soldiers who stood stone-faced behind him.

"What I'm doing is called science, Captain," said Dr. Mencken. "You forget that I am the Science Commander of this expedition."

Jack decided this must be the Captain Ardinger that Mencken had spoken of. That was some good deductive reasoning right there. He was definitely getting better at thinking.

"Nobody authorized you to interfere with these prisoners!" Ardinger barked.

"Maria Blutig demands results," Mencken said, and his voice took on a whining tone. "If she wants results, I must have test subjects."

"Well, not these," said Ardinger. "Not yet, anyway." He turned to Jack. "Is your name Jack McGraw?" he snapped.

"Yes!" Jack said, "Yes, it is!" He realized the truth of it just as Captain Ardinger spoke the words, and he found that astonishing. "By the way," he added, "I'm probably going to kill that man."

"I would be…obligated to stop you," said the Captain. "So, Captain Jack McGraw. And that makes you Dr. Dorothy Starr. Maria Blutig has a particular interest in these two, Mencken. You're not to do anything until she's informed of their capture. Then she will decide what is to be done with them. Do you understand me?"

"Are you in contact with the *Luftpanzer*, then?" asked Dr. Mencken with a bit of a sneer.

"We are scheduled to resume communications within the hour."

"Then by all means," said Mencken, "Let us make our report. I'm sure she will be interested to hear of your interference in the important work I'm doing here!"

Ardinger turned to the two soldiers accompanying him. "You, stay here and guard these two. Any further orders come directly from me. Do you understand?"

"Yes, sir!" they both shouted.

"With me, Doctor," Ardinger said, and he ushered Mencken out the door.

The two soldiers moved to the closed door and took up positions on either side of it. They stood like statues, glaring across their two prisoners and saying nothing. A few moments passed.

"Hey, do you guys have any licorice?" Jack asked. It was the damnedest thing. Suddenly he had the strangest craving for licorice.

- CHAPTER 20 -

Somewhere over Kashmir, a dark shadow slid across the mountains. It drove against the fierce winds blowing from the Khyber Pass and made its way steadily southeast. The *Luftpanzer* was a huge black shape slipping through high clouds. Few on the ground saw the great airship, but those who did instinctively knew it for a dark omen and made warding signs or muttered prayers to the spirits.

On the bridge, Maria Blutig stood at parade rest, feeling the faint hum of the steel deck through her boots. She looked like a carved ebony statue in her crisp, black uniform and short, black hair. Her demeanor told an onlooker that for all her beauty she was cold and unapproachable. In the Silver Star, she was considered efficient and effective, but lacking in emotion. It was a lie, of course, Maria was anything but unemotional, as her enemies eventually discovered to their horror. But it was a useful lie, and she went to great lengths to maintain it.

Around her, the flight crew went about their duties in silence under the watchful eye of Captain Ecke, the ship's commander. The only sound was the wind whistling around the edges of the hull. All was routine.

Maria was tired of routine. For months now, she'd been flying the same course between Shambala Base and a Silver Star provisioning depot on the Caspian Sea. This rebuilt *Luftpanzer* was meant for conquest, just as Maria herself was. Ferrying supplies back and forth was degrading to them both.

But the Shambala project was critical to the Silver Star's plans. And it was an amazing accomplishment to maintain an expeditionary base in such a remote, inaccessible place. Literally everything there had been carried deep into the Himalayas aboard *Luftpanzer*, then flown into the valley in breathtakingly dangerous flights—hundreds of them—by small planes never meant to carry passengers or cargo. It was a testament to the Silver Star's capabilities and to her determination.

And worth the effort, she reminded herself. Already, the science team had delivered powerful weapons and other discoveries that would help destroy the Silver Star's enemies and extend its power. Crowley was pleased. He had given the project his full support. And none of that would have happened without the new *Luftpanzer*. That built Maria's own power within the organization, and went a long way toward repairing the damage to her reputation from the loss of the original *Luftpanzer* a year ago.

A junior radio officer approached her and saluted.

"Mein Führerin," he said, a hint of nervousness in his voice. "We have established radio contact with Shambala Base. They transmit Code Falcon."

Maria showed no reaction, but Code Falcon meant Captain Ardinger was requesting to speak to her directly. Something had happened. Ardinger was a good soldier. Stolid, unimaginative, but he followed orders and he could be trusted not to do anything stupid. She almost felt bad for making him babysit Mencken. The Doctor was endlessly whining about one thing or another, usually the lack of resources to conduct whatever new experiment he'd dreamed up. Even in the most remote place in the world, he was incapable of understanding why she couldn't simply snap her fingers and produce a hundred pounds of refined mercury or a sub-micron filter. If Ardinger was requesting an audience, it could mean Mencken was causing trouble for him again.

But she needed to keep Dr. Mencken happy to maintain the flow of useful discoveries from Shambala and build her own power within the Silver Star. If she kept producing miracles for Crowley, soon no one would be able to prevent her from using the Silver Star's resources as she saw fit. And Maria had big plans. Crowley was a dissipated asthmatic, his body wrecked by indulgence and drugs. He wouldn't live forever. One day, she might control the Silver Star, and through it the world.

The radioman was growing increasingly anxious at her side. She looked him up and down, just for effect, then nodded. "Very good." She gestured and followed him out the rear door to the main access way. Whatever Ardinger's problem, it was better to take it in the privacy of the radio room.

She made her way down the metal catwalk, surrounded by aluminum beams, guy wires, and the ship's gas cells. A pair of technicians pressed tight against the railing to let her pass. They saluted, and she tossed off a perfunctory salute in reply. She walked on and turned into the ship's radio room. The senior radioman was there, furiously transcribing Morse signals on a pad. His subordinate stepped to one side and stood with his back to the wall to make room for her in the small cabin. The man on the radio finished his sentence, then tapped out a quick "stand by." He took off his headphones and snapped to attention. His expression was grim, Maria noticed.

"You have a report?"

The man handed her his pad with a crisp motion. She glanced over the report and felt her jaw tighten. No wonder Ardinger had wanted to report directly. Enemy contact. She'd worried about that since they briefly tangled with the *Daedalus* in the high mountains. Somehow AEGIS had found its way there, and that was cause for concern. But she knew there was no way an airship could make the passage into the valley itself, and the *Daedalus* couldn't carry winged parasite fighters as *Luftpanzer* did. But it appeared they'd gotten their hands on an airplane after all. At least there was only one, and she noted with satisfaction that that one had promptly been shot down.

But still, fourteen men lost? That was more than a quarter of the force she'd worked so hard to establish there and keep supplied. And killed by just two AEGIS agents? She expected better from Ardinger. So this was why he was waiting on the radio, to explain his failure.

She thrust the pad back at the radioman. "Give me Captain Ardinger."

The radioman flipped switches and offered her a headset. She held it against one ear as the radioman adjusted the signal strength and spoke into a desk mic.

"Shambala Base, Shambala Base. *Luftpanzer* sending. Falcon is on the channel."

The radio crackled and whined. Radio reception in these deep mountains was a tricky matter.

"*Luftpanzer*, this is Shambala Base," a voice finally replied. It sounded stretched and eerie. "Going to open mic."

The radioman turned to Maria. "Ma'am."

Maria let a hint of venom slip into her voice. "Captain. I've seen your initial report. Please explain yourself."

To Ardinger's credit he didn't try to deflect the blame. "When the aircraft appeared, I scrambled our planes and they were able to bring it down over the deep valley. I deployed my forces to search for the crew. They were located and trapped in a small tributary canyon on the southern edge of the valley. The terrain there largely neutralized our advantage in numbers. I made the choice to send my men into the canyon to root them out. They used explosives to destroy a glacial dam there, and the resulting avalanche and torrent of water killed all but two of the men in the canyon."

"And yet their quarry survived quite unharmed!" Dr. Mencken's high, reedy voice sounded even more unnatural over the radio channel. "The Captain seems unable to properly lead a simple military mission, much less a scientific expedition of this importance."

This again. From the beginning, Mencken had chafed at having a soldier in charge of what he considered his expedition. She needed to keep Mencken happy and productive, but she couldn't let him run amok and make a disaster of it. She had too much at stake for that. So she performed the delicate balancing act of stroking Mencken's ego while keeping him focused on his work.

"What matters is not the Captain's failure, but the capture of the two enemy agents," Mencken was saying. "I've told you repeatedly how critical human test subjects are to my work. I must have these two or I can't predict how much my work might be delayed."

"Don't try to threaten me, Doctor," she snapped. "That will go badly for you. I got you the man you said you needed, and you lost him. Have you recovered Dr. Rhys yet?"

"More incompetence!" Mencken practically screamed. "One of his pilots killed him! Weeks after his escape! Somehow he survived in the jungle for weeks! I've no idea how! I was very clear that I needed a blood sample as well as tissue and—"

"My pilot followed standing orders to kill the large predator species on sight," Ardinger interrupted. "My reports have made clear the problems we're having with aggressive wildlife. If I had a generator capable of powering an electric fence—"

"Without some indication of how Rhys survived on his own, the DL-95 project remains —"

"Be quiet!" Maria shouted.

Both men fell silent immediately. For a moment there was only the eerie hiss and moan of the radio channel.

"Neither of you is indispensable," she said at last. "Remember that. Now then. You've captured the two AEGIS infiltrators, and the dispute is whether they're to be kept for questioning or given over to Dr. Mencken for his experiments. Do I have the essence of it?"

It was Mencken who spoke first. "As always, Fraulein Blutig, you have a gift for seeing clear to the heart of the matter. I concede the possibility that they might be able to reveal some small shreds of information. But compared to their value to the toxin program..."

"We've identified the agents, mein Führerin," said Ardinger. "They are Dorothy Starr and Jack McGraw."

Jack McGraw. The instant she heard the name, Maria's world seemed to collapse down to a point. Nothing else mattered. She'd found McGraw at last. When he left AEGIS and disappeared a year ago, Maria had put out feelers and searched everywhere she could think of that McGraw might have gone. But she'd gotten back nothing. There was simply no trace of him for her agents to find. It was as if the earth had swallowed him up.

But now he'd returned. And to find him here! It was beyond belief.

The oath she'd sworn. The oath of vengeance that drove her. If it could be fulfilled after all these years. If that demon could at last be sated...

Ardinger and Mencken were arguing again, she realized. The radioman was staring at her, openly terrified.

"Bring McGraw to me," she said softly. "I will expect him immediately upon our arrival. Dr. Mencken, you may have the woman for your experiments. Am I clear?"

Even through the radio, the sound of her voice silenced them immediately. "Yes, mein Führerin," said Ardinger.

A moment later, Mencken added, "That will suffice for my initial tests."

Maria checked her watch. "We will arrive on station in just over four hours," she said. "I will expect a plane carrying McGraw to meet us. *Luftpanzer* out."

❧

Jack's head hurt. That was how he knew he was becoming himself once again. Whatever had been in the dart they'd hit him with had left him floating painlessly on a cloud. Now he was coming in for a hard landing.

Jack looked around. This place must be a makeshift lab. Doc lay on the metal table, not moving. He thought she was asleep. He was tied to a cot that he gathered was war surplus. A folding wooden frame with stretched canvas. His wrists and ankles were tied to the frame with plain hemp rope.

The guards were still standing by the door, silent. Jack had no idea how long they'd been there. His sense of time was unreliable at the moment. Memories came back to him slowly. Dr. Mencken, the madman who had created the poison, who had threatened to destroy Doc's mind. The man he'd promised to kill. Mencken wasn't here because another man interrupted him. A soldier. Jack presumed the commander of the base. He'd recognized them, and right now would be sending word of their capture to the *Luftpanzer*. Maria Blutig would be pleased to hear that she finally had him in her grasp. But whatever she had planned for Jack wouldn't be pleasant. He needed to come up with a plan, and fast.

One of the guards yawned, and the other one gave him a stern look.

Jack gently pulled against the ropes binding him to the cot. They were tight. But there was something different about his right leg. He tried it again. There was the slightest bit of give in the wood. He could flex the wooden cot with that leg where his other leg and his arms remained motionless.

There was a weakness in the wood, a knot or some other flaw. It was something he could work with.

The yawning guard turned to his comrade. "Cover me a minute," he muttered in German.

"No," the other whispered back. "You saw the Captain. He's in no mood today."

"I have to piss."

"Piss your pants, then," the other one answered. "It's nothing to me."

"Come on, just cover for me. I'll be right back."

Jack flexed against the rope, testing it, and decided he could probably snap the wooden frame there if he tried. But then what? He pictured the construction of the frame. If it broke there, what would he be able to do?

He could roll to his side, Jack thought, and get the free leg underneath him. That would let him stand. He'd still have the cot tied to his back, his wrists roped to the frame. But he'd be able to move. The guards had their rifles slung over their shoulders. It would take a few seconds to bring them to bear. If there was just one of them, he could charge and hopefully take the guard down before he could fire. It was a long shot, but that was all they had.

The other guard shook his head and sighed. "Fine," he said. "Be quick. If the Captain comes back, you're screwed, you hear me? I'm not taking the fall for you."

The first guard muttered something Jack couldn't make out, then slipped out the door. Jack took several deep breaths, tensing his body.

"Hey!" Doc snapped suddenly. "Big boy! You want to make it out of this in one piece, you better listen to me!"

Jack looked over at her. She was looking at the remaining guard. But she was flashing a signal with her tied hand, from a code they'd worked out with the rest of the crew. The sign meant "go".

The guard strode toward Doc's table, taking his attention away from Jack. Jack thrust his right leg against the ropes with all his strength and felt the wood give with a splintering crack. He threw himself to his right and powered up to his feet, dragging the cot with him.

The guard whirled and whipped out a dagger with blinding speed, but Jack was already lurching toward him. He spun his torso to turn the cot, using it as both weapon and shield. The blade glanced off a wooden crosspiece and slashed the tight canvas. Then Jack slammed into the guard, and they went down. He felt the broken frame giving way, but all he could do was kick with his right leg. He managed to get a knee into the guard and heard him grunt in pain.

Then there was bright light from behind him and a shout. A rifle butt slammed him hard in the ribs and knocked the wind out of him. Arms hauled him up, ripping the shreds of the cot away. The other guard had returned, and he'd brought two others with him.

Jack felt a cold muzzle thrust against the back of his neck. He stopped struggling and stood quietly as one of the guards cut the ropes binding his wrists to the shattered wooden frame, then pulled his arms out in front of him and slapped metal cuffs on his wrists.

One of the soldiers gave a vicious laugh. "You're going to wish we'd just shot you."

- CHAPTER 21 -

There were four guards, including the one Jack had just jumped. Two held guns on him while the others kicked away the wreckage of the cot, cut away the ropes, and rechecked the metal cuffs.

Then they turned him around and marched him toward the door.

"Hey!" Doc shouted from the lab table, "Hey, where are you taking him?"

The guards ignored her. Jack went rigid and glared at the guard trying to steer him to the door. "We're a team," he said. "I go, she comes with me."

Then his legs were suddenly swept from beneath him and he fell. But he didn't quite hit the floor. One of the guards caught his cuffs and pulled Jack's arms up behind him. He gasped in pain, and Doc shouted, "Stop it!"

They dragged him by his arms a few feet farther. "You walk, or you go like this," one of the guards snarled.

"All right! All right."

They let Jack get back to his feet. He glanced back at Doc and saw the fear in her eyes.

"It's okay," he said. "I'll be back for you."

"I know you will," she answered.

Then they opened the door and marched Jack outside.

He was in the middle of the Silver Star camp. The laboratory was a fairly crude building made of plaster poured through what appeared to be some kind of metal meshwork, all held up with metal framing. Everything here had come in aboard one of the small fighters, Jack remembered. They would have chosen materials that were as light and collapsible as possible. There were a couple other buildings nearby made of the same material, but most of the men lived in army-style field tents. They marched Jack past a row of them, and he saw a second row laid out in parallel on the other side of the metal and plaster structures.

Glancing inside an open tent as they passed, he saw two cots and did some math. Two men to a tent, two rows of about a dozen tents. So the place could hold about fifty men. If they'd really killed more than a dozen back at the canyon, that meant there were between thirty and forty enemy soldiers left. The airstrip was straight ahead, a couple hundred yards beyond the edge of the camp itself. The two small fighters were parked side by side at the end.

He wasn't sure what to do with the knowledge. He had no weapons and no plan. But if an opportunity arose, he meant to be ready to take advantage of it. Doc was in danger, alone, and afraid. She could take care of herself, but this was one of those situations where he didn't think she'd mind some help.

At the opposite end of the camp, they stopped at another metal and plaster building of about the same size and dimensions as Dr. Mencken's lab. One soldier knocked, and there was a voice from inside. They opened the door and marched Jack into what he realized had to be the Captain's office.

Dr. Mencken and the Captain were there. Ardinger was his name, Jack remembered. Mencken wore a nasty little grin. Ardinger stood behind a camp desk covered in papers and the remains of his breakfast on a tin plate.

"Captain McGraw," Ardinger said. "You do cause trouble, don't you?"

"I didn't start it."

Ardinger ignored him. "We have received new orders regarding your disposition. You are to be flown out immediately to rendezvous with the Silver Star airship *Luftpanzer.*"

"When Maria Blutig's done with you, you'll wish you'd stayed here and assisted in my research," said Mencken, laughing.

"What about Doc?"

"She will remain here," said Ardinger.

"She will be a martyr to science," said Mencken. "There's so much we can learn from her."

"Not really," Jack offered. "Because I'm still going to kill you." It sounded brave at least, but inside, Jack could feel cold terror taking root. False bravado was all he had right now. Unless he came up with something, and fast, Maria Blutig would torture him to death in vengeance for the lover Jack had shot down over France. And Doc...Jack couldn't think about what would happen to her. He would die before letting that happen. Even if it was a futile gesture, he realized, he wouldn't let them fly him away from her. He'd make them kill him fighting to save her.

"Well, I'd suggest you be quick about it," said Mencken. "You don't have much time left. Am I needed any longer, Captain? My work awaits."

"Go," said Ardinger. "By all means, Doctor, go."

Mencken gave Ardinger a final slight sneer, then turned on his heel and left.

When Mencken was gone, Ardinger turned to one of his aides. "Inform Lieutenant von Birken," he said. "He will fly this prisoner to rendezvous with the *Luftpanzer*, and transfer him to their custody."

"Yes, sir," said the aide, and hurried off.

"We have a few moments before the aircraft is ready," said Ardinger. "Do sit down, Captain." He gestured to a folding camp chair beside his desk. Jack glanced over at it, then at the armed men along the far wall. He sat down.

Ardinger removed a bottle of whiskey from his desk. "Not easy to get this in, believe me. Even for the base commander. Everything on every plane is accounted for, down to the number of screws to put something together."

He produced a pair of shot glasses and poured two fingers into each. "You are an honorable foe, Captain McGraw. You are vanquished and bound for a fate from which I cannot save you. But I salute your courage nonetheless."

Ardinger picked up a glass, raised it to Jack, and drank. Jack reached out with cuffed hands to pick up the other, and took a swallow.

"I can't save you from the rage of Maria Blutig," Ardinger said. "But I may be able to make your fate easier to bear. As one soldier to another."

"And how is that?" Jack asked.

"Mencken is a butcher and a madman," said Captain Ardinger. "Your friend's fate at his hands will be no better than yours at Maria Blutig's. Worse, perhaps. You are a soldier; you face your end with courage. But hers, this is a different matter, I think. I can spare her. I can remove at least some of your pain."

And here it was. "You want something from me," he said, "and your offer is to kill Doc if I give it to you. Do I have you correctly?"

Ardinger poured them each another shot. "Here, at the end, each of us must make the best bargain with death that he can," he said. "I want the airship. The *Daedalus*. It is legendary among the Silver Star. The man who captures it will make his career. Your fight is over. Tell me how to take the ship, without bloodshed if it can be done—I wouldn't have you betray your comrades' lives. Do this, and you have my word of honor, her passing will be quick and painless."

Jack enjoyed the last swallow of whiskey, felt it burn its way down his throat. "I'm afraid I can't do that," he said. "You see, Doc would never forgive me. And despite your lofty words of honor, and your excellent whiskey, you're still Silver Star. And that makes you a murderous son of a bitch I wouldn't turn my back on if we were surrounded by hungry crocodiles."

He raised the empty glass to Ardinger with both hands, then set it down on the desk with a sharp click.

"As you wish, Captain McGraw. As you wish." Ardinger capped the bottle and put it away in his desk. "I have tried. My conscience at least is clear. I suggest you look to your own."

He rose and nodded to the guards. Two of them strode over and lifted Jack out of the chair by his arms.

"Have a safe trip to the *Luftpanzer*, Captain," said Ardinger as they marched him out the door. "I do not think we will meet again."

Outside, they formed up in a line, a guard on either side of Jack, and marched him across the open field toward the airstrip. One of the planes had been warmed up and moved out of its parking slot. It sat at the end of the airstrip, the figure of its pilot waiting beside it.

The guards walked with one hand on the butts of their pistols and the other holding one of Jack's arms. They were wary, expecting him to try something. He wouldn't have the element of surprise by any means. But none of that mattered now. He calmed his breathing, pictured what he would do. A feigned stumble to break the grip on his arms, then he would swing both fists into the one on his right. He'd try to get that one between him and the guard on his left. Beyond that, if he was still alive, he'd improvise.

The space between the camp and the airstrip seemed to go on forever. They were about halfway across now. Jack was walking steadily, breathing deep. This was what it felt like to walk to your death, he thought. But the walk couldn't last forever. Ahead was a stone he might credibly stumble over...

Suddenly a rifle cracked in the distance. Jack heard the distinct smack of a bullet striking flesh. Then the guard on his right lurched forward and fell with a surprised grunt. Jack could see the entry wound between his shoulder blades.

For a brief moment both Jack and the other guard stood frozen in shock. Then the guard suddenly scrabbled for his pistol. Jack laced his fingers together and planted his foot. He swung his cuffed fists at the guard's chin like Babe Ruth swinging for the bleachers. He connected, and the blow lifted the guard off the ground and dropped him like a sack of potatoes. Jack stood alone in the field, still not quite believing what had happened. What was he supposed to do next? He hadn't expected to make it this far.

He heard a pistol shot, and a bullet whistled past him. He whirled toward the waiting biplane and saw the pilot sprinting toward him, firing a Luger as he ran. Jack dropped to the ground as another shot barely missed him. Then there was another rifle shot from behind him, and the pilot tumbled forward and fell in a heap.

Who the hell was firing? Was it Deadeye? Had the others managed to find another way into the valley? Jack had no idea and didn't care at the moment. All that mattered was that Doc was in danger. He was in no position to quibble over who his allies were.

That snapped everything into clarity. He had resources now. Until someone managed to kill him, he could fight.

Jack scrambled over to the body of the first guard as it began to smoke and hiss. He thrust his hands into the man's uniform pockets looking for the keys to his handcuffs. The smell was horrifying. It was chemical, but also something more, something that suggested incense and opium smoke. Jack gagged and coughed, but kept searching for the keys.

Behind him, he heard shouts, another gunshot. Then an alarm siren gradually spun up its mournful wail. His fingers found hard metal, and he pulled out a key on a brass ring. Jack rolled onto his back and looked back at the camp. Men burst out of tents, looked for an enemy, ran around in confusion. They didn't know what was happening either, Jack realized.

He fumbled the keys, and had to scoop them off the packed ground again. This was harder than it looked. Finally he managed to get the key into the lock, and one wrist snapped free. He popped the cuffs off his other wrist and grabbed the dead man's pistol from its holster.

Someone was running toward him from the camp, brandishing an MP-18. That would do nicely. He rolled onto his stomach, aimed the Luger carefully, and squeezed off three shots. The man fell. In a moment, Jack was on his feet, sprinting toward the body. He was hearing more gunshots from the camp now. Somewhere in there, someone was firing back at the sniper who had saved him. He had no idea if they knew what they were shooting at or were just firing blind, spooked by noise and the sight of their comrades turning to smoke.

He barely broke stride as he bent down to scoop up the submachine gun. With it and the Luger, he felt ready. Jack veered off and headed toward a row of tents. At the end of that row was the lab where he would find Doc.

Jack cut down a pair of confused Silver Star troops and roared with anger as he charged into battle.

- CHAPTER 22 -

Doc lay alone on the cold metal table. She'd struggled with the ropes until it was very clear she wasn't going to get out of them. So instead she used her eyes and her brain. She searched the lab and the equipment, looking for clues. Every object here had been brought here with great difficulty. They must be critically important to Mencken's work. She was a scientist herself, so she understood how a laboratory worked. What would lead her to choose these exact tools?

Everything on the bench told her a story. There was a titration setup for determining the concentration of a solution. The gray box with the connected hoses was a vacuum pump. Coiled next to it were hoses with complex valves and taps. Those were Schlenk lines, she realized, used for cannulation, transferring gas samples without exposing them to outside air. Was that to protect the samples from contamination, or to protect Mencken from the samples? The crude bamboo frame against the wall had spring clips attached. She counted them and worked out how many different hoses it was meant to support. The neatly arranged row of flasks at the end of the bench confirmed her count.

A picture began to form. She imagined how she would be able to use that equipment, what it would do for her. Plant samples, handled with the rubber gloves over there. Placed under the glass hood at one end of the bench. Heated somehow, probably with a compressed gas torch. She couldn't see it, but there was a spark lighter for lighting it. The toxin released as a gas, collected, separated into flasks at different concentrations. She could almost paint a complete picture of how it was made. But where were Dr. Mencken's notes? He had to be keeping detailed records of his work. That was what she had to find.

Then the door opened and Dr. Mencken's long shadow fell across the lab. Two soldiers followed him in and closed the door behind them. They waited near the door while Mencken gathered up the wreckage of the cot from the fight with Jack and put it in a corner.

"Now then," he said at last. "So much to do and so little to work with. But you're a start at least. A start."

He walked past the table and checked the ropes, making sure she was still secure. Then he moved out of her field of view, and she heard something like a drawer being opened. There. A desk, or a cabinet perhaps. She knew he had to keep his research notes somewhere. He shuffled through the pages, opened another drawer. Then suddenly he reappeared with a small leather case. He zipped it open and showed her three syringes nestled in tight fabric loops inside. Each was labeled and filled with a different color liquid.

"The baselines," he told her. "Reference samples. If the formulation should drift, these are the blueprint." He tapped each syringe in turn. "DL-26, the original toxin. You've seen its effects, I believe. Remarkable discovery. I'm still working out exactly how it does what it does."

He tapped the next syringe. "DL-95. The more controlled, slow-acting version. Held in check"—and he tapped the final syringe—"by DL-95-A in variable strengths of solution for varying effects and countdown times until fatal toxicity is reached. DL-26 is a chain saw. These two are more of a scalpel. Never forget that I wield both."

"Not likely," Doc said through clenched teeth.

"Good. I'm going to test a number of experimental formulations on you, and I need your cooperation. It will be painful, but not nearly so bad as these. So you must keep your wits about you, and faithfully report your sensations and symptoms. These will always be at my side if you are not of value to me. Do you understand?"

She took a moment to steady her nerves, then she nodded.

"Good." Mencken put the clip of syringes in his pocket. Then he turned to the guards. "Remove her from the table, please. Keep her hands tied behind her back. She's not to be trusted, this one, are you?"

The guards worked with strength and efficiency—they were, after all, elite forces of the Silver Star, which valued those two qualities above all else. They untied her ankles and one wrist, then rolled her off the table. One of them twisted her free arm behind her, and she gasped. Then he freed her other wrist and tied them behind her back.

She could see the rest of the lab now. There was the desk she hadn't been able to see before. A cabinet stood beside it. The door was open and she could see notebooks and sealed glass vials. That was it, she realized—

the research notes and samples of failed for-mulations. That was everything she'd need to develop an antidote. All she had to do now was stay alive and get her hands on it.

Mencken was rummaging through a collection of vials in a drawer of his desk. "Which one," he muttered. "What would have the least impact? Start there and work up." He turned to Doc and smiled. It wasn't an unkindly smile in its way. "We mustn't kill you until there's nothing at all more that can be learned from you, must we? Who knows when there will be another of you?"

He held a vial to the light and shook it. "Yes, this, I think. You'll still be able to speak."

Then the crack of gunshots came from outside. The two guards tensed and looked at each other.

A moment later there were more shots. Then the alarm siren slowly spun up and wailed.

The guards drew their weapons. "You stay here," one of them snapped to Mencken. Then they ran out the door. In the moment that it was open, Doc heard shouting and more gunfire.

Mencken moved like a snake and grabbed her bound wrists. He pulled her off balance and held her in front of him like a shield. One of his syringes was at her neck.

"Don't move," he hissed. "This is DL-26. If you so much as twitch, you'll die wishing you could scream."

Doc remained still and silent. They both stood motionless, staring at the door as the siren wailed outside. She didn't know how long they both stood there. It seemed like hours. Doc felt Mencken's cheek against hers. She felt the warmth of his skin, the moisture as he started to sweat.

There was a shot outside and Mencken flinched. Doc gasped as she felt the tip of the needle dig into her neck.

The door opened.

A figure was briefly silhouetted against the afternoon sun through the doorway. Then he stepped inside and closed the door.

"Jack!" she cried out.

Jack held a Luger leveled at Mencken. A submachine gun was slung over his shoulder, and his eyes were grim as he stared over the Luger's sights.

"Hold it!" Mencken snapped. "This is pure DL-26. Highly concentrated. A drop and you'll watch her die! Very badly!"

"I see you haven't really thought very far ahead, have you?" said Jack in a cold, steady voice. "What's your plan for getting out of the valley alive?"

"You'll fly us out!" Mencken's voice went high, and Doc felt his hand quiver.

"With you holding that needle to Doc's neck?" Jack said quietly. "You're forgetting a couple things. One, your planes won't carry three. Two at the outside, and that means you'd have to give up your hostage. Want to know the second thing?"

"What?"

"I promised to kill you," said Jack. The Luger cracked and Doc felt the bullet slash the air beside her face. She felt the needle slide into her flesh. She heard the slap of a bullet against bone and tasted blood.

Then she was falling.

℘

Jack strode through the door with the Luger in his outstretched hand. As his eyes adjusted from the bright sunlight outside, he made out a shape standing in front of him. Two people. Doc, with Mencken behind her, a syringe against her neck. He was shouting something about DL-26. Jack didn't know what that was, but he got the gist.

He exchanged a few words with the doctor, but Jack wasn't paying attention. He was lining up his shot. Then he said, "I promised to kill you," and pulled the trigger.

Mencken's head snapped back, and blood sprayed Doc's face. She fell to her knees, and Jack's heart leapt into his throat as he saw the syringe in her neck. He dropped the Luger and ran to her. She nearly fell over but managed to steady herself and remain very still.

"Get it out!" she cried. "Don't touch the plunger!"

Their eyes met and Jack tried to project cool confidence, but there didn't seem to be much of that inside him at the moment. He reached out with two fingers for the syringe's barrel.

"Straight out," she said. "Raise it up, just a little. There! Now, straight out!"

Jack slid the needle out, and they both let out a breath. Jack was going to smash the syringe, but she stopped him. "Baseline sample! We need that!"

Instead he cut her loose, and they held each other tightly. Jack felt himself shaking. "God, Dorothy, I thought I lost you!"

"I'm fine!" Doc said, her voice taut as she struggled with her fear. "Just help me. Mencken's notes are here. Samples. Everything we need! Watch the door!"

Jack trained his gun on the door as Doc emptied a canvas field pack and started filling it with notebooks and vials. Jack's guts were twisted into a knot. He'd fought alongside comrades before, and he'd learned how to deal with it when they died. But this was something different, and Jack didn't like it. He'd carefully honed his instincts for battle, but this new truth threatened to undercut all his hard-won experience. What if he hesitated at a crucial moment, or made the wrong choice and killed them both out of fear for her?

Then she closed the pack and thrust it at him. "This has to get out, even if I don't."

"Damn it, stop talking like that!"

"Language!" Doc said sweetly.

Jack forced down his fear. He would have to deal with it later. Right now, they were still in danger. He unslung the MP-18 and handed it to Doc. Outside the siren had stopped wailing, but they still heard gunshots. "Careful who you shoot out there," he said. "We've got an ally. Somebody saved me, and they're still fighting."

"About time we got some help," Doc said. She was mixing reagents and chemicals into glass flasks and stuffing the necks with cloth. "This should cause some trouble," she said, showing one to Jack with a nasty laugh. She packed several of the flasks into another bag, slung it over her shoulder, and picked up the MP-18. "Ready," she said.

"We go for one of the planes," Jack answered, and threw open the door.

Outside, Jack led the way down the row of tents toward the airstrip. There were fewer figures running around now, and the air held the chemical smell of dissolving Silver Star dead. Ahead of them the two airplanes sat side by side. But then one of them started its engine and edged out onto the airstrip.

"Oh, no," said Jack. "No, no, no." He started running. If that plane got airborne, the pilot could strafe the camp, fire through tents. Their chances of survival were about to drop dramatically.

The pilot had opened the throttle all the way, and Jack could hear the engine race. He snapped off a couple shots at it, but to no effect.

"Lighter!" Doc shouted. "Give me your lighter!"

Jack dug in his pocket for it and thrust it at her. She lit the cloth in one of her flasks. The plane was gathering speed, bouncing toward them down the crude dirt airstrip. Doc cocked her arm, ran a few paces, and hurled the flask. It tumbled in a long, high arc toward the plane.

Then there was a flash, and the plane seemed to simply erupt into a ball of fire. Jack knew how vulnerable the dope covered fabric was to flame. Even more than bullets, fire had been a pilot's greatest fear during the war.

The plane veered off course, bounced off the airstrip into the grass and came to a stop, already an inferno. There was no way the pilot could have made it out. Already the skeleton of the wings was collapsing. The plane was a pyre. Its twin sat intact at the end of the airstrip. It was now the only way out of the valley, Jack realized.

Doc turned back to him with a grin. Jack nodded. "Try not to do that to the other one," he said.

Then they turned and headed back into the camp, toward the sporadic bursts of gun-fire.

❧

Aboard the *Luftpanzer*, Maria Blutig returned to the radio room. This time the crew wasn't expecting her, and they hurriedly flew to attention as she stormed into the small cabin.

"Raise Shambala Base," she snapped.

"We have been trying, mein Führerin," the senior man said nervously. "They missed their last scheduled radio check and are not responding to us."

She bit the inside of her lip but kept her demeanor icy and calm. It was necessary that the crew see her as unshakeable, but this was bad. The *Luftpanzer* had been on station outside the entrance to the valley for almost half an hour now. The plane she had expected to meet them, the plane carrying Jack McGraw, had not been there. Now this. Something had gone wrong. Ardinger and a force of nearly fifty trained soldiers should have been able to handle one man, but Maria had learned that nothing went quite as it should when Jack McGraw was involved.

The junior man was on the headphones, adjusting his equipment and tapping out the recognition code on his key. Suddenly he turned.

"Voice channel! I have something!"

He unplugged his headphones and hit a switch. The sounds of gunfire erupted from the speakers.

"*Luftpanzer, Luftpanzer*, this is Shambala Base! We are under attack!"

It was a nervous, young voice, obviously unfamiliar with radio protocols. Where were the radio officers? Where was Ardinger?

"This is Maria Blutig," she snapped. "Who is sending? Where is Captain Ardinger?"

There was some kind of scuffle, then Ardinger came on.

"Ardinger here, mein Führerin. We are under attack, I believe by AEGIS reinforcements. Most of my men are dead. I have fallen back to the radio shack, and we are holding for now. But our situation is desperate."

"What about McGraw?" She felt a cold rage growing in the pit of her stomach.

"McGraw and Starr are free and participating in the assault," Ardinger said. "Both pilots on base are dead, and one plane is destroyed."

"How many attackers in total, Captain? How did they get into the valley?"

"Unknown, mein Führerin. Snipers are firing from the southern ridge. I sent a commando team to root them out, but have lost contact."

It was exactly as grim as she expected. There was one last thing to confirm.

"What is the status of Dr. Mencken?"

There was a pause. Maria heard shouting and a burst of gunfire in the background.

"Unknown, mein Führerin," Ardinger said again, in the tone of a man who knew he was calling down his own doom.

"Stand by, Shambala base," she said.

There was a pause, then Ardinger replied, "I understand."

She turned to the radio men. "Clear the room, please," she said softly. The two men saluted and withdrew, not quite able to hide the relief on their faces. The second closed the door behind him, and she was alone.

Someone was breaking down over the speaker. She heard fear, then Ardinger shouting, "Hold your position god damn you, or I'll kill you myself!"

She unsnapped a leather pouch on her belt and withdrew a carved metal medallion with several long, thin metal chains hanging from it. The medallion was very old. It was tarnished and marked both by time and by several failed attempts to destroy it. Maria quivered with anticipation as she pressed it to the back of her left hand and carefully wrapped the chains. This one around her wrist, this one around these fingers, one around the thumb and back to fasten here. It was a ritual she knew well, the movements almost automatic.

There was nothing else to do now, she knew. Mencken was Ardinger's primary responsibility. If he didn't know where Mencken was, then the doctor was surely dead. And with him, the project. They had gotten what they could from it. Crowley would be disappointed, as she was, but there would be new opportunities, new avenues of attack.

On the radio, Ardinger began to lead his men in the Silver Star anthem. They were ragged at first, but soon the words rang loud and clear—words of strength, words of revenge. The Silver Star could never fall for its strength was never truly lost.

Maria closed her eyes and murmured words of her own—ancient words in a language no longer spoken on this world. She made a complex gesture with her left hand, wrapped in its delicate filigree of chain, and she felt the medallion begin to tingle against her skin. The ancient chant built to its climax, and she let out a loud gasp as she drew her hand back into a fist that gathered everything into its grasp.

The radio fell silent.

A moment later, Maria Blutig gasped as she felt the rush of power and almost sexual pleasure wash over her.

❧

Jack and Doc crouched behind the corner of a storage shed, trading fire with the last of Ardinger's forces in the radio building. The only remaining Silver Star soldiers were inside there now. Jack estimated there were perhaps a dozen. They'd fought their way back here, killing several as they came. And their mysterious ally was still out there somewhere. Jack had no idea who it was, but he hoped it was Deadeye. Certainly he had Deadeye's skill as a sniper, and he'd been watching over them as they fought their way through the Silver Star troops. Whenever someone had gotten too close to them, rifle shots had removed the threat.

Now there was only sporadic fire from the building's windows, and it didn't look like their own shots were penetrating the plaster and metal mesh walls. It was a standoff.

Jack was considering how to get Ardinger to surrender when the building's door suddenly flew open, and a figure dashed out. Doc leveled her MP-18, and was about to cut him down, but then she stopped herself. The man was unarmed and paying no attention to them at all. He sprinted away, heading for a stand of trees a few hundred yards away. Doc raised the MP-18's muzzle and let him go.

Then, as they watched, the man seemed to erupt into smoke. One moment he was running hard for the distant trees. The next there was a puff of greenish smoke, and the man's bones clattered to the ground and lay there, wrapped in his Silver Star uniform.

"What in the world?" Doc said, uncomprehending. "Was he shot?"

"No," said Jack. "He just..."

The gunfire had stopped. Jack and Doc looked at each other. What in the world was going on?

"Captain?" Jack shouted. "Are you ready to give up? All of you throw out your weapons and come out with your hands up!"

The only reply was the wind. It banged the door of the radio shack against its frame.

Jack and Doc leveled their weapons and walked slowly toward the building. When they reached the door, Doc used the muzzle of her gun to catch the edge of the door and pull it open.

Then she looked inside and gasped.

Jack moved around the door frame and looked in himself.

They were all dead. Nothing was left of the last of the Silver Star troops but bones, uniforms, and dropped weapons.

"What happened?" Doc asked in a small voice.

Jack put away his gun. "We won," he said. "That's what."

Then Jack heard a whistle, loud and shrill. They turned and saw a figure approaching from the south. A lone man with a rifle. He thrust the gun away and dropped it as he walked into the remains of the camp. This must be the man who'd saved him, Jack realized, who'd saved them both.

"Oh, my God!" said Doc.

As the man came into view, Jack's confusion only grew.

"You two all right?" Christopher Rhys asked with a smile.

- CHAPTER 23 -

Doc rushed to embrace Rhys but then stopped short.

"Christopher?" she said. "How? We saw you…"

"I'm not sure where to start," said Rhys.

"You couldn't have survived that!" said Doc. Rhys didn't have a scratch on him, Jack noticed.

Rhys nodded. "I know. You'll want your . 45s, Jack. They're in Captain Ardinger's safe. This way."

"Uh, okay." Jack had indeed been wondering where his guns were. Rhys led them toward the command building.

"I remember the airplane," Rhys said as they walked. "I remember falling. I knew I was going to die." He stopped and let out a breath. "I remember hitting the rocks."

After a moment, he started walking again. "It was night when I woke up. I was covered in blood, and I hurt like hell. The Tarasque was next to me. Very dead. But I was alive, and I knew you needed my help so I came to help you."

"Well I'm glad you did," said Jack. "For a medical man, you make a hell of a sniper. My friend Charlie Dalton couldn't have done any better, and we call him 'Deadeye.' So thank you. I mean that. I don't mean to sound ungrateful at all. But this doesn't make any sense, and I'd really like to know what's going on."

"Can't fault you for that," said Rhys.

When they reached the command building, Rhys led them into Ardinger's office. A safe sat in the corner behind his desk, covered in boards to form a makeshift table.

Rhys knelt beside the safe. "I can't explain it," he said, "not completely anyway. Let me demonstrate. To be clear, I didn't see Ardinger put your guns in this safe." He closed his eyes and placed the fingertips of one hand gently on the door. "And he certainly didn't tell me the combination."

Rhys took a breath and held it. Then he slowly turned the dial. They were all silent, listening to the soft ticking of the dial. Rhys stopped and turned it the other way. Then he rubbed his fingertips together for a moment and turned it once more. Finally he stopped, opened his eyes, let out the breath he was holding, and opened the door.

Inside, on top of a stack of supply lists, was Jack's gun belt with his twin .45s secure in their holsters. Jack and Doc traded a look as Rhys handed the guns to Jack.

"When I came to, it was the dead of night," Rhys said. "I got out of the gorge by climbing those cliffs in pitch darkness. I just knew where to put my hands. And yes, I've fired a rifle before, in basic training. But I can assure you, my squad mates did not call me 'Deadeye.' Something happened to me. Something remarkable."

"Christopher!" Doc said suddenly, "When was the last time you had a shot?"

"The morning before we went hunting for civets," Rhys answered. "Don't worry, the poison's cleared. I'm in no danger."

He led them outside, and they looked around at the wreckage of the camp. The remains of fallen soldiers lay scattered on the ground, the last faint wisps of smoke rising from the bones.

"The mother of medicines!" Doc said suddenly. "The Long Walker talked about it. Did you—"

"He told you?" Rhys said in surprise. "He must have liked you a great deal. He hinted and talked around it for months with me."

Jack struggled to remember exactly what the Long Walker had said. "Enlightenment," he said, "and bodily perfection. Are you saying..."

"There's no way I could have survived that fall," Rhys said. "But I did. I don't know if I *can* die now. I heal with incredible speed. And I know things. I knew how to climb a cliff in the dark. I pointed a rifle at a man hundreds of yards away, and I felt the path of the bullet connecting before I ever pulled the trigger. I didn't miss a single shot. Missing never entered my mind."

It sounded impossible, but there Rhys was. He'd survived the fall. He'd gotten out of the canyon. He'd killed those Silver Star soldiers. Jack didn't have a better explanation.

"We have to get you to a lab!" Doc said. "Blood samples, tissue types. Were you tracking your solution levels over time? Christopher, do you have any idea how big this will be? We can save so many people!"

Rhys shook his head. "You don't understand," he said. "It's ironic, really. I had to purge the DL-95 to survive outside the valley. Now if I leave, I have no idea what will happen. And you have to leave now. There's no knowing how long you have before the Silver Star returns. And that plane won't carry three. Am I right, Jack?"

"Even two's hard enough," Jack admitted. "I can't fly you both out at once."

"Then you'll come back for him!" Doc cried. "Jack, we can't just leave him!"

"It's not that simple," Rhys said as they walked toward the airstrip. "The outside world's learning about this place. They'll be coming. Some will be like you, but a lot of them will be more like the Silver Star. Think about it, Dorothy! Say you figure out what happened to me. Say you cure polio and cancer and tuberculosis—say you cure everything! Do you really think it would stop there? Do you think the world's ready for what would come after that? I have to stay here. At least until I understand what's happened to me."

Doc was on the verge of tears. "What about the Silver Star? What will you do when they come to retake this place?"

Rhys said simply, "I'll stop them."

☙

Maria Blutig stood on the *Luftpanzer*'s bridge, looking out across the mountains. The only sounds were the drone of the engines and the occasional click of a switch.

Captain Ecke sat brooding in his chair. Ecke was the *Luftpanzer*'s Captain in principle, but of course that meant nothing when Maria was aboard. He was an old-school military man, gruff and stoic. She knew he considered it his duty to rein in her more aggressive impulses, to be the voice of reason, the angel on her shoulder. He was competent and loyal, so she tolerated it. But now even he was silent. Captain Ecke knew better than to deny her when Jack McGraw was involved.

She felt the faint bump as one of the fighters disconnected from its launch crane. A moment later, the small plane flew out from beneath the hull and raced ahead to join its fellows.

"All planes are away," Ecke said.

Maria's orders had been unequivocal. They were to destroy anything that moved. That specifically included the two fighters they'd left at the base. If either of those planes was airborne, it was no longer friendly. There were no friendly forces remaining at Shambala Base. She'd made sure of that herself.

Ahead, the four remaining fighters were forming up outside the canyon that led to

Shambala Base. When they were ready, the leader headed into the canyon and the others followed.

Maria had loved a man once. Love had filled her heart until it spilled over. She dreamed of the better world she would make for the child they would have. But the war had taken him from her, and now the world would know the strength of her love through the unfathomable depth of her rage.

The most guilty of course was Jack McGraw, the man who pulled the trigger. But that was only the beginning. There was the officer who ordered the sortie, the men who started the war, the women who birthed monstrous children that grew up to make a world of poison gas and carnage and airplanes falling in flames from the sky. From one end of the Earth to the other, nobody was innocent. In the end, Maria would punish them all.

Not even her own troops were innocent. Their loss was nothing to regret. It was just another small part of her grand vengeance. She'd seen the entire garrison of Shambala Base destroyed. What difference four more pilots and their flimsy airplanes?

"Move us closer to the canyon mouth," she snapped suddenly. A crewman actually jumped at the sound of her voice. They rushed to carry out the order.

If she couldn't reach into the valley and pluck Jack McGraw out, then she would make the place his tomb.

"Captain Ecke, prepare the field guns for firing."

⊂⊃

Jack, Doc, and Rhys had loaded the poison samples and research notes aboard the Silver Star fighter. Jack had confirmed that the fuel tanks were topped off and the flight controls were working properly. The radio was operable; even the machine guns' ammo bays were fully loaded. There was nothing else to do; the plane was ready to fly.

"Christopher, for the last time, come with us," Doc begged. "We can dump weight. We'll get you out somehow."

"Thank you, Dorothy," Rhys said with a smile. "This is where I belong now."

Rhys had found the spear he'd made in his first days in the jungle, and now he leaned on it with an ammunition belt slung across his chest and a pair of long-barreled Lugers in wooden holsters on his hips. If he could still shoot the way he had earlier, Jack thought, he didn't like the Silver Star's chances of reclaiming the valley from him.

"We'll come back and check on you, at least," said Jack. "Bring you supplies. We won't abandon you up here."

Doc hugged him one more time, then they helped her climb into the small cargo bay. She sat behind the cockpit with her head and shoulders jutting out of the fuselage.

Then Jack and Rhys shook hands. "Good luck," said Jack.

Rhys gave him an enigmatic smile. "Take care of her."

Jack nodded and climbed into the cockpit. He pulled the stick all the way back, opened the fuel valve, and shouted "Contact!" Rhys spun the propeller and the engine caught immediately. Rhys moved away to the side, and the plane started forward. Jack turned it down the airstrip and threw the throttle open. They accelerated into the wind, gaining speed fast. He felt the wheels lift off the ground, and they were airborne. Jack turned and headed for the canyon mouth.

As they approached the canyon, Jack took one more look back at this strange land. The last he saw of Rhys, he was standing with his spear thrust skyward in salute. Then they were into the canyon, and Jack's attention was focused completely on his flying.

Coming out wasn't the same as flying in. The canyon's narrow twists and gaps were different from the other direction. The short cave was actually much easier this way, with the light coming from behind them. He shot through with no trouble this time. The next two turns were equally simple. But coming up on the third, Jack realized it was going to be trickier in this direction. He'd have to turn blind, thread a narrow gap, then immediately climb for all he was worth to make it over the steep slope he'd come down on the way in. He considered how fast he could safely make the turn itself, and edged the throttle forward.

"Hang on," he shouted back to Doc. Then they were into the turn. Jack rolled sharply to his left, watching the wall of the canyon coming up fast then disappear right under the nose. He leveled out and yanked the stick back.

And nearly flew directly into an oncoming airplane.

Even before he registered that this was an enemy fighter, Jack was slewing to the right on pure instinct. There was nowhere else to go. He was already climbing as steeply as he could to stay above the canyon floor. He slid to the right, then steered back again, barely clearing the other plane.

For the other pilot, there was just nowhere to go. Jack had appeared at the worst possible instant. His choices were to fly straight into the oncoming plane or dodge into the canyon wall. Jack heard Doc scream, then the crunch of the airframe crumpling against the stone. He could only see out of the corner of his eye as the debris tumbled down the side of the cliff, the engine trailing a corkscrew of smoke.

"Look out!" Doc shrieked as they cleared the slope and the canyon opened up. Suddenly there were Silver Star fighters everywhere. Jack counted three waiting to follow their now dead leader through the turn. The first one passed right over them, barely missing the wing, and disappeared behind them. The pilot was already committed, Jack realized. There was nothing he could do but complete the turn and come out on the other side of the bend. It would take him some time to come around and get back into the fight. That meant, for a minute or so at least, he only had two to worry about.

The second pilot pulled sharply up to get out of Jack's way. But the third one had time to react. He lined up and opened fire. Jack heard bullets ripping through the fabric of the upper wing and slewed right, toward the canyon wall.

There wasn't much room to maneuver here. The cliffs were immediately in his windscreen again. He looked up and realized he didn't have much ceiling to work with either.

His instincts took over. Doc screamed again as Jack stood the plane on its left wingtip and pulled back hard on the stick. He braced himself for impact, but the wheels barely cleared the cliff, and he was leveling out and scanning the sky for the enemy planes.

He saw one high above him. The second one in line, he realized. The pilot was trying to do a loop to bring himself back around to fire. He was going for the high position, just like he'd been taught in the war no doubt. But this wasn't the place for that kind of maneuver. The pilot was focused on Jack's plane, not on staying within the shelter of the cliffs.

He's cutting it awful close, Jack thought. Too close. As Jack watched, the wings dipped into the fierce mountain winds above the canyon walls. The airspeed over the wings was suddenly doubled or tripled, and that meant lift. The plane seemed to fall upward at impossible speed, twirling out of control. Then it was simply gone, as if God himself had reached down and plucked it out of the sky.

Bullets spattered against the stone, yanking Jack's attention back to the remaining plane. He jerked the stick back and forth, making himself a tougher target. Looking over his shoulder, he saw the first plane, the one that had disappeared around the bend, coming back.

Jack pointed his nose back down the canyon and sped away. He had guns of his own, but there was no sense trying to dogfight in this confined space. He'd seen how that ended. Let them chase him.

A moment later another sound cut through the drone of the engine, a dull bass thump that no one who fought in the war could ever forget. An artillery barrage. That could only mean one thing. Jack opened the throttle to full and hoped they weren't already too late.

He raced the remaining two Silver Star pilots down the canyon, dodging fire as he went. Taking the tight turns would give him an occasional respite, but then the enemy planes would come around and line him up again. The plane had taken some damage, but nothing serious, and they were both unhurt. So far, they'd been lucky.

Jack came around the last bend and flew straight into a thick cloud of smoke and rock dust. Ahead there was an explosion in the cliff face and huge chunks of stone rained down. He could make out the dark shape of the *Luftpanzer* ahead and above, raining down fire. Maria Blutig would seal off this place forever and sacrifice the Silver Star's plans for the valley if it meant destroying him.

"Jack, what are we going to do?" Doc shouted.

"Only one thing we can do," he called back.

"I was afraid you'd say that."

"Hang on!" he shouted. Then a shell screamed in overhead and gravel rained down on the wings.

Suddenly, Jack seemed detached from everything around him. He was calm somehow, when he knew he should be too terrified to function. That was probably it, he thought. If he wasn't separated from what was going on around him, he'd be a gibbering mess, and then he'd fly into a rock wall.

Bullets slashed past, shredded part of the lower left wingtip. The Silver Star pilots were nothing if not persistent. In their place, he'd be less concerned with shooting him down than with getting out of this place alive.

Jack rolled the plane and shot sideways down a narrow gap. He heard Doc's wail behind him. Then they came out into a wider stretch, and Jack could see the canyon mouth. But he realized they weren't out yet. The barrage had been at its worst here. Huge fingers of rock were separating from the wall and falling against each other.

Jack dove straight into the mass of falling stone. On either side of them, enormous towers spun and toppled. He wouldn't be able to keep his promise to Christopher Rhys, he realized. Maria Blutig was sealing the canyon off for good.

He aimed the plane by instinct, pointing toward the light as shadow and stone closed in around him. A huge wall of rock had detached ahead and to his left. It was falling straight across the canyon like a brick wall someone had toppled over. Jack dove to pick up speed. They'd make it out or they'd die beneath those tons of stone. Jack had no idea which. That was up to fate now.

It was like flying through a hailstorm as pebbles and chunks of rock pelted the plane. To his left, one of the Silver Star fighters exploded into a rain of debris. He'd lost track of the other one.

Jack looked up and for a moment he couldn't see the sky at all. There was nothing but rock above, falling down to crush him against the canyon floor. There was a roar like the world tearing in two.

Then the plane shot free, into open air. Jack whooped with the sheer joy of it. The Himalayas lay spread out beneath him, snowcaps gleaming in the afternoon sun. He couldn't stop laughing. What a beautiful place to fly.

"Jack!" Doc shouted. "The *Luftpanzer!*"

The great airship was bearing down on them. The field guns had fallen silent, but the ship had plenty of machine guns that could tear them apart. Jack veered off, dove for speed, and raced away down the line of mountains.

He switched on the radio and heard Silver Star chatter. Someone aboard *Luftpanzer* was trying to raise their pilots. Jack suspected they wouldn't have any luck. He grabbed the mic.

"*Luftpanzer*, *Luftpanzer*, this is Jack McGraw calling," he shouted. "Is Maria Blutig aboard?"

A few moments later, he heard her voice. "Damn you to hell, McGraw," she snarled. "I swear I'll kill you!"

"You sure do try, don't you?" Jack called back. "But not today. Just wanted to let you know I'm alive and well. Going to have to borrow your plane here. Hope you don't mind. You have a nice day now."

He flew away, outpacing the huge airship as he dove down out of the high mountains. He let Maria rain curses and threats down on him by radio until the transmission faded. Then he switched frequencies.

"*Daedalus*," he called, "come in *Daedalus*, are you out there?"

For a few moments, there was nothing, then he heard Duke's voice, tight with excitement. "This is the *Daedalus*. Jack, is that you? Are you all right?"

"We're okay, Duke," Jack answered. "Though I don't know if Doc's going to want to fly with me after this. Be aware we're in a stolen Silver Star fighter, so don't go blowing us out of the sky or anything."

"Understood," said Duke.

"I don't know if this thing's got enough fuel to make it back to Almora," he added. "We may need a pickup somewhere."

"You got it Jack. We'll find a safe place to put down and we'll guide you in. Hey Deadeye, break out the charts! I've got them!"

- CHAPTER 24 -

Delhi, four days later.

"Now let me make sure I understand what I'm hearing," said Padger, sitting up in his hospital bed. The crew had rushed to Delhi as soon as they made it back. Padger still wasn't ready to fly, but they were happy to see that he was well on his way. Then they had to tell him what they'd done to his Bristol.

"First, while I was laid up and unable to stop you, you lot stole my airplane. Then you went and crashed it in the mountains."

Jack tried to look appropriately sheepish, but Padger's barely contained grin made it difficult. "Shot down," he said. "Not crashed, exactly."

"Oh, so you think stealing my airplane and getting it shot down is better than just crashing it, then?"

"Well, isn't it? A little anyway? I mean that's mostly on the Silver Star."

Padger dismissed the argument with an imperious wave. "The aircraft impacted the ground at a high rate of speed. It was rendered less than airworthy and must be considered a loss."

"I think that's fair," said Doc. Padger winked at her.

"So then you stole another airplane, one of those Silver Star jobbies they carry around in their zeppelin. Perhaps with the thought of bringing it back to me as at least *some* recompense, however inadequate, for the grievous harm you'd done me. But then you crashed that too. Is that the story?"

"Well, not exactly," said Jack.

"No, you never *exactly* crash, do you?" said Padger. At this Deadeye lost it completely and had to turn into the corner, shaking with laughter.

"But you ran it out of fuel and left it somewhere back in the mountains where there's no hope of recovering it. So when they finally let me out of this place, I'll be stranded here, without my livelihood and only means of support. Is that what you're telling me?"

"Well, it's not entirely bad news," said Jack.

"Right," Duke added. "Look at it this way. You don't have to worry about the RAF auditing the paperwork and figuring out you stole a much better airplane than the one you paid them for."

"Balderdash!" Padger snapped. "That plane was precisely as described in the purchase contract. Bristol F.2 airframe with a Sunbeam Arab engine."

Rivets snorted. "If that was a Sunbeam Arab, I'm Rudy Valentino."

"Go check the serial numbers if you don't believe me!"

"Nonsense!" said Rivets. "You swapped the ID plate from an Arab onto a Rolls Falcon engine, and you slipped it by some idiot quartermaster that didn't know an airplane from a farm tractor!"

"Prove it!" Padger shot back.

"Exactly!" said Duke, reaching out to take Rivets by the shoulders and calm him down. "They'll never find that airplane. The evidence is gone, and you're in the clear. We did you a favor if you think about it."

Padger feigned shock. "You villain!"

"We do have a peace offering," Jack interjected. "We feel bad about everything that's happened, so we talked to AEGIS, and there's a job waiting for you when you're back on your feet."

Padger looked suspicious. "What kind of job?"

"This is obviously a part of the world AEGIS can no longer ignore," said Doc. "We need eyes on the ground, and in the air. We need someone who knows the region, someone with mobility, and someone who can handle themselves in a fight."

"Well, that's kind of you to say, but I don't get around so well now that someone went and wrecked my Biff." He shot a look at Jack.

"We mentioned that to Mr. Edison," said Jack. "We told him without an airplane you're no good to anyone. You just lie in bed all day and complain."

"Why you—"

"So he pulled some strings, and we got you a new airplane." He took a folder from a satchel he'd brought along.

"Did you now?" said Padger with a raised eyebrow. "Well, what kind of plane are we talking about?"

Jack opened the folder and produced a thin stack of drawings and spec sheets. "Brand new Boeing Model 40-A," he said. "They're making them for mail service in

America, but they won't even go into service there until next year. Yours is an off the books prototype. It's on its way here now."

"Oh, let's have a look at that," Padger said, reaching for his breakfast tray and spreading out the papers Jack handed him.

"She'll carry two passengers and twelve hundred pounds of cargo,.." Said Jack. "Upgraded engine from the original Model 40 too. She's got the new Pratt and Whitney Wasp. Four hundred and twenty horsepower."

"Oh, my word," Padger murmured as he scanned the performance figures.

"Those are the official numbers, by the way," Jack added. "AEGIS made a few...enhancements before she left the states. You'll find she'll do a bit more than you see there."

"Oh, mate," Padger said, "all is forgiven!"

The others crowded around to check out the specs of the new airplane, but Jack hung back a moment and looked over the crew. His crew. They'd taken the fight to the Silver Star one more time, and won. They hadn't gotten away without taking a few punches themselves. Dr. Rhys was stranded in the valley, probably forever given the destruction of the only safe passage through the mountains. Rhys was a good man, and he'd been a valuable ally. Jack hated knowing he could do nothing to rescue him. But the source of the poison was gone now, and Doc had all she needed to create an antidote for any poison remaining in the Silver Star's hands. Overall, it was a victory.

It was a good note to end things on, he thought.

He drifted silently away from the group at the bedside and slipped through the curtains onto the balcony. He leaned against the rusting wrought iron railing and looked out over the building's courtyard. Below, a nurse pushed a patient across the grass in a wheelchair.

"Hey," Doc murmured suddenly at his side, "the party's inside. What are you doing out here by yourself?"

"I was just thinking how much I'm going to miss all this," he said.

"What are you talking about?

"We came back because Mr. Edison needed us, and I thought we'd see how it worked. But look what happened. We can't keep living like this!"

"Oh, nonsense. Is this because of Ellen? You didn't have a problem with us risking our lives before I told you she was yours."

She glanced over her shoulder and made sure no one would overhear them from

Padger's room. No chance of that Jack realized. They were all talking at once.

"It's different," Jack protested. "We've got a daughter now! She needs us."

"Well, *I've* had a daughter for years," she reminded him. "You think I didn't think about that? Believe me, I thought about it. And I'm sorry if all this is new and frightening for you, Jack McGraw, but it's nothing new to me, so you shut up and listen for once."

Jack recognized her tone. He shut up and listened.

"We didn't come back to try it out, or to do one last favor for Mr. Edison," she said. "We came back *because* we've got a daughter to think of, and she's got to live in this messed up world. Now there's a lot of good people in it, but there's a lot of vile, noxious sons of bitches out there too. The Silver Star not the least of them. So we're back because we owe Ellen a better world, even if we have to kill every one of those rotten bastards in it ourselves."

Jack drew back to look her in the eye and saw the steely determination there. She was right, he realized, but he couldn't help laughing.

"Whoa, what is it with your language lately? First I thought, okay, she's just scared, but...I didn't think you knew half those words."

Doc sighed and shook her head in exasperation. "I was a battlefield nurse, Jack! If scared, dying men scream it, I've heard it. I can curdle milk from across the room in five languages! Plus a few random obscenities in Hindi and Afrikaans. I just didn't use them around you before. I was minding my manners."

"Right," Jack said with a grin. "I remember now. You stopped because I don't rate anymore."

She playfully hit him in the shoulder. "You rate just fine, Jack. Maybe I don't feel like playing a role around you anymore. I did that for a long time. I hid the truth from you because I thought it was the right way to play it. But that didn't do either of us any good. So I don't want to hide things from you anymore. This is me, Jack. I'm not always very ladylike. I swear sometimes. When I get going, I'm actually pretty good at it."

He reached out and placed his hand gently against her cheek. "Sure you are. I've noticed you're pretty good at a lot of things."

She smiled back at him. "Damn right. So no more of this acting like I can't take care of myself anymore just because you love me.

Nothing's going to happen to me. I've got Captain Stratosphere watching my back."

Jack winced. "I deserved that, didn't I?"

"You did," said Doc. "But you deserve this too." Then she leaned in and kissed him.

"Come on," she said after she broke away. "Let's get back in and join the fun.

Jack nodded, then stole another kiss.

Duke and Padger were teaching the others some English drinking song as they came back inside. Even Rivets was getting caught up in the mood of celebration.

"Come on Jack," Duke called out, "Stop monopolizing Doc. We need an alto here."

Doc gave him a smile and squeezed his hand. She was right, he thought. It was a tough world out there, and they owed it to Ellen to do what they could to make it better. But they were together. They'd won this fight, and with their friends beside them, they'd win the next ones too. It was going to be a hell of a world when Doc was done with it, Jack decided. He couldn't wait to see it.

He took Doc's hand and they joined in on the chorus.

Well it's all for me grog, me jolly, jolly grog,

All for me beer and tobacco.

For we spent all our tin, with the lassies drinking gin,

And across the western ocean we must wander...

☙

As the *Luftpanzer* neared Samarkand, Maria Blutig felt an intense need for sleep and knew it wasn't natural. She left Ecke in command and retired to her cabin. She prepared a magic circle on the metal deck and sat down in the center. With her hands on her knees, palms up toward the heavens, she focused her energies outward and let the summoning take her. She closed her eyes and was asleep in moments.

She dreamed herself in a blasted stone circle atop a mountain. It was an ancient place, marked with age-old runes and lit by torches and lightning that flashed silently through the clouds overhead. She knew this place well. It was where she'd sworn allegiance to Crowley and the Silver Star in exchange for the power to take her revenge.

Crowley stood on the far side of the circle, waiting.

"My master," Maria said as she approached.

"This is a setback, Maria," Crowley said. "A significant one. Shambala was an important part of our plans."

"It couldn't be helped," she replied. "We underestimated AEGIS once again." Her unspoken meaning, of course, was that he had underestimated AEGIS. Under her command, Shambala Base had been producing powerful weapons. It was Crowley who had overreached in his plan to remove AEGIS and invited a counterattack before they were ready. But that criticism would remain unspoken. Crowley was still the master, for now at least.

"McGraw has resurfaced," she added. "He's working with AEGIS again."

"Your obsession with McGraw is becoming a liability, Maria," Crowley said.

She accepted the observation but wasn't threatened by it as she assumed he intended. "But not one large enough to outweigh what I bring you."

The closed line of his mouth moved into something not quite a smile. "Not yet."

"We can return to Shambala," she said. "*Luftpanzer* can land a team in the mountains nearby. They can make their way in overland." It was true. It would be more difficult than flying in, but it could be done.

"No, that avenue is closed to us," Crowley said. "At least for now. I've attempted several psychic probes since you chose to abandon Shambala Base. The valley has found its guardian. We must seek another way."

"What would you have me do, my Master?"

She studied his face, his expression shifting subtly. It was getting harder to conceal the insolent tone behind the words. Their alliance meant different things to each of them. To Crowley she was a tool, a weapon like any other in his arsenal. More capable, perhaps, and so more highly valued. But still a means to an end. He would discard her when it suited his purpose.

But she would never be the slavish acolyte he required. Most of Crowley's tools and weapons were broken when he picked them up. They devoted their very souls to him because he promised to make them whole again, to repair what the war, or just the world in its turning, had done to them. Maria was different. What she'd gone through hadn't broken her; it had forged her. Serving Crowley was to her advantage and as long as that remained true, she would be his weapon. But if that ever changed...

"AEGIS is the power that opposes us," Crowley said at last. "So I set my best weapon against them."

He paused a moment, and Maria noted the parallel with what she'd just been thinking.

How far into her mind had he managed to burrow? Did he trust her, or did he realize the danger she represented?

"But my best weapon has failed me," he said. She noticed his dream form growing taller, his posture more aggressive. "In my visions, I see you destroy my enemies. I see you shatter AEGIS to clear our path. Yet again and again you fail. And McGraw is always at the root of it."

His aspect was terrible now. She saw the leering expressions of Crowley's demonic advisers flash across his features.

"I see the flaw in you now, Maria. No matter how strong I try to make you, your obsession with McGraw makes you weak. If you're to be of use to me, we must first deal with that."

Crowley towered over her now. The rocks trembled, and Maria saw a darkness in his eyes beyond darkness. He was becoming something other than human, she sensed.

"McGraw is the keystone!" Crowley's voice boomed. "If he is destroyed, then AEGIS must inevitably fall. I've considered what motivates him, what makes him strong, and what makes him weak. I know how we can annihilate him utterly."

Maria looked into the abyss of Crowley's eyes, and smiled. This was why she followed

him; because he always saw the next step forward.

"I am yours to command, my Master," she
said in earnest.

☙

Christopher Rhys stood on a hilltop and
looked out over the valley. There was the river,
there the waterfall, there the broken grassland
where the Tarasques hunted, there the high
slopes with their pines and the nests of night
birds. Rhys leaned on his spear. He could feel
the energy of the place coursing through him.
He was part of this land, and he could feel its
strengths and its illnesses. The valley was a
living thing, and everything here was a part of
it. He had become its consciousness, the part
that recognized threats and defended the land.

He knew the canyon leading to the outside
world was sealed now. No aircraft would come
through it again. He was alone here, but he
was safe, and the land was safe. For now at
least. It wouldn't always be that way.

The sages who had once made their way
here and returned to the outside world had
written of the voices of the spirits speaking to
them. If Rhys closed his eyes and remained
very, very still, he could almost hear them. Not

voices, exactly. And not speaking words. But concepts would come to him and while his mind translated them into his own terms, he knew the ideas didn't originate with him. The destroyed canyon would keep the outside world away for a time, they said, but not forever. Eventually, outsiders would come again to explore and to plunder. Dangerous times were coming, when the valley's secrets could be hidden away no longer. It was important to protect the valley from the outside world, but it was equally important to protect the world from the dangers of this place. He might be called to leave the valley someday and return to the larger world for the good of all.

Rhys opened his eyes and looked up. A flight of vultures circled overhead. He knew they were interested in a goat carcass near the northern cliffs. All around him life began and ended, but the valley was eternal. Close enough, anyway.

He would protect this land, he thought, as the sun settled over the mountains. Yes, enemies would come looking for the treasures the valley held. And when they came, he would be ready for them.

The End

ABOUT THE AUTHOR

E.J. Blaine has enjoyed a writing career best described as "eclectic." While working as a trade journalist covering the telecommunications and energy industries, he moonlighted for a major media company, covering upcoming genre films for its print publication and writing movie reviews and other content for its website. He produced background material and scenarios for a number of role playing games, and occasionally published short fiction. He attended the prestigious Clarion workshop for science fiction and fantasy writers.

He lived in Vancouver, British Columbia for several years where he attended film school and worked in the Canadian film industry as a story editor. While there, he also wrote film and comic book scripts, and did development work for animation and live action television.

Currently, Blaine lives in Virginia with his wife and infant daughter, where he is massively overextending himself in an attempt to produce an ambitious array of novels and other fiction projects while dealing with a very demanding baby. *Assassins of the Lost Kingdom* is the first of these projects to reach print. His next project is *Smuggler's Log*, a space opera serial to be published by Waterhaven Media.

www.ejblaine.com

www.waterhavenmedia.com